BEN DOLNICK

You Know Who You Are

Ben Dolnick grew up outside of Washington, D.C.,
and currently lives in Brooklyn with his wife. He
is the author of a novel, *Zoology*, and his work has
appeared in various publications, including *The
New York Times* and *Five Chapters*.

Also by Ben Dolnick

Zoology

You Know Who You Are

You Know Who You Are

BEN DOLNICK

Vintage Contemporaries

Vintage Books

A Division of Random House, Inc.

New York

A VINTAGE CONTEMPORARIES ORIGINAL, MARCH 2011

Vintage is a registered trademark and Vintage Contemporaries and colophon
are trademarks of Random House, Inc.

Library of Congress Cataloging-in-Publication Data
Dolnick, Ben.
You know who you are : a novel / by Ben Dolnick.
p. cm.
ISBN 978-0-307-39087-5
1. Family—Fiction.   2. Domestic fiction.   I. Title.
PS3604.O44Y68 2011
813'.6—dc22
2010028364

Book design by Fritz Metsch

www.vintagebooks.com

Printed in the United States of America
10   9   8   7   6   5   4   3   2   1

For Elyse

and

for Sam

Acknowledgments

Thank you to Sara Crowe and Jennifer Jackson, for shepherding this project from its earliest days; to Katherine Lacy, Ben Solomon, Heather Kaye, Bob Koenig, and Alan Jacobs, for their patient explanations; to Elyse, Sam, Heidi, Ruth, John Burghardt, Josh F., Josh H., Scott, Nishant, Bryan S., and Adam, for early readings and for general book-related buckings-up; and to my parents, for all these things and countless more.

You Know Who You Are

Extra Life

Jacob and his brother, Will, had always shared the bedroom at the top of the stairs, and this had never seemed to Jacob any more unstable an arrangement than the one between his parents. Other siblings moved into rooms of their own, or had never shared rooms to begin with, but this, like having your parents divorce, was not something anyone could prefer. Jacob didn't think he would be able to sleep without his brother's presence across the room, and on the few occasions until now when he'd had to try it—when Will's class had spent the night at the Chesapeake Bay, for instance—he'd felt as if he were missing a pillow.

But Will had recently decided to move into the back bedroom, and so now Jacob trudged through his days weighted down by a shame and a mystery: his brother loved him less than he had just last week.

He and Will weren't the sort of brothers who used words like *love*, though, and in fact they often didn't get along at all. Jacob bossed Will around, though Will was two years older, and as often as not when Will's friends came over they ended up playing Nintendo with Jacob, while Will and Cara, their younger sister, shouted and cheered and pleaded, with equal hopelessness, to be given a turn. Where, then, had Will suddenly gotten the nerve for this rejection?

Jacob suspected that it had begun that fall when Will had been elected president of his class at their elementary school, Waggoner. Will now read the announcements over the PA in the morning and led the school in the pledge of allegiance before assemblies. These powers must have gone to his head. Rounds of applause, a special badge on his patrol belt, teachers calling him "President Vine" in a teasing but respectful way. Now he refused to hold up *Nintendo Power* while Jacob tried to figure out what to do with the soothsayer's enchanted flute. He no longer wanted to listen to Jacob recite the lyrics to "Good Vibrations."

And, worst of all, he had begun to date. Jacob didn't know what dating meant, exactly, but he expected that Will could be teased into renouncing it. No. Dating had swept Will's grade like pinkeye. None of the couples went anywhere, and they certainly didn't kiss, but they seemed to take very seriously the decision to be bound. Melanie Friedman, Julie Sutter, Emily Cobb—these were ordinary girls who now giggled when they passed Jacob in the halls, and who called and asked for Will with sweetly masked danger in their voices. They seemed to Jacob as if they wanted blood.

It was no wonder, then, that Jacob threw his alarm clock

at Will's head. It didn't hit him or come close to hitting him—instead it smashed thrillingly against the bookshelf, showering plastic splinters all over the carpet—but still Jacob had needed to do it. And still he was grounded. When it began to snow, Jacob begged his parents to reconsider, and when they wouldn't, even as kids from all over the neighborhood converged on Pinyon bearing sleds and saucers, he gave in to a fit of self-pity that felt like poison ivy emanating not from his skin but from his bones.

Now he sat, a prisoner with his head in the stocks, at the desk in the playroom overlooking the street. Open in front of him was the black-and-white-speckled journal that Mrs. Grillet would collect on Monday. Jacob had fallen months behind in his, and so, changing pens for each entry, he was re-creating the holidays and field trips of the fall. *So far in my life*, he wrote, *Montana is easily the best vacation I've ever been on. When I first arrived I came on a little plane which was a lot of fun.*

With the keenness of a dog he listened as his father and Will dragged the serious sleds up from the basement. These sleds were wooden, heavy as sandbags, with metal runners and a hairy length of rope that you tugged to steer. In the hallway just outside the playroom he heard Cara say, "I don't *want* it buttoned all the way up! It's choking me! It's choking me!" And then he heard the *whump* and latching of the door, and life carrying on away from him. He balanced his head on his fist and stared down at the page, so that his misery wouldn't be lost on them if they happened to look back. *Each rapid had a name, the first was tunnel rapid, the second was bonecrusher and the third my favorite was the repeater. After a little more drifting we stopped at an island. We were going to eat steaks but the instructor forgot the grill. There goes the lunch idea.*

No one in his family did look back, but in his imagination Jacob followed them up the hill. So many people were out—the atmosphere was like a street fair—that they would have to choose a path carefully. Arthur and Cara, piled like the beginnings of a snowman, would take run after run, their noses stinging.

Will wouldn't be sledding—Jacob felt fairly sure about that. Instead he'd be skulking around with Andre or Nicky, whispering about the weekend. Jacob was nursing the imaginary scene like a mug of bitter tea when the door swept open again, and voices came tumbling into the kitchen. His father, Will, Cara—and his aunt Judy too. She must have come for a visit, though in all their voices there was a note of either panic or excitement, rather than the usual jokey cheer. Judy's son Aaron was missing. Somehow Jacob had absorbed this even before he'd crept out to the kitchen.

His mother stood in her nightshirt and socks at the counter, holding the spoon over the canister of Quik. His father, still wearing his gloves, pulled the phone book out from the cereal shelf and flopped it onto the table. Judy was as little help in an emergency as a child, so it was Arthur who dialed the number for Michael Schloss's house, where Aaron had said he was spending the night but had never shown up. "Well, would it be all right if I gave you our number here in case he does turn up?" Then Teddy Macove. Matthew Picardi. Ian Kupchik.

Judy slumped back in her seat and chewed the insides of her cheeks.

"We'll find him," said Alice. "Don't you think he's probably just wandering around somewhere? Where was he last time, by the Giant?"

Jacob knew that what he was doing counted as "hovering." *Quit hovering. Don't hover when I'm reading.* His parents didn't shoo him away now, though, and in fact they seemed hardly to have noticed him. When his mother finally did look at him, she said, "I guess you'd better come. But be quick about it. And you're still grounded when we get back." Jacob went for his Celtics jacket before anyone could object.

Cars on Pinyon during snowstorms were treated like members of a presidential motorcade. At the sound of tires easing up the middle of the road at two or three miles an hour, shouts of "Car!" "Car!" "Car!" would pass up and down the street, and all the cold patient faces would watch seriously from the curb.

Judy, whose knees were forced up almost to her chin in the backseat, reached over and took Jacob's hand. "Hey, I haven't said hello to you. I love you. You guys are awesome for helping out like this. Your family is so amazing. I mean that."

She was as tall as Jacob's father and, like him, her body had the presence of a block of clay. She lived in the bleak part of Bethesda past the strip of shops on Bradley, and she seemed to Jacob proof that adults could remain funny and lively and crude.

She came to the Vines' for dinner a couple of times a

month, and she'd tower in the kitchen, her skirt like a curtain, her earrings long and jingling, her face a beaming slab. She was always stepping onto the back patio to smoke, and Jacob would go with her. He liked the smell, and he liked the pained expression she wore when she inhaled. "If you ever smoke, I'll kill you," she'd say. "I'm serious. You'd get sick. I'm not saying you're weak, but." She wore heavy makeup, and she laughed unlike any of his parents' other guests, throwing back her head and emitting something between a yell and a snort. She could also sing. Toward the end of dinners, when she had had more wine than his parents would drink in a week, Arthur, shining and stuffed, would say, with a look at the kids, "Judy, why don't you give us a little concert?"

"I hate people watching me," she'd say, turning her chair to face the bookshelves.

And then, after a rich pause, her voice would fill the room. The first time he'd heard it, Jacob wouldn't have been any more surprised if tiny fireworks had exploded over her head, or if she had transformed in her chair into a cheetah. The song was "Sometimes I Feel Like a Motherless Child," and she sang it so sincerely that in addition to delight and astonishment he felt a surge of alarm, as if she had burst into tears rather than into song. When she turned back toward the table she was flushed, spreading her napkin over her lap, and Arthur gave everyone at the table a knowing look.

Away from the dinner table, though, Arthur held her up as a cautionary tale. Her mistakes, her disasters, formed a fable whose moral the kids were always to keep in mind.

The seven-month first marriage for which she'd dropped out of college, the plan to move to Alaska and spend a year on a salmon boat, the jobs that she'd always quit just as she realized she was going to be fired. Don't live in your head, the lesson went. Don't rely on your talents, because other people will never think as much of them as you do. Learn to manage a budget, repair an air conditioner. Arthur owned, with a partner, a successful hardware and housewares store in Bethesda called Griggs', and this meant he had the right to pull down and recite from books about World War II in the hoarse, emotional voice of a teacher. He, Jacob understood, kept his talent like a gleaming spare tire in the trunk. Not Judy.

"Was Aaron upset about something, or—?" his mother asked Judy.

"I don't think so, I mean, we had a good week, I'm pretty sure he was having fun. What I really keep worrying about is what if he did try going to Michael's house—what if he didn't run away this time, what if somebody took him."

The mention of a kidnapping was enough to make Jacob wriggle forward in his seat. He kept his face an inch from the window, staring out as if he were on a safari. Every parked car, telephone pole, garbage bag was sharpened by the possibility of concealing Aaron—and the face of every person who walked by was charged with the possibility of concealing evil. He thought, fondly, of Aaron locked in a pitch-black closet (as Aaron had once locked him, not even letting him out when he'd cried and swore to God he couldn't breathe).

When they turned onto the web of streets on the other side of Piedmont, Arthur said they should split into two groups. Will and Jacob and Arthur would get out and walk toward the park, and Judy and Alice and Cara would drive around toward school. They'd all meet back at the Vines' house in an hour to see if anyone had called.

As they walked Arthur started a game. *"There once was a man from France, who didn't wear any . . ."*

"Pants?" Jacob said, with slight despair.

These streets, though part of Waggoner, were separated from the Vines' side of town by a stretch of gravel and a thicket of bamboo that seemed to Jacob as meaningful a boundary as the one between countries. Doug Winston and Leo Niack and Stuart O'Brien happened to live over here—these were boys who'd get into fights and then return to class with torn shirts and red, elated faces. Jacob both dreaded and craved running into one of them. Aaron was understood, even by these boys, to be fearsome. He was in sixth grade already, and smoked, and was widely believed to have been naked with a girl from camp. Being related to Aaron was the most, and possibly only, intimidating thing about Jacob.

"You do one now," said Arthur.

"A cat walked down the street, looking for some . . ."

"Meat," said Arthur. "Good one."

A pair of girls from Will's grade wrestled at the bottom of a steep lawn a few houses away. They didn't wrestle to hurt, as boys did, but rather to perform, to give themselves an excuse to shriek and dissolve in laughter.

"Hey!" one of them called out. "Hey! Will! Come here for a second! We have to ask you something!"

"I can't," he called back. "I'm doing family stuff." He kept his face pointed straight ahead.

"Stop flirting," Jacob hissed, once they were safely away. It was the first time they had talked since morning.

"Screw yourself."

"Hey!" Arthur said, a halfhearted bark.

"I hate you," Jacob said, wincing at the taste in his throat that told him he might cry. Doom seemed to settle over him, cold as the air. He hoped that whoever had taken Aaron would take Will too, and that Will would have to eat stale bread in a dripping basement. *I'll never talk to him again*, Jacob thought, and just then *never* didn't seem extreme or unlikely. It seemed, instead, like the shortest possible time in which Will could be made to feel the proper measure of regret.

On the night Will moved out, they got into bed just as they always did, and Will even listened patiently as Jacob described, in lavish and invented detail, that day's recess football game. But after their lights had been out for a few minutes—when Jacob's thoughts had just begun to tilt toward sleep—he woke up to the sound of Will rustling in his bed. He was gathering the blanket around himself, sitting up, and then, without saying a word, he was out the door.

Just outside their room was a space that they hardly used. It had a bookshelf full of basketball almanacs and Guinness books, a pair of wicker baskets full of coarse-haired or balding stuffed animals. Now—while Jacob watched from their doorway—Will made himself a bed in this area, laying together a row of the itchy blue pillows that stood stacked by the banister. He lay down on these pillows, sighed, and didn't move.

Was he sleepwalking? (Occasionally Will had "night terrors," during which he crashed around the house, sweating profusely.)

With his heart pounding, Jacob pulled the blanket from his own bed and went out to join Will on the floor. The carpet was stiff but thick, covered in a layer of Finney's pale hairs, and Jacob tried to imagine, as he settled down under his covers, that he was comfortable, and that, if need be, this could become a tolerable new arrangement. Will didn't stir.

After a few minutes Alice appeared at the head of the stairs. She came onto the third floor, their floor, only rarely. She wore her long white nightshirt, and she took a few steps onto their carpet, but instead of speaking she gave them both a pitying, helpless look. Jacob felt that he'd been caught at something shameful. "What are you guys knocking around about? You aren't going to get any sleep out here, are you?" She spoke quietly, almost as if to herself, and then she turned and headed back down the stairs.

Jacob had no doubt now that Will was awake. And he knew too that if he were to say a word, or even to breathe too loudly, then Will was going to stand up. Only if he kept absolutely still was there a chance that Will would actually fall asleep, and that their new arrangement would be able to settle into place. But after waiting for as long as he could bear, Jacob turned to scratch his side—and sure enough, Will stood up. Again he gathered his blanket around him, and then, before going back into their room, he looked down and met Jacob's eyes with an expression of unconcealed dislike. Jacob stood up, holding his breath, and followed Will back in.

"What are you doing?" Will said, as he spread his blanket over his mattress.

"I'm trying to go to bed."

"Why do you keep following me?" Will shook out his pillow.

"I want to sleep in our room if you are."

At this Will finally turned around. "Don't you get it?" he said. He spoke coldly, calmly, strokes of a knife. Without his glasses his eyes looked oddly naked. "I don't want us to share a room anymore. I don't want to be anywhere near you." Jacob felt, for the first time, the pain of hearing the words that he had most been dreading. The clarity, the chilly numbing flood.

Trying to act exactly as if Will had never spoken, Jacob went ahead and settled into his bed. Now he was crying, but quietly, and he didn't say a word or move—instead he held the blanket pinned to his throat—when Will gathered his bedding again and shuffled back out of the room.

Jacob heard, or imagined that he heard, someone at the top of Chapel Road. "Hello?" he called, sprinting up the street. "Aaron? Hello?"

The old man who lived in the last house on the street turned, not setting down his shovel. "Who?" he said. His Rottweiler opened his eyes where he slept in the snow. The man was known for running the annual Back to School Classic with furious slowness, as well as for writing outraged letters to Waggoner, demanding that students take recess indoors because the noise was keeping his wife awake. His thin bare legs poked out from a pair of sneakers underneath his coat. "What are you doing?" He glanced at his dog, who now stood staring.

Jacob watched him for a second, paralyzed by the dog's attention, before running back down the street to his father and Will, calling, "It wasn't him. It was some guy, but he hasn't seen anything."

"You didn't even ask him anything," Will said.

"Yes I did, shut up."

Did the old man keep a cage in his basement? Did he hold lots of boys in it, or just one at a time? Did he starve his dog, to make sure that the boys' bodies wouldn't lie around?

The wind had taken on a higher pitch, and, except for Arthur muttering as he adjusted his hat, they talked almost not at all as they walked on. The search had begun to feel like a march. The entrance to the park was marked by three waist-high wooden posts, each one softly capped with snow. It seemed impossible that in this landscape, as strange and forbidding as Pluto, Jacob's team held soccer practice every spring. The only life in the park was the people sledding down the hill from the parking lot.

They were, Jacob saw, probably high school kids, a few years older than Aaron, and to Jacob this meant that they were no less adult than his father. It was three boys and two girls, all trying to pile onto one plastic sled. Jacob didn't notice that there were bottles on the ground until one of the girls knocked one over. Will stood slightly back. Arthur walked straight toward them, undaunted.

"He's in, what, sixth grade?" said one of the boys. "Isn't he the kid who put Vaseline on Mrs. Tyson's car?"

"That sounds about right. But you haven't seen him?"

"No. Why would we have seen him?"

"He's been missing. He said he was sleeping at a friend's house last night but he didn't make it."

"Huh." And then, after a pause, "You know what, we did hear somebody screaming a little bit ago."

"Yeah?"

"Seriously!" the boy said. "Didn't we? It was like—*Ah! Ah! Ah!*" The sound the boy made was breathy and girlish, and his friends fell over each other laughing.

"Well, thanks for all your help," Arthur said. He led them out of the park the way they'd come, and he now walked a few steps ahead.

"Are they lying about hearing someone?" Jacob said, hurrying.

"I think they probably are."

"Why would they do that?"

"Trying to be funny, I guess."

"What's funny about it?"

"Wait," Will said, "shut up, was that our horn?"

"Don't tell me to shut up."

"*Shush.*" Arthur stopped and tilted his head. At the sound of three more bleats, he led them stumbling through the snow.

Afterward Jacob imagined it like this: Aaron slipping out the back door while Judy and whoever was her boyfriend then—probably Ray, the stumpy fireman—kissed and watched TV on the couch. Aaron might have called out that he was sleeping at Michael's, but he might not even have done that.

He would have hurried off looking for trouble, seeing the possibilities of trouble in everything, the way certain robots looked around and saw only heat.

He would have found it, Jacob thought, in someone's yard: an abandoned sled, or one that a little kid was using. He would have grabbed it and run (he was infuriatingly fast). And when he finally slowed down, having jumped fences and slipped through bushes, he would have come out on a street crowded enough to get lost in. He would have taken a ride or two, possibly trading his sled for a better one, laughing at his luck, bumping into people. And at some point, dizzy and cold, he would have stood up and seen the yard, the driveway, the house with its lights. And he'd have known exactly where he was.

They found the Volvo parked in front of the Buggis' house at the bottom of the street. Cara sat in Alice's lap in the driver's seat, wriggling and pressing the steering wheel.

Mrs. Buggi stood at the edge of her yard, talking to Alice through the open window. "It was just twenty, no, fifteen minutes ago. Right where you know that path goes between the FedEx and the photo place? Just right out of the corner of my eye." Jacob knew her from the Waggoner Book Fair, where she sat at the table with the money and said, "Well aren't *you* a serious reader!"

Once they were all back in the car Arthur reached forward and twisted the heat as high as it would go. "Do we think it was really him?" he said.

"It has to be," said Judy. "If we don't find him soon I'm going to blow my brains out. Peter's going to kill me so I might as well."

There was no one on the sidewalk in front of the FedEx, no one in the parking lot, no one on the path. "Shit," Judy said, looking around. "Shit. Excuse me, guys. Shit. I really wanted him to be here." The street looked like an empty stage.

"What's that down there?" Will said, and all the air in the car went still. Of course it was Will who'd seen it, Jacob thought. There was a dark lump in the middle of the road, fifty feet away. "That's just—," Arthur said, but he didn't finish, because the closer they got the less it looked like a traffic cone or a rock. Something unmoving, not yet covered in snow, just where Carlton crossed Euston.

"Where?" said Cara, squirming in Alice's lap. "Where? I can't see."

"Wait, we have to stop," Judy said. "You go. You go. I can't. I can't. Oh God. Oh my God." She bobbed in her seat and bounced her hands on her legs.

Arthur and Will stepped out of the car, and before Alice could stop him, Jacob leapt out to follow. He didn't feel afraid; he felt a narrowing of focus, as if he were walking across a wobbly bridge. *Be dead*, he thought. *Be dead.*

"Jesus Christ," Arthur said. A mound that could have been someone's torso—and something lower to the ground, longer, that could have been an arm. Turned so its back faced the car. Jacob chattered mindlessly with every step. As they got closer, he thought of running back. He glanced over his shoulder but the car was too far away; the space between him and it seemed to be stretching out.

The shape had so clearly become a body, Aaron's body, that when they finally came upon it, it seemed as if someone must have made a switch at the last second. Someone must have taken Aaron away and put this torn bag of road salt in his place. No one could ever have mistaken this for that. The bag, folded over on itself, made of thick brown waxed paper printed with the words MAGIC SALT, had almost certainly been bought at Griggs'. An arc of bluish crystals had poured from the rip and left a fan-shaped place where the wet road showed through.

"Now how the . . .," Arthur said. He gave the bag a light kick, and a gush of salt slipped out.

Back in the car they were quiet the way you are after nearly tripping on a steep set of stairs. While they drove toward home, Judy lit a cigarette without apologizing and blew toward the roof.

At the Vines' house the adults sat around the kitchen and the kids lingered, hoping for stray voltage. Arthur uncorked a bottle of white wine and poured three full glasses. "Can I just give you the number one more time, please, to make sure?" Arthur said into the phone. Judy finished her glass and then went to the fridge to refill it, but she suddenly stopped as if she'd been kicked in the stomach. She leaned over the sink and wailed and let a long clear tail of drool hang out. "Oh, what the *fuck* did I do?" she screamed, and Arthur and Alice's eyes ticked toward each other. *"What the fuck am I doing wrong?"* She kicked the cabinet hard enough to leave a crack.

"The only thing we can do right now is wait," Arthur said. "Wait and then if we don't hear anything, go back out. Let me pour that."

Will slipped off upstairs, and within a minute the light on the living-room phone showed that he was on.

Cara planted herself in front of the playroom TV, knowing that no one would bother her about having already watched her half hour.

Jacob went down to the basement, to think how he might transform the space into not just a new room but into a kind of house within a house. He would bring down a box of cereal and a few bowls and eat his breakfast every morning over on that corner of the Ping-Pong table. He would put all his folders and markers and notebooks on that shelf, and he'd do his homework lying on the couch, which he would also use as a bed. His boom box would go here. He'd tape up a row of drawings all along the wall by the stairs with enough room to add a new one every week. And on this shelf in the closet here he would hide his safe and his—

As Jacob remembered it later, the pair of eyes shone in the dark like a raccoon's. "Shhhh!" Aaron lay curled on his side, his jacket balled under his head, his body hidden by the half-closed sliding door to a closet that usually held nothing but empty picture frames, old oven racks, a shopping bag full of used tennis balls.

"Don't. Say. Anything," Aaron told him. *"Close the door, see how long they take to find us. Come on."*

Jacob felt oddly, almost unbelievably, calm. "Why are you down here?"

"Shhhhh!"

Upstairs in the kitchen Judy had her face in her hands at one end of the table, and his parents sat with the phone between them at the other. From between Judy's fingers came a steady murmur that may not even have been words. "Mom?" Jacob said. "Dad?" He had to say it a few times before anyone looked up.

Did Judy ever think, really, that Aaron had been kidnapped? At the time Jacob would have said yes, of course. But afterward, once the angle from which he saw her had shifted—once her gaudy decorations, her colorful lies, had faded and begun to tatter in his mind—he didn't know. The dramatic disasters she was always at the center of were probably, he thought, as real to her as her made-up face or her boyfriends' promises to propose. Real enough to live by, but not real enough to provide warmth.

He occasionally imagined a scene, once he was grown, that he was fairly sure had no memory as its basis: Judy in her bedroom alone at the end of a day, caught in her closet's cracked mirror, staring straight ahead. Desolate and yet self-aware in a way that Jacob would never, in ordinary life, have given her credit for.

Once Aaron had been dragged up from the basement, once he'd been grabbed and hugged and shaken by the shoulders, Judy seemed to want everyone to take turns remembering just how terrified she'd been. "I was shaking like a fucking...like a buzzer, wasn't I? Jesus! What did I look like? Jacob, I'm sorry. You must have been freaked out when I screamed like that!"

His parents, to Jacob's surprise and dismay, seemed hardly to remember his role in all this. A hero without a parade. As soon as they'd understood what he was saying, they'd rushed down to the basement and he might as well not have been with them at all. Aaron had been down there all last night and all today, like a monster under the bed. He described, smiling proudly, how when Arthur had come down to get the sleds he'd been crouching right behind the boiler holding his breath. And how in the middle of the night he'd snuck up and eaten some leftover chicken from the fridge. "You didn't notice?!"

Now Jacob stood in the doorway to the kitchen feeling invisible and electric, and when his dad put on his coat to take Judy and Aaron home, Jacob insisted on coming along. After they dropped them off he was sure his father would tell him he'd done good, that if he hadn't been with them tonight, well, he didn't like to think about it. Judy and Aaron rode in the backseat, and she held him mashed against her chest as if they'd been separated by a shipwreck. Aaron had a slyly pleased look, and Jacob kept glancing over his shoulder with hate in his eyes. Arthur waited to see them go into the house, and on her stoop, just before she opened the door, Judy spun around and blew a kiss, looking dazzled by her luck.

"Well" was all Arthur said once they pulled out.

"Do you think if I didn't find him he was just going to stay there?"

"I don't think so," Arthur said.

"For the night, though?"

"Maybe, maybe."

"Did you really think, when we got out of the car before, that Aaron was—"

"Yes. For a second I did."

"What would have happened?"

Arthur shook his head and sighed. "*A boy can run from home, but he'll never . . .*"

"Be alone?" said Jacob. "Dial the phone?"

"I was thinking 'eat a bone,' but yours are better. You're too good."

When they were stopped at a light Arthur looked over and, just when Jacob expected to be bathed at last in recognition, he said, "You know, it's a very scary thing, how much we love you guys." Jacob understood that there was something new in Arthur's quick, clotted voice—something other than recognition, but no less important. A tone that sounded almost like an accusation.

They didn't talk again, and a feeling hovered over them like the feeling at the end of a much longer drive than this—mild but broad exhaustion, some hint of disappointment or defeat that could usually be washed away by the first sight of the hotel bed or a good dinner.

The feeling lingered now, though, and followed Jacob up to his room—where the pillow was missing from Will's bed and the clothes were missing from Will's drawers and the lamp was missing from Will's bedside table. All this space was Jacob's now, however little he wanted it. He turned on the radio loud enough for Will to hear in the back bedroom. The eleventh person to call WAVA would get a choice of a fleece or an umbrella. "Turn that down!" Arthur shouted up the stairs, so he turned it off. He felt a sweet painful splinter of resentment. Betrayed and forgotten on all fronts. He hadn't brushed his teeth or even undressed, but as soon as he lay down he didn't feel he had the energy to stand up, and though he dreamt that he was reading his book and considering turning out the light, he had fallen asleep.

A pair of boys outside shouted and laughed, running up and down the hill, and Jacob wove the sound into his dream. He was sledding on his stomach, as frictionless as a bowling ball, down hills and across fields—he could have gone on forever. In the dream the shouting was encouragement, amazement. But when the sound stopped, his dream seemed to stub its toe. He woke up and found that hours had passed, and found too a startling idea waiting for him:

someone had died there in the road, but it wasn't Aaron, it was him.

He would have known, if you'd shaken him awake, that this made no sense, that he was warm and safe at home. But so long as his thoughts could remain half-dipped in sleep, he felt the wet road underneath him and saw the headlights passing by.

Ordinarily he couldn't summon an especially vivid picture of his own face, but now he saw himself perfectly, truer than in a mirror, his face girlish and pale in the streetlights, his hands dirty and trembling. It was an almost unbearable sharpness, like skin through a magnifying glass. He knew that the wind was too loud for anyone to hear him. He understood that he would wither away here—that in fact he had already begun.

The Jacob in his bed turned and nestled into the covers. The Jacob in the snow thought, *So dying isn't really as bad as all that. It's just a giant unbuckling.* The ground had stopped feeling cold now, and the wind no longer hurt. He was a cluster of balloons being snipped free one by one. Good-bye feet, he thought with curiosity but no real pain. Good-bye legs and stomach. Good-bye Will, good-bye Cara, good-bye Mom and Dad. The snips were coming faster now. Good-bye ceiling fan, good-bye taste of backpack straps, good-bye smell of sneezing, good-bye Cheddar cheese microwaved onto a paper towel. Years of having been told to be careful—*stop, drop, and roll; don't touch that knife; don't swim where I can't see you*—had taught him to regard himself as a particularly precious bundle, so the ease of letting it all go alarmed him. He would have to keep it secret. When his head, his mind, the thing he called Jacob, finally went, he felt the same careless joy as when he'd once flung a deck of cards into a swimming pool—good-bye, good-bye, good-bye.

Intimate Letters

At ten years old best friendship is like marriage. Jacob's first best friend, and the one he imagined, without enthusiasm, that he'd spend his life with, was Marek Bondarchuk, a boy with fine black hair and a complexion the color of chicken fat. Marek appeared at Waggoner in fourth grade, and for those first weeks, Alexandra Kohn or Sarah Gross, beaming with virtue, would invite him to pull over his desk at lunch and then he would sit there silently, not participating in or even seeming to understand the conversation, slurping the leftover juice from the tinfoil in which his food had been wrapped. Mrs. Sobolesky spoke to him in the same voice she would have used with a dog.

The class was learning to write letters. Date in the upper right, sender's address in the upper left. A comma after the city. *What are the initials for Maryland again? What about California?* (This was Ira Maccary, whose father lived in LA and who wore Lakers colors every day.) When Mrs. Sobolesky told them to write invitations for imaginary parties, Jacob addressed his to Marek, because no else was certain to receive it without embarrassing him. Jacob understood his mistake as soon as he lay it on Marek's desk.

Marek began to follow Jacob around at recess. He turned out to speak English well enough. "Let's play four-square." "Let's race, on the count of three." "Watch, I can jump over the fence with no hands. Can you?" On Halloween he invited himself to trick-or-treat in Waggoner—he said his parents had insisted on it—and after an evening spent following Jacob and Cara from porch to porch, he handed over all his KitKats and Snickers, his eyes huge with hopefulness. Jacob wasn't such a hard catch. He had begun to fear that he was destined for nothing but conditional friendships, to lingering on the edges of other people's happiness. He fought back his better sense and forged ahead. Suddenly he had a name to call when Mrs. Sobolesky asked for partners.

"This smells like Marek!" Alexandra Kohn shouted, holding up a clear bottle of vinegar during a science lab. This was near Thanksgiving break, after Marek had become something of a pariah.

"This looks like Alexandra!" Marek shouted back, holding up a picture in his textbook of a perfectly ordinary-looking woman using a hair dryer.

Their friendship consisted mostly of carrying out various of Jacob's schemes. They turned the Bondarchuks' living room into a fort. They recorded a radio show in which Jacob was a detective and Marek was a criminal, accused of having killed his neighbor. Jacob tended to lose interest in these ideas halfway through, and Marek would be left to clean up or to explain to his parents why their bedding was draped over the dining room table and covered in masking tape. Marek's parents—his father was an engineer, his mother a day-care teacher—were so happy about Marek's having a friend that they didn't dare complain. Mrs. Bondarchuk told Jacob to invite his parents over for dinner, and asked him about his brother and sister, and sent him home with pockets full of the sticky, dented candies they kept in a heavy glass bowl on the key table.

On weekends, they'd lie in the dark in Jacob's room, Marek in Will's old bed, and Marek would say, "Who do you think is Mrs. Sobolesky's favorite kid?"

"I don't know. Vincent?"

"No. I think she likes you. She's always joking with you. She hates me. She thinks I'm so annoying."

Jacob agreed, but he said, "No. The only person she really doesn't like is Isaac."

"I know! Did you see when Isaac spilled glue? Mrs. Sobolesky said, 'Damn it, Isaac.'"

Jacob hoped this was an acceptable place for their conversation to dock for the night, so he let himself not answer, let his eyes fall shut, let his cheek drift to the pillow...

"Are you awake?"

"Yes."

"Good. I thought I heard you snoring. My mom snores so much my dad sleeps in the study."

"Huh."

"Does anyone in your family snore?"

"I don't know."

"Do you want me to shut up?"

That spring Marek joined Jacob's soccer team, and he was prepared to bear it—to pair off with Marek for all the dribbling drills—until, entirely without meaning to, Jacob fell in love with someone else. He'd known Owen Polo ever since kindergarten and had always thought of him as a not particularly funny class clown, but one day Jacob happened to be standing nearby when Owen was impersonating their coach, a Brazilian man named Viktor. Viktor had a spongy head of white hair and teeth like raw corn kernels. None of the boys would have been surprised to learn that he was eighty. His body was spry, though, and he talked about having played against Pelé in a tone that wasn't overly impressed. He regularly worked himself into a spitting rage.

Owen had turned his feet inward, beaten his hands together like claws, and said in a hoarse, accented voice, "Owen! You are a stupid shit! Go home and never disgust me like this again!" The laughter hit like a revelation. That afternoon Jacob began mooning around after Owen, asking him to do Viktor again and learning that he had many others just as good—Louis Armstrong singing "What a Wonderful World," Mrs. Macomb asking weepily why no one had signed up for her dancing club. Eventually, with a shy smile, he did his Marek impression too—"Vy is everyone battering me? Go to hell! All of you go to hell!"—and Jacob found himself breathless. Owen was short and solid and had a gap between his front teeth that made him seem to be joking even when he wasn't. He was the only boy Jacob knew who already had longish hair.

One day at recess, as Marek and Jacob tossed back and forth a Nerf football with a chunk bitten out, Marek said, "Why is Owen such a show-off?" Jacob murmured and shrugged. "He acts like he's the only one who knows any jokes," Marek said. "He looks like a girl."

Marek realized before Jacob did that Jacob really would abandon him, that such a thing was possible. "Why do you act like that now?" he said. "You're Owen's little toy. I saw you following him after school. You look so stupid. You look like a dog." It was true, but in Owen's company Jacob was happy; it felt as if someone had thrown open the curtains. When they were together they talked easily, with delightful freedom, about which girls in the class they would kiss if they were forced, and about how far their siblings had gone, and about how ridiculous Ethan Blunck was, who cried whenever the Redskins lost, and Sharon Cross, who kept her patrol badge in a plastic bag so it would never get scratched. *Playdate* seemed much too meek a word for their afternoons—they snuck into neighbors' backyards, spied on Owen's brother, wrote other people's initials in wet cement. One day Owen announced that Jacob could put anything he found in the kitchen into a tablespoon and he would eat it for fifty cents. Jacob held out a spoonful of peanut oil, anchovy paste, vinegar, and Marmite (Owen had English cousins), and Owen slurped it into his mouth, then squeezed his eyes shut while he choked it down. Afterward he ran around the house shouting and banging into walls, like a cartoon character with smoke pouring out of his ears, and Jacob thought he would burst from glee.

At the beginning of May, Jacob stopped dragging his desk over to Marek's at lunch. Marek didn't have the sense—or the cowardice—to accept this fate calmly. "You don't want to sit with me anymore?" he said, standing with his lunch above Jacob and Owen. The windows were open, the trees were drooping with green, the air was bright and chaotic with hope and pollen.

"There just wasn't room to move my desk," Jacob said, flushing.

"Woof woof," said Marek.

When he wasn't with Owen, Jacob was replaying conversations they'd had, even muttering the things they'd said, thinking about jokes he ought to have made or jokes he had made that had gone over especially well. Always there were a handful of recent memories—impersonations Owen had done, snatches of a song, faces—that Jacob could touch in his mind to make laughter come spilling out of him like coins. They started calling each other "my liege," or sometimes "liege lord." These were phrases Owen had picked up from a Social Studies unit on feudalism, and Jacob knew only that they had something to do with horses and fields and knights, but he knew that they were absolutely right. Saying them or hearing them gave him a jolt, like tuning forks against his skin.

Marek appeared one afternoon at the Vines' front door. "Here," he said, and shoved a piece of paper into Jacob's hand. "It's yours. I don't want it. I hope you fuck my mother and die."

Dear Marek,
I would be so happy if you would join me next week at my
party. There will be dancers, and magicians, and so much
macaroni and cheese—

Marek stood at the bottom of the porch stairs, watching Jacob read. "You are an asshole to me!" he shouted.

"Marek," Jacob said, with no notion of what else he might say.

"It's too late! I'm not your friend!" Marek took off up the street running.

The clearest signal, in retrospect, that something was wrong with Jacob's mother that spring was the uptick in his freedom. His parents gave in easily when he suggested that he eat leftover spaghetti for dinner in front of the TV, and when he came home late from Owen's house, armed with excuses, he found that they hadn't even wondered where he was. When he climbed into his mother's lap while she sat working at the table, instead of playing with his hair she told him that he was hurting her and nudged him off. He thought at first that this might have to do with Marek and Owen—they were preparing to tell him that he'd done a terrible thing and needed to apologize. Testingly, he said to his mother one day, "I think me and Marek might start being friends with other people now."

"Is that right? That sounds smart."

She was so listless, so frustratingly unreachable, that he asked if she was sick.

"I'm just not feeling very good."

"Why not?"

"Oh, I don't know, I've just got a little something, I guess."

That afternoon Will took Jacob onto the porch and told him, in a voice of strained patience, that their mother's cancer was back. The air was warm and still and there were little brown birds hopping from the patio onto the lawn. They're not sure how serious it is yet, Will said. He told Jacob to picture a smaller version of the bubbly lump on the tree in the front yard. Jacob knew—that is, he could recite the fact—that his mother had had cancer once before, but until now he'd never thought seriously about what it meant. He'd touched the shiny pink scar on her chest; he knew that cancer was something adults took seriously and had fund-raisers about; but he didn't understand that it killed people, or that it might kill his mother. It seemed to him, like tampons and hemorrhoids, one of the disgusting but not necessarily important features of the adult world. "Can't she just take it out, though?" he said to Will.

"That's what they're always talking about. It's not that easy, because sometimes there are little lumps you don't know about in other places. Don't say anything, they don't want you guys to know yet." Jacob decided to hear this as if Will had said that their parents didn't want *Cara* to know, and he silently pledged to protect her. As soon as he was back inside he led his mother by the hand into the pantry and slid the door shut. There, under the bare bulb, between family-size boxes of Cheerios and canned kidney beans, he asked whether it was true.

"Yes, but we're doing everything we can to get me better. You shouldn't waste one single minute worrying about me."

They hugged and, before she opened the door, she pulled a pudding pop from the ice-crusted freezer and promised Jacob that they were all going to take care of each other.

The next day Jacob told Owen about his mom and Owen shrugged and said that his grandfather had lung cancer and that it wasn't such a big deal except he had to drag around an oxygen tank. "Is she going to the hospital?" Owen asked.

"No, she's home."

"Oh."

This was significant to them because they were spending most afternoons then on the Vines' third floor, looking through a book they'd recently discovered. Cara always did her best to detain them downstairs. She'd hop onto the couch beside them and talk out loud to herself as she did her coloring exercises.

"Wait," Owen would suddenly say, during a commercial. "Didn't you leave some homework upstairs?"

"That's right! Let's go get it."

One of his parents might call out from the bedroom as he and Owen hurried up the stairs, but usually not, and anyway they wouldn't come into his room without knocking.

The book, *Changing Bodies, Changing Lives*, was a large white paperback, and though they'd found it on Will's shelf they now kept it in the drawer in Jacob's bedside table. Jacob had looked at it a few times before, and on his own he'd found nearly all of it not only boring but off-putting—there were chapters about birth control and fallopian tubes and self-esteem that were best flipped past entirely. But now, with Owen, Jacob found a handful of pages that seemed to have a direct effect on his heart, as if he'd injected something.

On one much-consulted page were side-by-side drawings of the male and female genitalia. The perspective was startlingly frank, legs spread, hair realistically filled in, even the sad little anus given its wrinkles. A page later were these same two people standing facing forward, their faces expressionless, as forthright and shameless in their nudity as Neanderthals. And then, farther down the same page, the same couple joined in intercourse, to demonstrate how the parts fit together. It seemed impossible that all over the country people were doing this to one another.

But they were, anywhere from one to four times a week. This and many other facts like it they got from the long *"Exploring Sex with Someone Else"* section of the book. They read these pages compulsively, in no particular order, so that they would still, after months of study, stumble onto passages they hadn't yet memorized, words they hadn't yet decoded.

Linda, fifteen, from Michigan: I was over at my boyfriend Mike's house and we were lying on his bed kissing and everything, and he took my hand and put it down his pants so I could feel his penis. But I didn't know what I was supposed to do, I had never done that before.

David, seventeen, from California: I can't stand to ask the guy in the drugstore for rubbers. He acts like he's my priest or something.

The thought that he might eventually have such problems froze Jacob inside—he was terrified but giddy, and he couldn't imagine speaking to anyone about it except Owen.

By fall they had graduated to a magazine called *Intimate Letters*. Owen had taken it—this didn't bear thinking about—from a box in his mother's closet. It was the size of a *Reader's Digest*, printed on grayish paper like newspaper, and it was full of actual snapshots with heavy thighs and tufts of hair and bald men snarling in ecstasy. Around these pictures were thousands of words sent in by people all over the country who felt the need to confess what they'd been up to. There was the stewardess from Milwaukee who snuck under a blanket with a passenger when their plane was grounded in the snow. The man from Phoenix who arrived home on his birthday to find that his wife had hired twins who were waiting in the bathtub ("one birthday I'll *never* forget"). Jacob found the stories almost too compelling—he couldn't look straight at the page, as if something in him might burst or come unglued. He didn't dare let *Intimate Letters* inside his house.

The Polos lived in a smaller, unrenovated house, on a street with carports rather than garages. Their kitchen was cramped and yellow with a peeling linoleum floor, a dingy sink, a small table covered in a red oilcloth. The house had two floors, but Owen shared a room with his younger brother (Jacob nodded solemnly when Owen complained about this) and from anywhere in the house you could clearly hear the conversation of anyone who was home. Owen's mother, dreary and enormous, always was. She lay beached in her easy chair, reading *TV Guide*, shouting for someone to bring her the mail. Everything about the house seemed to Jacob to broadcast the message, *This is a family without a father.*

"Owen, who is this?" Mrs. Polo said the first time Jacob came over. "Are you and Peter having a falling out? Is this a new friend? Come in here and talk to me. Don't just disappear up the stairs, I won't bite, come here. Who are you?"

After a few minutes ("Oh, all right, your father's the Griggs' guy. Does he fix dryers?"), she told Jacob he could go just as soon as he handed her the remote.

"My mom's insane," Owen said once they were upstairs. "I usually come in the other door."

They spent their time there in Owen's room—whose door had a hook-in-eye lock—reading *Intimate Letters* in silence on Owen's bed, pausing occasionally to compare their trembling erections. Each page of dense type was a hideous gift. Owen had shown Jacob how to masturbate, and so when they read something especially potent they'd retreat to separate corners of the room and rub themselves to dry, half-painful spasms after which they'd want the book away from them, buried in the woods. "Let's not look at it for two weeks and see what happens." "Let's do four weeks."

Once they had gone through most of the stories, they started working on one of their own. They wrote on Owen's older brother's word processor, a gray machine about the size of a book. *David took his huge hard dick...Karen squeezed her boobs and said...* They had the vague idea of sending it in to the New Jersey address in the front of the magazine, signing it with Marek's name. They called the story "Orgasms in the Mist" and printed out their progress each afternoon on paper with perforated edges, which they kept underneath a stack of binders on Owen's desk.

Eating dinner at home after working on the story seemed impossible to Jacob, as if his skin were stained by what he'd done, and the only way he could manage it was by making himself into two boys. There was the Jacob who sat with his parents at the picnic table on the patio and who preferred milk to soda, who had been so moved by the sled dog's death in the fourth-grade reader that he had wept into Finney's fur, and there was the Jacob who that afternoon had paused to ask whether *blow job* has a space in it.

Jacob had the feeling that Owen had a second self to settle into as well, and, although they never talked about it, this was the purpose of the long walks they took just before separating at six o'clock—on these walks they never, or almost never, said a word about sex. First Owen would walk Jacob the seven minutes back to his house, then Jacob would turn and walk Owen back to his house, and often, since they still weren't done talking—and since Jacob still didn't feel fit to be alone—Owen would walk Jacob home again.

"Do you ever think we're too perverted?" Owen asked one day.

Jacob's heart picked up and he said, "Too perverted for what?"

"I don't know, why aren't most people like this?"

"I think we're just mature. I think most people probably get this way when they're thirteen or fourteen. And we're not that perverted."

Sometimes during the evenings, sitting at his desk filling out his multiplication tables while his parents murmured in the other room, Jacob promised himself that starting tomorrow he'd stop reading and writing these stories, stop pulling down his pants, stop masturbating, stop living a life that shamed him as much as if he'd been a murderer. Just thinking of those pages sitting in Owen's room made something cold plunge in his chest. He needed to throw out his life, return to the self he'd had when he'd been friends with Marek. He needed to play Mouse Trap and fall asleep in front of Robin Williams movies; he needed to find a basketball court far away where he could spend his afternoons learning to dribble between his legs. He thought of how recently his penis had been for nothing but sending apple-juice-colored pee arcing into the toilet. He thought of Cara racing through the sprinkler in the front lawn and the blameless miniature butt she had in front. Enough with obsessing over the hair and spasms and squirts. His resolve would last all the way until the next morning, when a phrase—*wet pink pussy, hot throbbing cock*—would appear and turn his mind into a ballooning sail, pushing him helplessly to the place where he least wanted to go.

One night that fall a friend of Jacob's parents named Sandy came over for dinner. Sandy had once been his parents' doctor, but now that he'd given up his practice he and Arthur stayed in touch mostly by playing tennis once every month or two. In spite of being shaped like a medicine ball, Sandy was vigorous in a way Jacob associated with his being European (he'd grown up in Belgium). He seemed always to be traveling— bike trips in China and hiking trips in Italy—and whenever he came to the Vines' he handed over gifts—wooden puppets from Prague, spiced Gouda from Amsterdam—with slight irritation, as if he were passing them along on a stranger's behalf.

Sandy had no children and no wife, and he was (this fact towered above everything else that Jacob knew about him) extraordinarily rich. Around him Arthur seemed to Jacob slightly shorter than usual. Sandy's wealth had something to do with medical devices. Jacob and Will and Cara had once gone along to a party at his house in Georgetown, and it had been the only time Jacob had ever seen his father in a tuxedo or his mother in a long dress. They were like strangers. Waiters had slid through the crowd wearing white suits and carrying silver trays, and the size of the staircase curving up to the second floor had made Jacob think not of any house he knew but of the Kennedy Center.

Tonight Sandy brought with him to the Vines' his on-again off-again girlfriend and travel partner, Meg. She had long black hair and bright lipstick and laughed too loud at her own jokes; the kids liked her more than their parents did. She always let them take Hershey's Kisses and gummy worms from the cool depths of her purse. She spent the beginning of the evening—when the adults usually sat on the couches in front of the fireplace—in the kitchen with Jacob and Cara, showing Cara how to put on makeup. A tampon fell out of her bag once, and Jacob had to pretend not to know what it was while she stuffed it out of sight. Will now sat in her place in the living room, saying nothing but listening intently, sipping his glass of water as if it were wine.

The reason for this particular dinner, though Jacob didn't know it until afterward, was his mother's sickness. Sandy had given his parents the name of a specialist at Penn, and this conversation had led to their saying they had to get together.

Through the wall, while he ate his Stouffer's macaroni and cheese straight from the microwavable tray, Jacob heard the evening mostly as Sandy's low voice, a steady accented murmur. When Jacob eventually wandered in, a postmeal trawling for fondness, he found the living room oddly quiet—no music on the stereo and no great gusts of laughter. It was as if he were interrupting a séance.

"Why's everyone acting so weird?" Jacob said to his father's back, just louder than a whisper.

"We're not acting weird. Come here. Why not show everybody that thing with a quarter?"

Jacob pulled a quarter from his pocket and, after a couple

of fumbles, made it disappear. All the adults applauded. It seemed to Jacob that there were times when he was asked to act out someone else's idea of being a child—when a relative would appear with a video camera and demand that he repeat something; when his father would tell him to ask his mother to dance—and these times both pleased and unsettled him. He could do it, of course, and he was glad to have the attention, but he knew there was something untrustworthy going on, some mutual deception whose terms he couldn't quite make out. He wished they would either tell him why they were acting so strange or stop.

Instead the adults stood slowly up from the table and, after Sandy and Meg had feebly offered to help doing the dishes and put on their coats, they all stood in the open doorway, noticing the rain. Will held Finney to keep him from running for the street. Jacob sat quietly on the stairs, shuffling a deck again and again, trying to leave the aces undisturbed.

Sandy said, "I did really mean it about Christmas. The place will just be sitting there. It might be just the thing. Colonialism by the seaside."

"You're very nice," Arthur said. "I think we'll have to see if—"

"Really, thank you," Alice added. "We'll talk about it. You-know-who can get strange about tradition sometimes, so—"

"*Who* can get strange?" said Jacob, mugging helplessly. Only Meg laughed.

They lobbed farewells at one another as the door swept

slowly shut. "Dinner was great!" "Drive home safe!" "Keep practicing that trick!" "We'll call you soon!"

"And I'll call with the name of the man who gives the massages," Sandy said, "People have told me it makes a huge difference." *Click*.

"So," Arthur said, leading Jacob into the kitchen, "how does Christmas on the beach sound? Their place is probably awfully fancy. Here, let's clean up, so Mommy doesn't have to do it. You hand me the dishes and I'll load." The water turned Arthur's hands pink. "Saint Bart's is near where we went on our honeymoon. We were on a boat, so we went to a bunch of places. That's where that picture of us in the goofy white hats is from." He was silent as he scraped off the last plate, meaning he was about to change course. "Don't give us too hard a time if we're acting funny, okay? This is scary stuff with your mother." He took a large spiny handful of silverware from Jacob and dropped it into the rack. There was another voice adults used, one just as clear as the invitation to make yourself into a cartoon of a child, but much rarer. *I know this isn't how we ordinarily talk*, this voice said, *but I'm exhausted, and here I'm going to tell you something real. Please don't make me regret it.*

Jacob bragged to Owen about the Caribbean. He told him that Sandy lived on his own island, accessible only by helicopter. He insisted, so confidently that he wondered eventually if it was true, that a certain TV commercial— a dolphin leaping arcs along a white beach—had been filmed at the very place he was going. He had no idea what side of the country the Caribbean was on, or even if it was part of America, but he knew enough to promise that the local women went topless and that children drank piña coladas and that the sea turtles lolled just offshore, waiting to be ridden.

(The unwelcome memory arose in him of Marek, when he was first securing Jacob's friendship, saying that in Latvia his family had had a pet lion and hundreds of servants.)

Owen, though, failed to be properly impressed, so Jacob said, "What if you came with us?" They were sitting in Owen's room, and Owen was plucking an acoustic guitar that for months had been missing its two highest strings. Jacob felt as if he had drawn a magic wand out of his pocket.

"Mom?" Owen hollered down the stairs. "Can I go on vacation with the Vines?"

"What? When?"

"Christmas. His parents said it's fine. *Mom*?"

"I don't see why you couldn't. Don't you like going to Uncle Barry's? Oh, I guess it doesn't matter."

Owen bounded across the room and lay on top of Jacob and kissed him loudly on the forehead. Jacob grinned and blushed and said now all they had to do was get tan so they wouldn't get laughed at on the beach.

Jacob managed not to realize right away the position he'd put himself in. And when he did realize, he swallowed hard and lied yet again, this time to himself: his parents would give in and let Owen come. Either that or Owen's mom would at the last minute forbid him. The same forces that protected Jacob when he biked without a helmet or when he glanced at Russell Moyer's reading quiz would keep him from harm.

Owen peppered him with questions every afternoon. Were there sharks there? Could they bring Luke's word processor and write a special Caribbean edition of "Orgasms in the Mist"? Would Jacob draw on this piece of paper exactly how their private hut looked? (Jacob drew a suite with indoor and outdoor pools, two enormous beds, a shower with a retractable roof.) Would there be girls their age there? In bathing suits? Would *they* go topless?

One afternoon Mrs. Polo called out, "Jacob! Jacob! Come down here and talk to me." All the color left Jacob's face and it didn't return when she turned off the TV and hauled herself up to sit with him at the kitchen table. "Don't look so miserable! You boys really need to learn how to act around adults, you're like squirrels.

"I want to get your parents a gift, and I want to ask you what you thought they'd like. Do they like chocolate? I've got a place I go that has amazing fudge. Or else I could get them a big bunch of flowers. I just need to know. I don't want them to think I'm not grateful for you guys taking Owen away like this, even if I wish they'd called to ask me first."

"I don't think they want anything," he said quietly. "I don't know, I could just tell them thanks if you want."

"Right, let's just have you be the messenger—my God, serves me right. No, I'll do it. Go back up and goof off."

(Jacob thought he heard *jerk off* and for an instant he froze.)

Upstairs Owen was still at his desk, with the lamp on in spite of the sunlight coming through the window, working on the cover of "Orgasms in the Mist." He'd been drawing for days, and the page was now so dense with figures that from a distance it looked nearly black. There were breasts hovering like clouds, men with penises twice as long as their arms, women floating spread-legged down winding rivers. (In college, when Jacob first saw a painting by Bosch, he thought immediately of Owen.)

"What did she want?"

"Nothing. She wants to get my parents something."

"Really? Why?"

"For the Caribbean."

"I think she's worried I like your family better than her," Owen said, not looking up. "I guess she's right."

For the first time Jacob saw a bit of Marek in Owen, just as he saw a bit of bleakness in the cramped and gym-short-smelling bedroom, and it gave him a start. Pleasures go suddenly stale all the time—a wild water fight becomes, when you try to repeat it, as inert as a game of checkers—but Jacob had thought that his and Owen's friendship was different. Maybe not. Maybe sex and silliness could go flavorless too, could leave you bored and embarrassed and checking your watch.

"Wait," said Owen, suddenly serious. "What is that?"

"Where?"

"Over here. Come here. Quiet. Look."

Jacob crept across the room, all senses straining, but it wasn't until he was nearly over Owen's shoulder that he saw the joke: Owen wasn't wearing any pants. His bottom half was naked in his seat, his butt bare against the plastic, his penis like a purple thumb pointing upward. Owen broke into his gap-toothed grin, spun a full circle in his chair making his Dr. Claw face, and Jacob burst into laughter so powerful that his stomach burned. He fell back on the bed, tears on his cheeks, his worry washed away like a spiderweb under a hose.

Jacob parents referred a fair amount to Christmas around him, but it was like an argument in which they weren't allowed to spell out the exact disagreement. Arthur wondered aloud whether it might not be fun to bring the Nintendo along. Alice asked, quietly, how the pilot of the little plane was going to know where to find them at the airport.

When Jacob's mother suffered—even when she just had a headache—she became like one of those Indian fishermen in a *National Geographic* photo, poling out to the center of a lake, majestically alone. The chemo once every two weeks left her feeling, she said, as if she had a low-grade flu: she would pause to gather herself before every trip up the stairs or even across the room. As soon as dinner was over she would make her way creakily to bed.

Jacob knew that she was getting sicker, knew that for a few days after each treatment they were not to bother her, but it still didn't seem possible to him that this might not be temporary. Even the new seriousness of his family—the constant grave-sounding calls from his grandmother and aunts and uncles—seemed proof only of adults' strange love of drama. They lived for calling to check on one another, giving advice, comparing stories. It was a dance, like the chatter when they ran into each other in the grocery store. His parents had sat them all down, Cara included, and explained that she was sicker than they'd thought at first, that people died of this. (But not *us*, Jacob thought.) Arthur said they would answer any questions they wanted to ask. All Jacob could think of was, if she was so sick now, why didn't she stay in the hospital until they made her better? His father sighed and stood up to rub his face.

Arthur was a doting nurse. It was the same role he played when one of the kids was sick: a large but light-footed angel, slipping into the room to deliver a warm washcloth or to carry away a cold mug of tea. She kept the lights off in their bedroom, and sometimes Jacob would follow Arthur in to see her. Arthur would sit down beside her, a hand lightly on her back, talking in a voice just slightly different from the one he used with the kids. "This is miserable," she said one afternoon, her mouth pressed against the pillow. Her bedside was piled with books and a week's worth of water glasses.

"I know. I know. But I talked to Dr. Ostro this afternoon. He gave me somebody's name at Columbia."

"I don't want to go to Columbia."

He rubbed her back as gingerly as if she were a sack full of feathers. "Say hi to Jacob—he's here."

"Hi, sweetie."

"Hi, Mom."

Jacob hung from the cold brass footboard and stared at her body under the covers. He daydreamed sometimes about discovering a cure, rushing into their bedroom with a bottle of potion, watching the color come back to her face, her hair grow thick. When she was up she usually wore Will's Vikings cap, but now it lay on the floor and he could see the places where her hair had become pale fluff, like combed cotton candy. Her face, when he saw it directly, reminded him of a mask: eye sockets and cheekbones and jawbones all pressing out from under skin as dull as tracing paper. The whole room had begun to smell like ointment and unwashed sheets. She seemed as fixed in their bed as a lizard in its case.

But one afternoon when Jacob and Owen were upstairs reading *Intimate Letters*—Jacob had let the magazine inside after all—they heard such light footsteps on the stairs that they nearly missed them. The doorknob turned and there, in her cap and a long blue sweater, Alice stood smiling in the door. She had days, rarer and rarer now, when she woke up feeling like her old self only thinner. She wanted to do something fun, she said. (Jacob stuffed the magazine into the crack between the bed and the window, and he saw his mother realize that there was a secret on their faces, and he saw too that out of kindness or discomfort she was going to let it pass.)

Her idea was to have them make paper turkeys for the table at Thanksgiving. Jacob felt about Owen seeing his mother, especially in daylight, the same speechless mortification that he felt when his father, in the pool locker room, used to step out of his bathing suit and reveal his hanging hairy balls.

Once they got downstairs it became clear that these turkeys were Cara's project—she sat in the middle of a rug spread with construction paper and safety scissors—and that Alice, in a moment of hopefulness, had thought they all might join in and make a memory of it.

"Owen, why don't you be in charge of cutting these," she said. He took the brown pages stiffly and began to cut, frowning at his hands. Owen's charms were completely untranslatable to the adult world, and Jacob watched helplessly—coloring eyes onto each of the turkeys that Cara glued—as Owen failed to respond to his mother's questions with more than a word, failed to smile, failed to behave even for an instant as if he were anything other than a prisoner.

Jacob stood up and said, "Come get a Coke," and then led Owen into the kitchen, where they stood by the fridge and whispered.

"I think you should probably go home," Jacob said.

"Okay. My coat's upstairs, though."

"I'll bring it to you tomorrow."

"Do you think your mom noticed anything?"

"No, we're fine."

Just before he let himself out the door, Owen turned and said, with a hint of apology, "You know, at least your mom's way less fat than mine." Jacob nodded and headed back into the living room, where his mother was sweeping scraps into piles with her hands while Cara squeezed dots of glue onto Popsicle sticks.

"Did Owen go?"

"Mm-hmm."

"He's shy, huh?"

"I guess."

"Well I certainly didn't mean to ruin your afternoon. I hope he wasn't spooked by me. I just figured we ought to spend some time together."

When Jacob's father gathered them to say they wouldn't be going to the Caribbean after all, he didn't need to explain that it was because of their mother. She'd been home all that week from work, and it had begun to take serious effort to imagine her dragging bags through the airport, or even just to imagine her lying in the sun in her bathing suit. She was never the one who wanted to travel, and the understanding had made its way to all of them that for now, and probably from now on, her wants were the ones that mattered.

Jacob didn't tell Owen that the trip was canceled. This would have been as hard to confess as the fact that Owen had never been invited at all. Thanksgiving passed, full for the Vines of tearful toasts to family; night began falling at five o'clock, then four-thirty. Jacob and Owen had finished "Orgasms in the Mist" and moved on to a story, less successful, about sex in a submarine. They still spent every afternoon together—they no longer needed to ask whether the other had plans—but some storehouse of joy in their friendship had sprung a leak. One night in December, just after the Vines had finished dinner, the phone rang. It was Owen, sounding agitated and possibly thrilled. Something had happened. Jacob needed to come quick. Meet in front of my house. As fast as you can.

Jacob was out the door in under a minute, and at Owen's in under five, but nonetheless he had time for dread to pool in him. This was, he thought, the knock at the door. The sky was nearly black, the air smelled like snow, the trees had been bare so long that it was impossible to remember them with leaves. Even the houses with Christmas lights and Santa masks looked empty. Jacob's sweatshirt had bits of hair clinging to its insides—he'd worn it for a haircut—and it itched terribly.

Since Owen wasn't yet outside, Jacob walked up to the Polos' front window, over which the blinds had been three-quarters lowered. He peeked in at Owen's older brother playing poker with two friends at the coffee table. They used checkers for chips. Luke was seventeen and as fearsome to Jacob as a lion. The window to Owen's bedroom was ten feet from the living room window, and the moment Jacob crept over to it—anyone watching would have thought he was a burglar—he found himself face-to-face with Owen, who gave him a stab of a look, and pointed toward the side door by the kitchen.

"My mom found 'Orgasms.'" Jacob's skin instantly chilled. "I came home and it was just gone. I was looking all over for it, and she made me come into her room and she was holding it."

"What did you do?"

"I didn't say anything, because I thought maybe I could blame it on Luke. But I forgot we put Marek's name on it. She said she knew it was mine. And she said if she ever caught me writing anything else like that, I'd be grounded the rest of the year."

"Jesus. Fuck. What's she going to do with it?"

"I don't know. I don't think anything."

"But what if she tells 'my *parents*?" A squealy desperation had come into his voice.

"I don't know."

They were walking unusually quickly, as if they were being chased, and they didn't stop until they came to the Town Hall tennis courts, empty and netless. The only light was the sodium security lamp in the parking lot.

"What the hell are we going to do?" Jacob said a few times. He considered the mechanics of running away.

(*David put his purple-headed warrior between Karen's boobs and said "Oh my god I'm about to cum," and she smiled and drank his steamy juice.*)

"I don't know. We can't do anything. I think we just have to hope she forgets about it."

Owen picked up a bald tennis ball lying in the parking lot and tossed it against a low brick wall. "I could try telling her Marek really did write it," he said, beginning to smile. "She probably knows he's too stupid, though." Jacob stood watching with his arms crossed. (*She put her fingers inside her sticky box and then waved them all around.*)

What Jacob felt, though he couldn't figure out how to say

it, was something like, *It's really catching up with us, huh?*
The secret shudders and itchy aches, this was what you got,
this was what they ought to have known they'd been court-
ing. If, by pressing a button, he could have done away with
Owen and their terrible, too-close friendship—made the
parking lot open up beneath him—he would have done it
without a second thought.

(*Afterward he smiled and looked at Karen and thought
I'm almost ready to do that again.*)

But there was something else to Jacob's feelings, something nearly unspeakable. Jacob's family was *good*—his
parents loved him, his father hadn't left. Owen's house had
sticky counters and gritty floors, and his mother heated up
dinner in the microwave. Grown-ups liked Jacob, teachers
asked him to deliver messages to other classrooms, gave
him special roles in assemblies. With Owen he was slum-
ming. Hadn't this been in the groundwater of their friendship all along?

Jacob walked Owen back home, where they didn't say
good-bye, and then he trudged up Pinyon, apparently the
only person outdoors in the entire neighborhood. Just as
someone who's been shot in a movie can keep moving for a
few minutes, telling everyone how fine he feels as his shirt
soaks with blood, Jacob walked into his house and went
through the rest of the night in a state that would be easy to
mistake for a quiet mood. Easy for anyone but Will.

"Girlfriend break up with you?" he said.

"He's not my girlfriend."

"Sorry. Boyfriend break up with you?"

"Shut up."

"Don't act so sad. Mom's feeling sick again, so no one cares if your friend won't jerk you off anymore."

That night, once the rest of the house had gone to sleep, Jacob crept out of bed and called Owen. This was in the room where Will had once built himself a bed of pillows, and where the oldest phone in the house—the buttons clicked rather than beeped—sat on an empty shelf.

"We aren't going to the beach. My parents said."

"Because of the story?"

"No. We just aren't. I don't know. I think it's because my mom's sick."

"Bullshit."

"What's bullshit?"

"I'm asking your parents. Say swear to God."

"I swear to God! Ask them! They hate you anyway."

Owen was silent for a few seconds, and Jacob wondered if he was going to peek out from behind his mask and say something funny. Jacob was greedy for it. But instead Owen said, in a voice full of ugly satisfaction, "You know I blamed it all on you, right?"

Jacob was suddenly aware of the pulse in his teeth.

"I told my mom you wrote it. She thinks you're a pervert."

"No you didn't!" Jacob heard Will getting ready to open the door in his room, so he turned to face the bookshelves.

"I swear to God."

"You're lying," Jacob said, but he knew that he wasn't. "I can't believe you, you're such a *liar*!"

"Well, we're even."

Jacob hung up on Owen, something he'd never done and would have thought he'd never do. He sat amazed in the dark, looking around at these bookshelves as if something on them—the travel alarm with no batteries? *James and the Giant Peach?*—might help.

He lay in bed that night feeling flayed, staring at the ceiling, too astonished to cry. He saw Karen and David more clearly than he ever had when he'd been writing about them, and he felt that they had betrayed him too. David had tidy brown hair and the ageless face of a game-show host. Karen was young, pink-skinned, quick to smile. They stared bashfully up at Jacob, naked, like Adam and Eve. He hadn't been able to keep his hands off her sparkly underwear. She hadn't been able to believe how big his thing looked in his pants. They knew not what they did.

The day that the Vines would have left was the sort of day that makes the Caribbean, or any mildness, unimaginable. Fingers throbbed in just the time it took to scratch an itch; the faded Maryland flag over Waggoner cracked and snapped. This was Christmas as Alice always said she wanted it—fire in the fireplace and soup on the stove.

Late in the afternoon she stepped onto the porch to bring in the mail and she nearly tripped over a box the size of a soccer ball. "All right, now who thinks I should open a present early?" she called out. Since canceling the trip she seemed to have been feeling better, a reedy sort of liveliness.

Inside the box, under a layer of shredded cardboard, was a brick of almond fudge, wrapped in clear plastic. The card read: "Capitol Fudge wishes you a Happy Holiday!" Underneath someone had written: "Thank you guys! I mean it! Erin Polo."

"Who's Erin Polo?" Alice said, wandering back into the living room. Arthur, sounding proud, said, "That's Owen's mother. Why?"

So here, Jacob thought, is what the end feels like. He stared down at the deck of cards in his hands, feebly cutting the deck.

"That was awfully nice of her—but what is she thanking us for? Jacob?"

Every detail of the living room felt awful. The dog hairs on the sofa waving and shaking, the wet-looking black-green of the coffee table, the pale spot on the couch where Cara had once ground a piece of Silly Putty.

"Did you give something to Owen?"

"No! I didn't!"

"Huh. Well, I feel bad. I'd always thought she was a little bit of a kook. Isn't she? This is awfully nice. Here, you guys, eat it."

The taste of that fudge, chalky and sickly sweet, would always be connected for Jacob with the realization that he couldn't bear it—anything—anymore. That winter, just as his mother went into the hospital, he had something like a breakdown. He would have expected a breakdown to mean hallucinations or ripping the wallpaper from the walls, but there was none of that. It was more like a car breaking down. He lay down on the couch that evening after eating nearly the whole brick of fudge, claiming to feel—and actually feeling—sick, and he stayed there through dinner, and slept the night there, and then stayed there all the next day and the next one. Whenever he did stand up he felt dizzy, having lain down so long, so he stood up less and less. While Maria, their twice-a-week housekeeper, vacuumed and shook her head, he watched Maury Povich, *The Price Is Right,* breathless documentaries about Super Bowls played long before he was born. The sun rose and fell, rose and fell, and only mattered to him in that it became easier or harder to see the TV.

Mrs. Bruce sent classmates to drop off his homework in a manila envelope sealed by a string. Arthur took him to doctors—medical ones, who tested him for things he didn't have, and psychological ones, who wanted to play board games and talk to him about his mom and whether he had ever thought about hurting himself. He stayed on the couch for nearly two months, in the end. Ordinarily he wouldn't have been able to get away with all this, but now nothing in the house was ordinary. Arthur would sit down beside him sometimes, then lay a heavy hand on his leg or shoulder and say, "You poor duck. This is too much. It's too much for me too." Will, rigid with worry and tact, would sit in the chair at the end of the sofa as if he were visiting Jacob in the hospital and quietly watch the TV. "Are you *dying*?" he said one afternoon, in the middle of their sitting in silence, and when Jacob said no, he saw that Will had been trying not to cry.

Jacob knew this couldn't last forever, but he couldn't imagine either how it might end. He had visions of himself as an old—or anyway older—man, left alone on his couch, accepted for his disability just as a blind person would have been.

One day in February it was Marek who brought him his homework. Jacob recognized his voice saying, "Finney, down! No!" Marek came and looked down at Jacob on his couch as if he were a body in an open casket. "Everyone thinks you're faking," he said.

"I guess I am," Jacob said.

"Well, you should stop it. And if you come back I think you should stop ignoring me."

"Okay," Jacob said.

"I'm friends with Adam now," Marek said. "But I don't like him really."

Jacob nodded.

"Here's some cards we made for you. See if you know which one is mine."

Jacob shuffled through the cards, which, because of Valentine's Day, were full of hearts. They had been drawn on red and pink construction paper in markers with glittery silver and gold ink.

Come back soon so you can make me laugh (in a good way).

We miss your weird stories.

You were always good at math.

I want to be sick. Cough on this and send it back.

On his card, which Jacob had no trouble recognizing, Marek had written:

I hope you feel better. I still love you even though you're mean. From, your best friend.

As Jacob read, Marek hung over the couch, staring challengingly down at him. Whatever internal gravity it was that kept Jacob pinned to the couch now strengthened. Suddenly he couldn't have lifted his head even if he'd wanted to. He thought of an afternoon more than a year ago when he and Marek had made a fort around this couch. Between where he was lying and the coffee table had been the entrance, between the table and the door had been the lounge where they'd put Cara's beanbag chair, beside that had been a room for Finney (though Finney had balked and refused to go in). He remembered sitting back in it after they'd finished, and the sunlight coming in through the glass doors and turning the yellow blanket a gauzy gold, and the thought of it made him so sad that he had to shut his eyes.

"What's wrong? Are you having a heart attack?"

Jacob didn't answer.

"Are you going to be my friend again or not?"

Jacob decided to pretend to fall asleep, and when he opened his eyes—having fallen truly and deeply asleep, though he couldn't say for how long—the room was dark and Marek was gone.

The fact that Alice spent these same months in the hospital, receiving grimmer and grimmer news, felt to Jacob like a coincidence. And in fact Jacob went on thinking that it had been a coincidence for years, until sometime in high school, when he began to wonder if some current of real and unbearable feeling for his mother had been diverted, an electrical misfire. Family friends and relatives, when they talked about it at all, referred to those months as the hard time he'd had about his mother. He hadn't been able to bear having her in the hospital, and so he'd lain down himself, it was as close as he could get to being with her. That was how Jacob eventually told the story too.

In May, when uncles and aunts and cousins and grand-parents made their first round of solemn visits, Jacob got back up. Through the tall glass doors looking out onto the backyard he'd watched winter end and spring begin—the patio was suddenly covered in little green-white flowers. Now there was the hum of the air conditioner, and way up above the slow revolutions of the ceiling fan. It wasn't that nature's vitality inspired him, or that he suddenly wanted to be a part of it all again—it was just that he'd had a vision of the world moving on without him, and he'd realized that if he didn't force himself to get up he was going to miss out completely. He'd seen his life pulling away from him like a train.

Owen hadn't visited him when he was at home (Jacob had known he wouldn't) but after a day or two back at school, he approached Jacob, shyly, by the bulletin board where the class was stapling up the poems they'd written about their favorite things to do in summer. There were only a few weeks left in the school year, and in elementary school.

"You look like a Feed the Children commercial," Owen said, looking ahead.

"I know. I just wasn't ever hungry."

That afternoon, as if they'd planned on it, they walked out of the classroom together and then down the stairs and out of the building. They walked stiffly, silently, as if it weren't a sidewalk beneath them but a wedding aisle.

"Did you watch anything good when you were sick?" Owen asked.

"Not really."

"Did you see that Philip shaved his head? He says his mom did it while he was asleep."

"Really?"

This was enough to carry them to the crest of Pinyon, where they paused and looked out, although the view—the wide asphalt river of the street, the green blur of the trees, even the parked cars—was so familiar that they could hardly see it. "My liege," Owen said, but in a tone so strange and forlorn that Jacob hardly knew afterward if he'd really said it.

"My liege," Jacob said, starting to walk.

They entered a phase of best friendship then that really was like marriage, although it took them a few months to settle into it. A ramshackle house with warm dens opening onto collapsing hallways, cobwebbed ballrooms and wings sealed off behind heavy doors—but one in which you nevertheless decide to live.

That afternoon they stood on the patio talking—taking turns tossing the use-smoothed ball through the rim, laughing at jokes that seemed to have come from another era—until just after six when Arthur, shuttling between the hospital and home, pulled into the driveway and, taking no note of Owen, told Jacob to hurry up and get in the car already, visiting hours were nearly over.

Wife and Mother

Jacob wondered, occasionally, whether the fact that his mother was dying was a help or a hindrance, on balance, when it came to his getting a girlfriend. He had plenty of time for this sort of thinking, sitting on the hard green hospital lounge furniture, or waiting in the car while his father picked up that week's stack of library books. He had plenty of time for all sorts of thinking. He would count the squares in the pattern on the wall, having decided that only if the number came out odd would his mother get better. He would try to remember one important thing, one dramatic or serious happening, from each year of his life. He would occasionally try too, as if it were a memorization exercise, to think about what his mother had been like before all this. He didn't want the forgetful, waxy-skinned woman, the one with the tube hanging from her mouth, to be who he saw when he thought about her. He didn't want to cringe in his memory as he cringed now when at the end of each visit Arthur made him lean over to kiss her oddly hot cheek.

These preoccupations stood between him and the frenzy that had lately consumed the seventh grade. Sarah Marks and Thomas Yip spent all recess walking around with their hands in each other's back pockets. David Fowler was dating both Tory Reyes and Monica Haldell (both girls seemed reasonably happy with the arrangement). Jacob wasn't in the class of, say, Johnny Ragusa, who had a purple blotch on his cheek, or Kyle Ledyard, whose breath smelled like rotting fish and Tic Tacs, In fact, for certain girls, he was probably more appealing than he would have been if his mother had been perfectly fine. But he felt set apart nonetheless, as a superhero feels set apart.

Jacob was twelve now, although he thought of himself as a teenager. He'd switched in sixth grade to private school, Vernon Day Middle, just as Will had done. He had grown his hair long enough that it hung over his eyes (and long enough that store clerks and substitute teachers regularly mistook him for a girl); he had started to wear jeans that, had he undone his belt, would have slipped straight to the floor. His voice hadn't yet changed and to compensate he spoke in a gravelly mumble, a voice he meant to sound dangerous and emphatically male. His favorite band was Nirvana, and he copied their lyrics on the covers of all his notebooks. He was entitled to gloom and to anger in a way that no one else was (except for Patricia Strauss, whose perky blandness had somehow held up after her older brother had hanged himself).

That whole fall, while Alice's death loomed, Jacob was

half in love with Emily Barley. A girl to like was as necessary as a favorite band, and at first she had seemed a natural, if uninspired, choice. She was compact and soft (in elementary school she'd been fat—people said this even when she was in the room) and had brown curly hair that was so healthy it looked wet. Her mother's father was from France, so she looked to Jacob vaguely foreign, and she showed off sometimes by speaking a rapid-fire French that she would refuse to translate (she deliberately gave the impression that she'd said something scandalous). Although she wasn't especially popular, she belonged to the class of the approachable, of liaisons: she was the type of girl you might ask about a girl you did like. Her best friend was her neighbor Cynthia Logue, tall and volatile—and unaccountably popular. Emily acted as Cynthia's handler. When Cynthia, weeping, dragged a knife against the door of Ted Rider's bedroom (he'd called her a bitch) it was Emily who led Cynthia away from the party and into a guest room to calm down. Emily's smile—a staple of Vernon Day brochures and yearbooks— was the type that made male teachers pause in their lessons and forget their ages. It reminded Jacob of an expertly arranged plate of cookies, and until it bewitched him he'd thought of it as cloying and phony. He thought of it now, being the one responsible for it, and felt a commotion in his chest, a calling to attention.

Since Jacob had come to Vernon Day, he and Emily had been part of a group that spent Friday nights at United Artists, the movie theater on Wisconsin. The movies themselves—*Mrs. Doubtfire, The Fugitive, The Firm*—

were merely backdrops, secondary always to whatever drama took place inside the theater. Exchanges of seats, trumped-up shoving matches, pieces of melting ice lobbed at the bald spot on a grown-up's head. And there would be commotion outside the theater too—fights and urgent conversations in the bright bathrooms where wet toilet paper lay wadded on the floor, or by the concession stand whose tanks of candy were never refilled. After the movies the excitement moved out into the large stone courtyard. Along the edges of the courtyard were a shoe store, a frozen yogurt store, and a card and novelty store permanently on the brink of reopening. They clung to this space as intently as pigeons. Even on freezing nights, they'd stand shivering above the warm Metro grates, determined not to call their parents. Often Jacob brought along Owen, who—in spite of the automatic regard paid anyone who went to public school—had no notion of how to talk to girls. He had a crush on Cynthia, but he turned sullen around her and was known, by her and everyone, mostly for the unusual bloody-looking pimples he sprouted on the tip of his nose.

Jacob and Emily and Cynthia, like everyone at Vernon Day, had heard stories about Owen's school, Spillerton-Courson, that made it sound like a city mid-riot. Teachers were hounded out of their classrooms, cash registers disappeared from the cafeteria, the bathrooms were full of couples and noncouples in every state of sexual misbehavior. Vernon Day Middle was a mild, dull, quietly self-satisfied place, with carpeted hallways lined with drawings and poetry, small classrooms full of well-behaved students, and an air of meekness that could seem alternately suffocating and comforting. Nearly all the students had known each other since kindergarten, and many of the teachers—gray-haired women in long skirts—acted like mothers, hugging children in the halls, making time for serious talks over lunch. No cafeteria, no school buses. To Jacob it felt more like a summer camp, or a religious commune, than like a school. The clearest difference between Vernon Day and Spillerton-Courson, though, came down to money.

Spillerton students were by no means poor—they lived in houses of two or three stories, had basketball hoops in the driveway, took summer trips to rental houses in Rehoboth or Bethany Beach. A handful of Vernon Day students, though, lived in houses with driveways that looped through woods, with art collections and walk-in closets and, in the kids' rooms, TVs and massaging chairs and footballs autographed by the 1991 Redskins. These kids' parents were friends with important D.C. figures—ambassadors, department secretaries—or else they were important D.C. figures themselves. Having a father who owned the area's biggest local hardware store seemed suddenly a quaint curiosity. In these houses, as clean and bright as executive conference rooms, you almost never saw a parent, unless you stayed for dinner. Signed photographs of Bill Clinton stood in golden frames on polished pianos. In the daytime a housekeeper presided—nearly always Spanish-speaking, briskly competent, burdened and beloved.

All this bred a certain softness, compared with which the kids from Spillerton-Courson seemed to possess an intriguing edge of wildness. They were much likelier, Jacob thought, to have been in fistfights, tried drugs, and, most important, to have gone well past first base. But even among them, French kissing was a major preoccupation. Often the only thing anyone remembered on Monday morning was who had Frenched who over the weekend, how noisy it had been, how it had started. Somehow everyone in the courtyard had come to believe that a kiss ought to last as long as possible. A couple would stand at the center of a circle and kiss, their arms encircling each other's waists, their mouths in greedy sloppy motion. Friends would stand and count, sometimes with a watch in hand. When the couple finally pulled apart, their mouths glistening, their eyes glassy and relieved, the timekeeper—often it would be a tiny boy, someone who'd seen that he couldn't be a romantic protagonist and so had turned himself into an elf, a mascot, willing to be dropped into trash cans or pushed into swimming pools—would race around the courtyard announcing, "Thirty-two seconds! Pete and Ellen just went for thirty-two seconds!"

Emily spent a lot of time watching the Spillerton groups, and although she kept a cautious distance, Jacob felt her fascination. She would never dare to have a crush on a boy from Spillerton, or even to initiate a conversation with any of them—interschool couples were nearly as rare as interracial ones—but when someone walked over to ask for matches or to talk to Owen, she handled herself in a way that none of the rest of them could. Even Cynthia turned spastic and laughable, but Emily could have gone away and carved a place for herself among them. Jacob saw it with envy and dismay.

He and Emily held hands for the first time at the end of September. It was during *Jurassic Park,* while Jeff Goldblum stood mumbling beside an SUV. Jacob and Emily sat next to each other and slumped so that their heads were well below the tops of the seats, their knees pressed against the seats in front of them. At first they just let the backs of their hands touch. This was both awkward and astonishing. Knuckles against knuckles, a strange nonaccidental sort of contact that nevertheless promised nothing. Minutes passed. A half hour passed, during which Jacob's entire being was concentrated in the back of his left hand; he had no clue even what movie they were watching. Her face was fixed on the screen with artificial intensity. Lips slightly open, eyes unblinking, she didn't so much as glance at her watch (she wore a calculator watch: a reliable, though worryingly stale, thing for Jacob to tease her about). In twenty seconds I'll take her hand. In thirty seconds. The next time they show the brontosaurus. Now. It was as if he'd landed a flying cartwheel, that vibrating dizzy second afterward. She squeezed *Okay.* He squeezed back. Her face still didn't change, but he glanced toward her, even let his eyes fall on her cheek. She resisted his look, as he knew she would. Afterward they unclasped, she wiped her hand on her jeans, and they filed out into the courtyard, where she paid him no special attention.

This scene played out again the next week and the one after that. Eventually they took each other's hands almost as soon as the lights went down, and Jacob didn't sweat quite so much. They started clutching each other tighter during scary or meant-to-be-scary moments. She'd trace a circle on the back of his hand with her fingertip. But still nothing further, nothing spoken. It was November now, and the year was turning dark and unpromising. Jacob listened to Pearl Jam, lying in his bed with a stiff jaw, imagining the various forms of his future happiness, wishing years could be skipped like tracks on a CD.

At sleepovers he and Owen—determined to stay up all night—would sneak out of the house and walk in the unearthly 3 a.m. light all through Waggoner, past leafless bushes and perfectly empty streets, and Jacob would mull over what he called his "Emily situation." Was it possible that she meant nothing by taking his hand, that she did it merely because she knew that he wanted to, or because she was bored? (No, this wasn't possible, Owen said, she wasn't like that.) But then why wouldn't she do more? Why, the one time when he'd said, Emily, I have something weird I want to talk to you about, had she grabbed Cynthia and run into the bathroom and then avoided him for the rest of the night? (Yes, that had been weird. Maybe she was like that after all.)

And then, to further complicate things, just before Thanksgiving the phone calls began. The phone, until then an instrument purely for making plans or checking in with parents, had in seventh grade been transformed. Many nights now Jacob went to bed with his right ear red and scorching. For hours after he got home he would lie on the ledge outside his and Will's rooms and talk—mostly to Owen or to Charles (a friend from Vernon Day whom he liked even more, he sometimes thought, than he liked Owen). But sometimes he talked to girls—forty-minute shapeless conversations about whose parents were abusive, who was about to be dumped and didn't see it coming. Often these conversations would end with no good-bye, just a sudden click: a parent or sibling had walked in, no time to explain.

Jacob's most important asset in these conversations was the serious business that was happening with his mother. No one quite knew the details—Jacob didn't talk about them—but it was a dark glow behind his silhouette. "What's it like when you go see her?" Emily would ask, tentatively and late at night.

"It's weird. It's like visiting a really old person. She's just in bed, and she's incredibly fragile, so we're not supposed to touch her or anything, and she's always tired. A lot of the time she's just sleeping. And she throws up. She'll just be talking really quietly about something and then all of sudden she throws up on her sheets and the nurses have to come and clean her up. She doesn't cry very much, but my dad does."

"Do you?"

He paused for a deliberately long stretch. "Sometimes. Mostly when I get back and I'm alone." (He had cried a couple of times, but in both cases he had been less sure than he would have liked that he wasn't pretending.)

These conversations with Emily had a giddy, therapeutic shape. They made Jacob feel, as almost nothing else did, that in fact his mother's death would be survivable. She told him that her neighbor Martin, hero of her childhood, had once shut them in his garage and shown her his bulging penis. She talked about how when she was little she'd believed that a particular fork with bent tines was bad luck—even now she shuffled through the silverware drawer to avoid it. Jacob would hang up after these conversations and go into his room and mash his face into his pillow and howl with wild joy. Or he'd go downstairs, where Will would be doing homework and Cara would be gluing pieces of dry pasta to construction paper with their babysitter, Michelle, and Jacob would feel temporarily invulnerable, both close to his siblings and soaring above them. Will had a girlfriend of his own—a straight-haired, faultlessly polite girl named Kate Maves—but they seemed to Jacob laughable, hopelessly formal. Will, now a freshman, had joined the tech crew for the school theater, and he and Kate had met working together on *Guys and Dolls*. Even when they kissed they looked as if they might as well be bowing. Will approaches girls, Jacob thought, just the way he approaches PE: as an ordeal to be navigated with as little embarrassment as possible.

Alice died on a Friday in December, a night when Jacob would ordinarily have been at the movies with Emily. Forty degrees, gritty puddles along the curbs, the sky pigeon-colored. That morning before breakfast Arthur had come home from a night at the hospital—unshaven and stale-smelling, wearing glasses because he hadn't had his contact solution—and sat all three kids at the table. "They think today might be it," he said. "They sound pretty sure of it, actually. We're down to talking days, anyway. So don't you guys make any plans. We're going to the hospital and we're sticking it out." Trying to maintain his composure, he sounded as if he were trying to maintain his dignity in the face of humiliation.

All morning the Vines shuffled in and out of her room. They sat in the chairs by the bed and watched her breathe—at the hinge of every breath was a moment of panic, a pause in which it seemed possible that her ribs would this time fail to lift. Arthur massaged her dry, thin hands, and Jacob, in a silent, unshareable terror, tried not to look. It was not his mother in there. The monitors and tubes and wires around the bed seemed to have more life than she did. Her face was cartoonishly puffy, and made Jacob think of a loaf of bread in which his mother's features had been buried. Her hair had fallen out again. The only thing that seemed capable of stirring her to consciousness was if she felt too hot or too cold—all day the nurses were pulling the blankets off her and putting them back on. When friends came to say good-bye, Arthur would step outside and tell them that she wasn't awake and wouldn't want to be remembered like this. After a second they'd understand and, leaving flowers against the door, turn away. Jacob was surprised that his dad let him and Will and Cara stay, then—would she want them to remember her like this? did it matter?—but they sat for hour after hour watching her wheeze and whisper and occasionally groan. A thick-ridged plastic tube poked out of her mouth like a cigar. She didn't respond to questions, so Arthur eventually just kissed her forehead. "She's pretty far away," Arthur said at one point, as if he were apologizing. Alice's sister Louise and her husband Bill (stiff as the Tin Man, nearly deaf) arrived straight from Chicago and tucked their suitcases and coats in the corner of the room. The serious conversations happened at the end of the hallway by the water fountains. *Dr. Stone says you can give up on solid food but then that's it. The pain would ease up but they can't let her blood pressure get that low.* Louise kept saying to whoever she was talking to that Alice had been this close once before, they'd all flown in and she had pulled through, remember? The doctors had been shocked. "They're really just covering themselves," she said. No one who looked at Alice could have believed that. Even Jacob wanted to cry out, *No! Stop lying! It's not possible!*

All day they waited, and then into the night, and it seemed as if she might not die after all. As with anything that one sits around and waits for, each of them came secretly, confusedly, to long for it. The clock on the cable box seemed to be stuck. They took turns saying, *Well, maybe we'd better go home for the night and come back first thing in the morning.*

You need your rest, they all told each other.

A vigil like this had happened months before, as Louise had said, and at the time it had seemed almost as dire. That had been the end of July, when her left lung had nearly collapsed. The doctors had pulled the curtains around her bed and the machines had chirped as fast as a drumroll, but she'd lived. "This doesn't look good," she'd said that night, waking up to find her entire family gathered around.

By fall she was so nearly inanimate that it seemed a miracle that her body could still generate such pain. But it did. And that was when they gave her control of the red morphine button on her IV machine, when her appetite, vanished, when her personality, along with most of her awareness of her surroundings, disappeared behind a layer of blurriness and drift. Whenever she expressed a desire for anything, it was news all through the hallway, it was a cause for great joy.

"She said she wants a *milk shake*!"

"Did she? Ask her what kind! Oh wait, don't ask her, don't bother her. I'll just get her a few. Does she like cookies 'n' cream? I'll get her that and then I'll just get her plain chocolate. This is great! When did her appetite come back?!"

Louise, who had stayed with the Vines for two weeks that fall, would be gone for twenty minutes, speeding along Euston, ordering two enormous shakes, carrying them (damp through paper cups) proudly into her sister's room, where . . . Alice had fallen asleep. And when she woke up she took a sip of the chocolate and winced and coughed and then let both full shakes melt completely on her table, leaving wide sweet pools for the nurses to wipe up.

So there was reason to hope now, and a feeling—which they didn't dare speak aloud—that by taking absolutely seriously the imminence of her death they could stave it off.

Alice's heart stopped just after ten o'clock that night. Louise and Bill had already gone to the hotel. Cara was asleep in her chair in the lounge, and so it was just Will and Jacob who looked up when Arthur walked in. They had struck up a cautious friendship with a pair of red-haired brothers at the hospital visiting their grandfather, and the brothers now squeezed out into the hallway. *Hot Shots* was on the TV. "Well, boyos. She's gone," Arthur said. A cold itching started on the outsides of Jacob's arms. Without intending to he stood up and said, "What happened?"

"She died? She's really dead?" Will said. His lips screwed up and he closed his notebook. He'd been writing a letter to Kate and even now the protective part of him continued to make its demands. "When?"

"Just a few minutes ago. I was right next to her. I was with her." He leaned against one of the child-size pieces of furniture in the dark lounge. "Come here." Cara woke up and saw her brothers hugging Arthur and she hurried to join them, though she could only get at his shoulder. "Mom's dead," Jacob whispered to her. The TV was still on and the voices in the hallway carried on undisturbed. Jacob buried his face in Arthur's sweater and let its itch and smell fill his senses while his mind put on something like a fireworks show, pile after pile of disbelief bursting into sight. His mother, that all-touching tangle, was gone.

"Are we supposed to leave?" Jacob said, and Will hissed at him to shut up. Will drank from the water fountain in the hall and Jacob tapped the back of Will's head so he banged his teeth. Their momentary hatred for each other was as consuming and complete as if each of them had grabbed a handful of nettles.

When they got home late that night Jacob could hardly wait to tell Emily his terrible news: he felt supernatural.

He lay in bed with the bulky portable phone and said, "My mom died tonight," in a flat, astonished voice.

"Oh my God," Emily said. "I'm so sorry. That's such a worthless thing to say, but I'm just so sorry."

He described for her, as if he couldn't quite fathom it, the sequence of the afternoon and evening. He'd been working with half his attention on math (would he always remember *page 281, 9–25 odd*?). He'd walked up and down the hallway, counting his steps. He'd decided that she wasn't going to die tonight, that this was some sort of mistake.

And then he told her how much he wished he'd been with his mother when she'd died, and to his surprise he started to cry. A vibration that started in his chin spread into his cheeks and erupted in gasping, sniffling yelps. He thought of putting down the phone for as long as this lasted, but he just cried and cried.

Will opened the door and said, dourly but sincerely, "Are you okay?"

Jacob turned away so that he was facing the window and Will left. Turning onto his side seemed to bring Jacob under control—breath by breath he felt his crying slow down. There Emily was, still on the phone—it was as if she'd been standing when a storm came up, and was still standing in just the same place after it had lifted and left a landscape plastered in leaves.

They were silent for thirty seconds, a minute, longer than either of them had ever been silent on the phone.

"Jacob, you mean so much to me," Emily said, and now she started to cry too. It seemed possible that she was faking, or rather that she'd decided to make herself cry, in the hopes of rising to the emotional occasion. But then she said, "And I'm such an idiot, because I don't have anything to be upset about and your mom just died and now you're comforting me, I'm so stupid. I was going to— I was going to ask you tonight if you wanted to go to a movie just us this weekend. I had it all planned out." She blew her nose loudly—something else she would never ordinarily have let herself do.

"I've liked you for so long," Jacob said. "You should ask Owen. You're the only thing I talk about. I have a little notebook where I write down everything we say. All day the only thing I think about is what I'm going to say to you."

"Cynthia calls me 'Mrs. Vine'. She made a rule that I can only talk about you for twenty minutes whenever I'm with her. She looks at her watch and she's like, 'Okay, time's up, now no more talk.' I have the corniest dreams too."

"Me too!"

The conversation wove on, with long sleepy stretches— each of them actually fell asleep, and at one point Jacob noticed that the phone had fallen off of his pillow entirely— until he bolted awake and noticed that the sky outside his window was turning gray. He'd dreamt that he and Emily were sitting in Algebra while his mother waited in the hall. "What time is it?" he said. It was five-thirty. Jacob felt as if his head had been scraped hollow.

"Hmm?" This was another voice of Emily's he hadn't heard—a private uncute slightly deeper voice, the voice he imagined she used when she talked to herself. "Oh. Okay.

We should hang up. Wait. So are we dating? Are we like boyfriend and girlfriend now?"

"Yes. Let's be boyfriend and girlfriend."

"Really?" In her voice Jacob heard Emily stretching, remembering herself. "Good. My boyfriend Jacob. Okay. I'll see you in a little bit."

Each morning for the next few weeks Jacob woke up with a feeling of general momentousness. That his mother had died didn't arrive for a second or two—until then he just knew that something important had changed, and his newly exposed nerves blinked in the air.

On the morning of the funeral, he stood waiting for the shower to warm up—the floor was so cold that he balanced on the tips of his toes—listening to the rest of his family downstairs. He was especially aware of his grandmother, whose presence made him feel as if he were a guest in the house. She went to bed before nine and woke up before dawn, and needed help to use the toaster and the coffee-maker. At dinner these past few nights they'd sat quietly at the table, the kids silently shrieking with boredom, Arthur and their grandmother speaking stiffly and only to keep the quiet from becoming overwhelming. "Now, who would like a clementine for dessert?" their grandmother would say.

Jacob and Will stood now in front of the full-length mirror in the bathroom, each wearing a dark blue jacket with brass buttons, Will's fingers undoing the knot around Jacob's throat.

"Did Dad ask you to say anything?" Will said.

"No. Did he ask you?"

"He said I should if I want to. I hate doing the whole Tiny Tim thing, though." He stood back from Jacob as if he were a painter inspecting a canvas. "That's still too short. Come here."

The Vines arrived at the funeral home at nine and passed through a side door into something like a dressing room, separated from the sanctuary by a heavy red curtain. Against one wall stood a table with a coffee urn and boxes of Lipton tea, and a few relatives, arriving now from the hotel, discreetly served themselves. Arthur took a seat on the long wooden bench at the front of the room and kept as silent as a boulder, facing the white coffin whose lid was piled with roses. Every word you spoke (though almost no one spoke to him) had to travel through an invisible jelly to reach him, and even then he might only squint or nod, even if the question had been "What time are we starting?"

Cara asked Jacob if the cookies had nail polish in them. "Taste this, they're disgusting. Taste it."

"Please come in," Rabbi Sumner whispered, sticking his head through the curtain, and the organ became louder. Jacob felt the same impulse to giggle that he always felt when he made the silent walk up the aisle and onto the stage at a piano recital. There's a type of daydream in which everyone you've ever known is under one roof, all gathered to praise or to condemn you. Here were all of Jacob's cousins; Mrs. Lanigan, who in first grade had taught him how to use a computer ("Now everyone flip over your disc . . ."); Mr. Isaacon, who played the cello at assemblies; the Meinekes, who lived in the log cabin that was the oldest house in Waggoner and who gave out popcorn balls on Halloween; the purple-nosed man who swept the floors at Arthur's store; the disconcertingly cheery woman who answered the phone at Alice's office.

The rabbi talked about coming to know the Vines these past months—"Perhaps the sole blessing of this terrible misfortune"—and then began, with his eyes gently closed, to sing. *This is your mother's funeral*, Jacob thought. *This is really it. Pay attention.*

A cousin of Alice's named Caroline spoke first. Alice and Caroline had grown up near each other in Wellfleet, and they always described themselves as being like sisters, although Caroline—mousy and short-haired—looked much older, and much more prim. She took so long straightening the pages in her hands that Jacob wondered if she was going to be able to read her speech at all. She had been famous, in his childhood, for being dyslexic—in fact she was the reason he first learned the word *dyslexic*.

"Since you're all here," she began, "I know I don't need to tell any of you this, but Alice was a remarkable woman. She was my best friend, she was my hero. She'd done all sorts of things, she'd read more than I had, she'd seen movies I hadn't seen—but she never made you feel like you didn't matter because of it. And as I think everyone here knows, Alice wasn't a very religious person"—there was laughter, a honking nose—"but I don't think she would mind it if we all took a second right now and imagined that she's sitting in a comfortable chair somewhere, the newspaper piled up in her lap, that little smile on her face, and she's looking at all of us and thinking, You know what, I had quite a family. And quite a life." Jacob had a feeling, hearing the murmurs around him, that everyone but him had silently agreed to participate in a play. They would laugh or cry, in keeping with the script, but no one would say anything sharp or funny, no one would curse or mention how strange her face had looked toward the end.

Now a dean from Alice's school settled himself at the podium, and a hum of static from the speakers rose up and crackled away. The dean was British and had perfectly symmetrical wattles, and Jacob knew that he was especially beloved in his mom's office. He wore a bow tie and had a habit of raising his upper lip so that he seemed to be ready to bite out of the air whatever he intended to say next. "Alice came into the department one morning—I had recently been transferred—muttering to herself, trailing bags, her hair still wet, her papers falling out from under her arm...And I stood up to help, thinking I might make a good impression. And I'll never forget: while I helped her off with her things she just stood there like a scarecrow and began to talk about the application she'd been reading, as if it were the most ordinary thing in the world for this strange Brit to be peeling off her coat. And I knew just then that this was a woman I couldn't help but love, and I was right. We love you and miss you, Alice dear, terribly, terribly much."

Arthur grabbed Jacob's and Cara's hands—they happened to be sitting on either side of him—and held them both against his chest, shutting his eyes like a child at the doctor waiting to get a shot.

When Jacob noticed that everyone behind him was standing up he figured that it was for another prayer, but the organ began to play again, and people started reaching for their coats. Over already. Songs, stories, death like a dimmer switch in the sky. He stood still, along with the rest of his family, and let himself be hugged by one sobbing person after another, but he didn't cry. People said how beautiful the service had been and how much they loved him and he just nodded.

Outside in the eerie silver daylight the crowd walked— slowly, slowly, to keep from passing the casket—up the smooth road to the cemetery, past the rows of parked cars stained with months of salt, past the hundreds of glossy black tombstones. Jacob had come here once before to see her plot, and the sight of the orderly rows of graves—so unlike the crumbling cemeteries he'd seen in movies—had made his heart race with shame. These tidy hills, just a few hundred feet from East-West Highway, looked like a farm for growing VCRs. Will appeared from behind Jacob and, with a gesture that seemed nearly accidental, he linked his arm with his brother's and they walked slowly along together.

And then there it was: a mound of dirt and beside it, straddling the hole, an apparatus like a bed frame. Green canvas straps, a metal crank. A pair of men in overalls and gloves who looked as if they might as well have been unrolling a pool tarp. Four men from the funeral home lowered the coffin onto the straps, and the burliest of them began turning the crank, then went on turning it for what felt like minutes. The coffin touched down (Jacob glimpsed a smooth-walled pit) and the men expertly disassembled the bed frame and hurried away, leaving the rabbi to preside as if the coffin had appeared at the bottom of the hole by magic.

More than a hundred people were quietly angling for places around the grave, and finally someone said, "Is it all right if we stand on other peoples' graves?"

The rabbi drew in his lips. "It's probably not preferable if you can avoid it, but there's no prohibition against it."

Upright in the mound of dirt stood three ordinary workman's shovels. The rabbi said a few prayers, and then one by one, stepping around the folding chairs that had been set in the grass for the people who were too old or too grief-stricken to stand, everyone took hold of a shovel, lifted a full load, and, with a hesitation that was like a curtsy, dumped the dirt down onto the coffin. First Louise, then her husband Bill, then Judy, then Caroline. The noise of the dirt seemed to Jacob shockingly loud and indelicate, like buckets of slop being emptied. He thought that they must be doing something wrong and that the rabbi would soon correct them. But the rabbi just looked calmly on, hands together at his waist. Will stepped up, wearing a tearful grimace, a yarmulke perched on the top of his head like a beanie. Then Cara, who made everyone smile by straining to lift the shovel. And suddenly it was Jacob's turn. He felt dizzy with self-consciousness and he bumped into one of the empty chairs. He wasn't sure he'd be able to stay on his feet. He got his balance by staring down into the grave for a private second, holding the heavy shovel, and then he said, just barely out loud, "I'm sorry," as he let his dirt slide down with all the rest.

Suddenly, again, everyone was standing up. "Can we drive with you to the reception?" "Do you have extra directions?"

The atmosphere in Lawrence and Sylvia Copes's house (they were old friends of Alice's) was practically festive—restrained but relieved. That was what Jacob saw on people's faces as they walked from the cars to the driveway, that's what he heard in the low-grade chatter. His father looked to be doing better now too, less pale. The house felt dark and warm and on the dining room table there were platters of berries and melon, smoked salmon and red onion, cheese quiches, miniature roast beef sandwiches, sickeningly sweet lemon squares. The Vines' corner of the living room, where Arthur and the kids stood in front of an enormous striped armchair, became the house's center—all the guests made their way over and told them how much they missed her, how proud she had been of all of them. Each of the kids practiced their fake smiles, and Arthur again and again narrowed his eyes and said, "I know Alice would be so glad you made it."

When Judy came over, a cup of black coffee in her hand, Aaron standing sullen behind her, honesty swept over them like a chill. Her mascara had smeared in black arcs under her eyes, and she kept turning away to blow her nose. She looked like she'd been caught in a hard rain. "You know," she said, "I know you're not supposed to say it, but you know what I keep thinking? Thank God last week is over." She stared off as if she were talking to herself, and she might have been. Aaron had grown the beginnings of a goatee and smelled like cigarettes. "Since a few days ago," Judy said, "since Thursday...No more. If we treated people half as good as we treat animals—" Now she looked for Arthur's eyes. "It was just *bad*, you know? It got so bad, and I don't think most of these people even know!" With that she started crying again, and Aaron—as if he'd been waiting for just this moment—handed Judy a stack of paper napkins.

Not long after that, the first trickle of guests began to leave, and the more the door opened and closed, the colder and sharper the air in the house became, and so the more people thought of being home. At two o'clock, as if by some secret signal, everyone who was still there began to gather their coats and bags and to find Arthur to give him one more hug, and soon the Vines—with Jacob's grandmother and Louise and Bill and a scattering of family—were driving slowly back home, the rest of the afternoon blank before them. There were clothes to change out of, cards to open, beds to make, but they found themselves, at stoplights, reduced to saying things like, "That rabbi really was good, wasn't he?"

The strangeness Jacob felt, over the following days and weeks, had a lot to do with time. Nights would seem to last three or four times as long as usual, and he'd often find himself remembering dreams only to realize that they were real and vice versa. When had he been standing in a public

bathroom drying his hands and heard an old man at the uri-
nal fart freely and with apparent pleasure? Dream or real?
When had he let Finney out in the middle of the night and
stood freezing in his boxers looking up at the sky? At some
point recently he'd been sleeping on the couch, or trying to
sleep, and he'd heard Judy say, "I didn't ever get over Dad,
you know. When he died I thought, okay, I'm going to have
to fake it from now on, because I don't have anyone I care
about impressing anymore." At another point—this was a
weekend morning when he was lying in bed—he'd heard
Cara in the shower, singing so clearly that she could have
been holding a tube to the wall. *The worms crawl in, the
worms crawl out, they turn you in-to sau-er-kraut.* Surely
life wouldn't feel like this forever?

It wouldn't. At some point during those bad months—as his
father seemed almost visibly to fade, as his grandmother
took over the house's daily operations—Jacob found himself
able to focus again, and what he decided to focus on was
composing, in his mind, a handbook titled *How to Have a
Girlfriend.*

    *How often should a boyfriend and girlfriend talk on the
phone?*

    As often as possible. The boy should, at various points
in the evening, shut himself in his room and call the girl
to tell her that he just heard a song on the radio that made
him think of her, or that he can't stand his family and just
wishes he could be with her, or to ask her, in a casual but
significant tone, what they—a unit, a couple—should do

that weekend. Before bed he should call and say good night (ideally he should be lying down, eyes closed so as to better imagine himself beside her) and, if he can get over his embarrassment, he should audibly kiss the phone.

What if, after a few of these calls, one of the girl's parents answers, sounding irritated?

The boy should hang up immediately.

How should they behave at school? Are they going to be one of those couples that's always all over each other?

Yes, to their surprise, they will be one of those couples. When they see each other in the hallway between classes they should step aside from the the flow of students and, under the coat hooks or leaning against the doors to the art room, cautiously but proudly kiss, hands around each other's waists. Whenever they find themselves sitting idly—in the back of the auditorium during a performance by a Japanese dance troupe, or lying on the cold metal bleachers during recess—they should hold hands. She should even rest her head in his lap while he, exaggerating his incompetence, tries to braid her hair.

What if teachers complain?

Ignore them. The boy and girl should react indignantly if they are scolded, like protesters for civil rights.

Should they start going on dates, just the two of them, or should they continue hanging out as part of a group?

They should stay with the group, but at movies they should sit a few rows apart from everyone else, both to kiss and to grope and to emphasize to their friends their intention to kiss and to grope. At friends' houses they, along with any other couples present, should sneak away to little siblings' tree houses or unlit basements or guest bedrooms and make out, before returning to the group with red lips and smug smiles and disheveled hair. Their only dates, for now, should take place on their one-month "anniversaries," when they should go to The Cheesecake Factory and share fettucine Alfredo by candlelight and feel, generally, a little awkward.

But what should they really do in those bedrooms and basements? They're only thirteen! Surely they're too young to have sex?

Yes, they're too young for sex. But they should kiss until their mouths ache. They should paw at each other through their clothes, rubbing bra straps and pocket seams and zippers. Eventually the boy, in a fit of boldness, should lift the edge of the girl's shirt, and the girl should astonish him by undoing her bra and then responding to the boy's every clumsy move with such sighs and shudders that the boy will think he has accomplished something extraordinary.

How often will they fight?

They won't fight, yet. Sometimes he'll be jealous when, for instance, she lets a boy in her History class undo one of her braids, and sometimes she'll be frustrated when, for instance, he keeps calling to see how her English paper is coming. But these feelings are nothing that a long, silent hug or a baby-talked apology can't fix. Occasionally they should refer, with pride and amusement, to how lucky they are not to fight, and how strange are the couples that do.

And how often should the boy and girl mention the

death of the boy's mother? Should the girl ever be the one to bring it up?

Very rarely. And no, the girl must never be the one to bring it up. This subject must be mainly confined to the matter of the boyfriend's "moods." He should be occasionally entitled to a few hours of portentous staring when, for instance, they are sitting in a friend's living room watching *Saturday Night Live* reruns in the middle of a weekend afternoon. The girl at these times should come sit beside the boy and lay her head on his shoulder or place a hand on his knee, but she must not ask him what's the matter, and she must never, under any circumstances, tell him to cheer up.

While Jacob created and lived by these rules, he noticed, and tried to tell himself he wasn't noticing, that his father was failing to live at all. Arthur's suffering was as plain as his new silver beard. He went into the store only occasionally, and most days when Jacob came home from school, a note from Emily tucked into his back pocket and the memory of kisses fresh along his neck, he would encounter the still presence of his father in the living room. Although he had lost weight, Arthur gave off an air like a hippopotamus in a zoo—massive and unmoving and pitiable. The sight made Jacob's back prickle.

"Don't you want these lights on?" Jacob would say, switching on one lamp and then another. It was dark already at four-thirty.

"Thanks. I was just reading and I think I must have drifted off."

But there was nothing to read. And he was no more likely to drift off than he was to begin whistling. He was like a child, eyes large and without comprehension. It was a face of such absolute vulnerability that Jacob began, at first unconsciously, then guiltily, to turn away from him. *There's nothing I can do to help*, he told himself. *He'll get better on his own*. Sometimes Jacob would try tempting him back to life with a question about something he was reading for school ("Does *ere* just mean before?" "What's a parish?") and Arthur would say, "I'm not sure I feel like talking, okay?" in a voice of effortful politeness. At the dinner table Arthur would eat slowly and without hunger, like an invalid complying with a nurse's regimen, and conversation, such as it was, usually consisted of Cara recounting in microscopic detail the plot of a book she was reading or a conversation she and one of her friends had had at school.

Will had withdrawn from his theater job and had quit Yearbook too. "Why are you doing all that?" Jacob asked. "I want to" was all he'd say. Will had just turned old enough to get his learner's permit, and many afternoons now he asked their father to drive with him up to the elementary school's parking lot. They would return home (announced by the clink of keys in the basket) cold and enlivened.

On weekends Will would tell Arthur he felt like doing a little work at the store, and Arthur—moving like a retired athlete in the site of his former glory—would take him up to the storage area and show him how to inventory the boxes that stood piled near the loading bay, or he'd set Will up alongside Danny at the paint counter downstairs.

Jacob told himself that Will was only doing all this because he didn't have any friends. This wasn't true—Will had two friends from the theater, and he still had some sort of relationship with Kate Maves. But it may as well have been true, Jacob thought. Will and his friends didn't drink (for most ninth graders, every weekend night was a complicated pursuit of alcohol); they talked regularly about where they might apply for college; they played sports less ably than many girls. When had Will become this person? There had been a window, between the ages of ten and thirteen, when Will had tried his hand at ordinary popularity, when he had carefully placed Soundgarden stickers on his binder and gone to the eye doctor for contacts, but something about high school had empowered him—was it an empowerment or a defeat?—to take up the tuba, to study Latin, to hurry around the theater's elevated walkways in enormous headphones, wearing black.

It seemed to Jacob that by rearranging his life for their father, Will was violating an understanding the Vine kids had reached. They could continue in their lives (Jacob growing his hair and plotting his next effort behind a closed door with Emily; Cara walking around the house wearing striped socks, practicing cradling a lacrosse ball) only if they didn't slow down and they didn't look back. There was a baffled, wounded, weepy version of the Vines always on their heels, and if that version caught up—as it threatened sometimes to do—then these Vines, the ones who could bear life, would never get moving again. They would be doomed forever to mull over the awful and embarrassing facts of Alice's death, how she'd thrown up in a plastic bowl and then shut her eyes in relief, how her mouth had hung open, how they had been unable to protect her. No one else would be allowed in the house. Time wouldn't pass. It would be, forever, the day of the funeral but also the day Alice's doctor paused during the CT scan and the day she fell in the driveway and the day last November when she said, "I'm sorry, but this just isn't fun anymore." Jacob felt he had lost a partner in keeping this possibility at bay.

One night when he was already in a bad mood—Emily had found out that he'd described the moles on her breasts to Charles, and now she was refusing to talk to him—he and Will got into a fight. Jacob was on his bed, staring at the portable phone and considering whether enough time had passed that he could call her again, and Will walked in— smugly, Jacob felt—and began going through Jacob's sock drawer.

"What the hell are you doing?"

"Looking for my sock."

"I don't have your socks. Get out!"

Will carried calmly on, pulling pairs apart to inspect them, and finally, smirking, he found the gold-toed sock he'd been looking for and turned to leave.

Afterward, when he and Will remembered it, the sock incident became laughable, a ready answer to the occasional friend or relative who wanted to know if, different as they were, they were the kind of brothers who fought. But there was no lightness in Jacob's mind when he leapt out of bed and launched himself at Will, gritting his teeth, aiming his knuckles at the bony center of his brother's back. Jacob was going to beat him until he gave up his act as a saintly stork.

But Will spun around, and with arms that were thin but surprisingly strong—Jacob hadn't fought him in years—he grabbed Jacob by the throat and dragged him to the ground. It was like being held down by a sculpture made of yardsticks. Will sat on Jacob's chest, pinned down his arms with one knee apiece, and then—a flash of inspiration behind his glasses!—he took the sock he'd been holding and forced it like a gag into Jacob's mouth. Jacob roared and groaned and tried to spit—his tongue worked frantically to keep the cloth from blocking his throat—but Will just stared murderously down. For all the violence of the moment they were oddly quiet. Will lowered his face so that his forehead was practically touching Jacob's (Jacob tried, unsuccessfully, to butt his head) and hissed into the damp sock, nearly speaking into Jacob's mouth: *"Dad. Needs. Our. Help."*

"FYHAAA!" [Fuck you!]

"You can't just think about you all the time. You're not a little kid anymore."

"YSFYHAAA!" [You're such a fucking asshole!]

"Will you help?"

"GETEFKHYA!" [Get the fuck off me!]

"Will you?"

"GETEFKHYA!"

When Will finally let him up, Jacob gave one face-saving kick to the back of Will's thigh (Jacob's toes hurt for the rest of the night). No, he would not help. He would lie on his bed and cry with shame and fury into his pillow and not answer the phone, even when he knew it was Emily, forgiving him. And when, that week, Arthur realized he couldn't carry on like this—he had never made any progress at all—it would be Will whose doorway he would appear in, Will who would stay calm and call their aunt Louise and together find Arthur a doctor who would see him in the morning. It was Will who would miss his Latin class to drive Arthur to his first appointment, and Will, a few weeks or a month later, whom Arthur would finally tell, in a voice that was oddly sheepish, that he was going to make it, he was going to be all right, he wasn't going to get over this—no way—but he was going to survive it. For the first time he felt fairly sure.

Troublemaking

Vernon Day High held dances on the first Friday of every month, sponsored by a club or tied to an inoffensive, which is to say nonreligious, holiday. Students regarded the dances half-ironically—they were no one's first choice for the night, and yet everyone ended up at them. The lobby and the first-floor hallway were incompletely transformed, the lockers hung with crepe ribbons, the front windows papered with hand-drawn posters. Just past the entrance Principal Batey stood behind a folding table with a metal box of neatly piled dollar bills, wearing an Orioles cap over his white hair and the same dourly amused expression as during the day. Some of the senior boys tugged the brim of his cap or told him how surprised they were to see him up this late, and he obliged by ignoring them completely. He only acknowledged students to apply a faint red stamp to the backs of their hands—this was so that no one could leave to get drunk and then come back and infect the night with disorder.

Jacob and Emily's first dance was Homecoming, which was a self-congratulatory joke on the school's part, since Vernon Day didn't have a football team or even a proper home field. Jacob and Emily had come in a cluster—no sensible freshman would have showed up without a pack—and as they walked in they talked to each other to keep from looking around like travelers in Oz. The senior boys wore store-bought football uniforms and had black smears under their eyes; the girls, who presided over the school with the security of being lusted at, wore cheerleader costumes. A few sophomores took turns rolling an orange cooler down the empty hall. Emily had her hair pulled back to highlight a face that was shiny, eager, attractive. She shimmered with the desire to dance.

She and Jacob had now been dating for a year and a half, which seemed to them a surreal, geologic stretch of time, and which put them in the rare class of couples whose couplehood was well known to students who had never spoken a word to either one of them. They had fought (more since coming to high school, Jacob noted uneasily); they had talked, lightly but meaningfully, about getting married someday; they had, unlike almost everyone else in the grade, been completely naked together. It was to this fact in particular that Jacob clung on nights when he was feeling dubious.

At some point in the past year—Jacob couldn't say precisely when—his lust, which had previously burned politely around Emily, had become a torch, nearly impossible to carry. The thought that hand-holding, flirting, even kissing, had as recently as last year satisfied him for an entire weekend seemed quaint. Each morning at 8:15 he would take his seat in Spanish class and, while Mrs. Bunter taught the distinction between the preterite and imperfect, he would, in mild shock, in still-uncertain sunlight, relive a growing handful of moments from his and Emily's relationship.

When she had pulled the yellow blanket all the way over her head and—

When she had led them to a bench in Norwood park and—

When she had cleared the clothes off the bed and—

He'd hurry to the bathroom and, at 8:45 on a Monday morning, stroke himself to a burning spasm of relief. He'd be clearheaded for a few minutes, awake to the smell of lemon Pledge and toilet water, astonished at himself. And when he sank back into his seat in class he'd be prepared to redeem himself and catch up on all he'd missed. Yes, yes, this was nothing he couldn't master. Preterite was like a bolt of lightning, imperfect a rolling wave. Just a simple matter of figuring out whether Felipe was talking generally about playing baseball or if he meant a particular game. Mrs. Bunter welcomed him back and asked him to look on with Roberto and read the next example aloud. All was well. (Mrs. Bunter was not from any Spanish-speaking country at all; she was from Montana. She had long black hair gathered loosely into a ponytail, and she seemed constantly to have injured herself while coaching lacrosse, so that one body part or another was forever in a cast. She was cheery and forgiving and clearly put great effort into her lessons, and yet something about her class caused such deep despair in Jacob that by the time it got to be about nine o'clock it was all he could do not to bash his head against the nearest wall.) Nonetheless, he made himself do the work. He conjugated one verb correctly and then another. But later on, during American History or Drama he remembered how vividly he'd earlier remembered the yellow blanket, the bench, the clothes on the bed...

Jacob knew that Emily wasn't quite so helpless or hungry as he was, so he had to be careful when they were together. If they were eating dinner at Emily's house, for instance, he couldn't be the one to propose that they go down to the basement (whose smell of damp dust was enough now to undo him). If they were with all their friends, he couldn't steal her away. Under no circumstances could he ever take her hand and direct it. And yet it was Emily who, when they were in fact alone together, when no parents were around, would bring up sex. "Ready?" she'd say. "I want to."

"No."

"Come on. Please. I have condoms upstairs." And, in a teasing but urgent voice, "I thought we were in love."

"Stop. No."

Jacob couldn't say what it was that stopped him, but he wouldn't do it, the temptation had absolutely to be resisted. And there was something in Emily's manner, a boldness and an insistence, that put Jacob off. Like the occasional cigarettes she smoked, or the beers she and Cynthia shared at sleepovers, there was something in her desire for sex that seemed to Jacob a product of *fashion*. He was frightened and disapproving in equal measure.

On the night of the dance, Emily's expression announced that she was in a public mood and that she wasn't going to propose or submit to anything. On the car ride over—they had driven with Charles's father, a man who loved his convertible and who listened religiously to Howard Stern—Jacob had put his hand high on Emily's leg and she, without looking at him, had removed it. He'd done it again, and this time she'd given him a single icy pinch on the back of his hand. Now they weren't in a fight, exactly, but a stalemate in which they each interacted only with their friends and pretended not to notice each other. Emily and Cynthia and the couple of other girls they'd brought swept off laughing into the auditorium, and Jacob felt the insult in this, as he knew he'd been meant to.

The dancing took place in the school's cavernous black auditorium, which had been filled for the purpose with balloons and speakers and a smoke machine. It was too loud inside for anyone's voice to be heard, which meant that mundane conversations—"Do you want something to eat?" "*Sure!*"—were conducted slowly and at top volume. Jacob settled against a wall with Charles, who had now been dating Cynthia for four months. Jacob and Charles had a passionate if slightly uncertain friendship. They hardly ever talked on the phone, but should one of them feel like skipping class he would seek the other out. Most weekends they had sleepovers, along with Owen and a semiregular cast of friends who would cover a basement or bedroom with mattresses and sleeping bags and stay up until three, four, five in the morning. They rented porn from the video store on Connecticut where the man behind the counter didn't check the cassette inside the case. They made too much noise and then giggled helplessly when a parent, furious and unkempt, stood in the doorway and told them to shut the hell up or they were all going home. They ate steadily, constantly, at all hours—cold eggplant Parmesan, Chips Ahoy!, cinnamon Life, mint-chocolate-chip ice cream. They all regarded girlfriends, the acquiring and retaining of them, as the most and in fact the only important thing in their lives. For a few minutes at a sleepover Jacob or Charles would, having received a page (Emily's code was 585), retreat to another room and call his girlfriend. This would be a conversation in a different key than the rest of the night. None of the antic pleasure of the sleepover, none of the silliness. It was practically like a call home.

"I don't know, we're just watching TV and eating and stuff. What are you doing?"

"Nothing. Being bored. I think I might go to bed."

"Okay. I love you."

"Good night."

"I said I *love* you."

"I know you did. Good night."

And so Jacob might return to the group a little disturbed, possibly even needing to go back and make another phone call a few minutes later, to apologize or accuse or just to retry.

Sometimes, before going to bed, Emily would send "I

love you"—4°5683°968—and Jacob would shut his eyes for a second as if he were leaning back into something warm.

The main engine of Jacob and Charles's friendship was their agreement that girls were crazy, and their ability to admit to each other, on long walks around the school's parking lot or the soccer field, just how miserable a fight could make them. Cynthia would sometimes not talk to Charles for days at a time, stalking past him in the hall, sprinting away from him at the end of the day—and right until she would reveal that it had all been a test, or that she had just been "PMS-ing," Charles would wear a sickened, grave expression. He functioned for Jacob as a jester— a bold, funny, unembarrassable sidekick. He was plump and baby-faced—a group of seniors called him the Pillsbury Doughboy—but he had a surprising diabolical streak, a genuine lack of conscience.

Back in the auditorium, Emily and Cynthia stood dancing cautiously, close to a table scattered with condoms (Juntos: World HIV/AIDS Awareness set up such a table at every dance). Their dance was simple but adaptable to almost any song that came on. The center of the movement was in the hips, which passed a wave from the shoulders to the legs. The girls' hands, every few beats, would tuck their hair behind their ears, and occasionally one of them would lean toward the other to shout something that made them both laugh. It was a variation on the dance that almost every girl in the auditorium was doing, and one that, so far as Jacob could tell, they had all been born knowing how to do.

Some of the older boys—Peter Chanen and Cesar Stoop,

boys who wore cargo pants and performed freestyle rap at talent shows—had relationships with the girls in their grade that were at once permissive and unserious. Peter, wearing a snow hat, walked up behind Rebecca Exel, a long-legged blond junior, and ground his crotch against her ass. She giggled and stuck her ass farther out and contributed her own bouncing and thrusting, so now, with happy defiant looks on both of their faces, they were miming sex in the middle of the floor.

Jacob was speechless and aching—he saw his look mirrored exactly on Charles's face.

Something, the crowd or the flashing lights or the smoke machines, made the room unbearably hot, so that after a few songs Emily and Cynthia needed a break. Charles and Jacob followed them out while trying to seem not quite concerned with them. Out in the hallway the girls' faces were bright red. Emily fanned herself with a notebook she'd picked up from the floor.

"They might not want you touching their notebook when you're so sweaty," Jacob said, the first thing he'd said directly to her all night. Emily turned her head crisply away.

"Cynthia, let's go find a beverage," Emily said, and they walked off toward the lounge with their arms linked.

"Women!" Charles said, in the voice of a sitcom dad. "Screw this. Let's go . . . troublemake!"

They found a door standing half-open at the end of the hall and climbed the silent, student-painted stairwell to the third floor, empty and dark except for a line of dim security lights. Just as important as the rule that no one leave a dance and then return was the rule that no one sneak into the closed parts of the building. If they were caught, they agreed, they would say that one of them had forgotten something in his locker. (A curious fact of Vernon Day was that it was difficult to get into any sort of real trouble. You could get scolded, called in for meetings, told you were squandering your potential—but nearly everything was reversible and subject to negotiation.) The walls were lined with bulletin boards on which teachers had pinned assignment sheets and optional readings. Down the hall was a display of black-and-white student photography—things like hubcaps and lightbulbs shot in close-up. Charles, arching his back for distance, shouted, "Cynthia can suck, my, giant, purple, hairy balls!!!" and spat a glob of yellow snot into the middle of the carpet.

Jacob, after glancing up and down the hall, lowered his pants and rubbed the crotch of his boxers all over the science office door. A lightness, a happiness, had opened up for them. It was the way Jacob imagined drunkenness, in that consequences had ceased to matter, or ceased to matter in the ordinary way. Charles took a running start and gave a flying kick to an open locker door. The ricochet caught him in the back of the head, springing tears to his eyes, and they both laughed until Jacob felt that the meat of his ribs might rip.

The doors to the science and computer labs were locked, as were the classrooms and closets and even the bathrooms. Charles grabbed a square cushion from one of the low wooden couches in an alcove—this was where teachers sat between classes with students and had long, earnest conversations about papers or personal crises—and stuck it between his legs and rode it like a horse. He tripped, or made himself trip, and again they stumbled with laughter.

The door to the art room was open.

The art room was a large, industrial-looking space that was less a classroom than a narrow hangar full of tables and paint-spattered stools and student projects in every state of completion. The women who taught Photography and Painting and Sculpture made up an odd subculture within Vernon Day—unintellectual, unconcerned with getting into college or competing with Sidwell. The head of the department, Mrs. Rice, had dyed red hair and a haggard, hungover face. She drank coffee out of mugs that were sometimes used for holding paintbrushes; she showed up to meetings with fingers crusted in gray clay; she was rumored to occasionally take in older girls who had run away from their parents. It would have to have been her who had forgotten to lock the door.

With some difficulty Jacob pulled open one of the windows along the room's back wall—it looked out over the school's front entrance and parking lot—and, kneeling, unzipped his fly and sent a burning jet of pee out the window. The pee pooled just a few feet below on a sill covered in smooth, whitish rocks. The night air was cool and Jacob had the half urge to climb out onto the ledge and see if they could get up onto the roof.

Charles placed on the floor a large blank canvas from a stack under a table, and he squeezed most of a tube of blue paint onto the middle of it. Jacob picked up a yellow tube and a brown tube and squeezed most of those on too. "It's art!" Charles said, and with shining eyes he turned backward, undid his belt, and dropped his pants and boxers to reveal his long-cheeked, squarish behind. Jacob glanced at the door, glanced at the window, kept his mouth open in anticipation and delight. With surprising delicacy, Charles lowered his ass into the piles of paint and smeared the canvas and himself until both were a blackish mess.

"I'm a painter, Mommy!" he shrieked, looking up with his bare ass pressed to the canvas, his pants smeared in blue and green, an expression of pure joy on his face. Every few minutes after he stood up and pulled on his boxers and pants, he reached in and gave himself a shake, or announced in a funny frantic voice that the paint was hardening, and Jacob laughed with a warmth that felt like love. They walked along the back wall of the room—the area reserved for sculpture—and one by one they plucked the sheets off to reveal the works underneath. Sculpture was open only to juniors and seniors; for a few weeks at the end of the semester their works stood on display in the lounge.

Jed Butler had made a surprisingly realistic clay bust of a man with jowls and a broad bald head.

Alex Tristen had made a skyscraper out of matchboxes, complete with scaffolding made of matchsticks.

Rena Taleb had made, from what looked like Styrofoam, a naked woman on her back with real-looking pubic hair and a mess of bloody cuts along her chest and arms.

At each sculpture Jacob and Charles would nod and

hmm and discuss the brilliant periodicity or the powerful critique of Darwinian industrialist society.

The last sculpture they revealed was by Simon Korm, and it was a half-size model in chicken wire of a man standing behind a DJ's turntable. The model wore a snow hat and a wristband and a pair of Nike sneakers. Simon himself was a DJ, and Jacob and Charles loathed him despite never having spoken to him. He was a junior who showed up to assemblies high, with eyes red and distant, and made public, nearly tearful pronouncements about the need for more sanity and peace in everyone's daily lives. "We are a school full of talented and wonderful people, and we are going at each other like...wolves, like lions, like animals that don't care anything for each other's well-being."

Charles reached into his pants and retrieved a glob of blue paint to smear across the model's wire face. Jacob felt ecstatic. He took the model's hand—positioned carefully just above a turntable—and bent it so that now the man was resting his hand on his heart, as if he were pledging allegiance. Charles twisted the head so it seemed to be looking out the window. Jacob, his heart racing, picked up a metal stool and in one glorious, emphatic motion, bashed the sculpture in the head so that it partially snapped and fell backward, an enormous cave pressed into what had been its neck and chest.

"Go, go, go!" they shouted in a British voice they sometimes used and, without remembering to turn off the lights or close the window, they ran down the hall and down the stairs and, not quite ready to face the world, emerged panting at the far end of the first-floor hall, away from the thumping and heat of the dance.

"Let's never speak of it again," Jacob said.

"Not a word. Not even to the wives."

"Not even to the wives."

They walked back through the rear hallways, tiled rather than carpeted, toward the auditorium's second entrance, and they heard the music loudly but muffled by the walls. "Do I have paint on my face?" Charles asked.

"No. Do I?"

"No."

They stepped back into the auditorium and found it the same as before except possibly even hotter. And yet it had been robbed of its dangerousness; it had come to seem, in contrast to the third floor, like the domesticated part of the school. There was a bigger crowd now, such a mass of people that you didn't have to worry so much about where you danced or how. A group of freshman girls who didn't have boyfriends, who had gotten more dressed up for this dance than they ought to have, danced in a triumphant circle, pointing at one another. In the middle of the floor a space had been cleared, and once they got close enough, Jacob and Charles saw that it had been cleared for a senior named Kendall—an elfin but popular boy who was both the best athlete and the best student in the grade, as well as an odd paragon of school spirit. He was breakdancing impressively, flipping himself again and again so that he held himself up with just his left hand, and when he stood up panting and grinning the entire circle roared and applauded.

What had happened was that sex had gone out of the room. It was like realizing that all the food is gone at a party. The prettiest senior girls, the beefiest guys, the dances that would require a chaperone to come lay a gentle hand on someone's shoulder—all of it had stopped and the energy had apparently moved elsewhere. Where were Emily and Cynthia? Jacob wanted to find them and confront them with his and Charles's delight and then not share it. One lap of the dance floor showed that the girls weren't there. They weren't in the hallway either, and for a terrible instant Jacob thought that they might have followed him and Charles upstairs and witnessed their every action. Emily would have been horrified by him, and made him tell Mrs. Rice (whose painting class she loved). Separation fell between Jacob and Charles; they were each now enclosed in a curtain of anxiety.

Charles led them into the lounge—which looked from the outside to be empty, a mostly cleared room with a few couches and vending machines and unsteady wooden tables on which no one ever did any work. The girls sat in the farthest corner from the door, the seniors' corner, with expressions that were absolutely foreign. They were expressions that cared nothing for Jacob and Charles, nothing for boyfriends at all. The girls sat, or slouched, side by side on one couch with their feet propped up on a low table, and on the couch beside theirs Jerome Koss and Mitch Sundra sat back, smiling, doing something with a pair of empty liter bottles. There was a second before Jacob and Charles stepped forward and got the girls' attention in which they could have been watching through one-way glass: the girls wore looks of pleasure, bemusement, delight in being singled out.

When they saw Charles and Jacob they sat up and, in spite of trying to retain some bit of cheer, their faces fell. "Hey!" Emily said casually. "We thought you guys left. Come sit."

Jacob and Charles walked over. "Do you boys," Jerome said, "happen to know the difference between a farting duck and a spring wedding?"

Jacob didn't smile. He didn't look at Jerome or Mitch. He said, "Emily, can I talk to you outside for a second?"

"Do you have to?" she said, still not entirely, or not exclusively, addressing him.

They walked out of the lounge onto the concrete terrace and she sat down on a picnic table with her feet resting on the bench. She shivered—dramatically, Jacob felt—and gripped her own elbows. It had rained at some point during the night, and the table and benches were wet. The sky had turned an unpleasant yellow. Jacob was trembling too, although he wasn't cold.

"Why were you talking to them?"

"Because they were talking to us."

"You just happened to walk into the lounge and there they were."

"No. We just happened to be dancing, because this is an event at which people dance. And because our boyfriends can't be troubled to be seen with us, other people saw that we were alone and starting dancing with us."

"Stop talking like that. I hate when you talk like that."

Jacob did at that moment hate Emily with a passion almost as powerful, and as transformative, as lust. Her doughy body and her mousy face with its absurd makeup, her jeans and her lacy top.

And then suddenly she began to cry. He had heard her cry many times, but never before at school, and almost never with such conviction. Her eyes were red, her mouth was misshapen, her entire face was scrunched, and a muffled wail rose from her. Instantly Jacob's anger turned into alarm. He wanted nothing but for her to stop.

"Emily."

"I don't understand why you have to do this to me every time I talk to anyone else, I feel like I'm in some kind of jail, it's so awful, it's so unfair, I can't even just do completely normal things like when I meet someone and start talking to them I always have to be asking is this okay, is this right, would Jacob be mad about this—"

"Emily."

"*And it never is!* You're always mad, and I'm so fucking sick of it I can't stand it. I don't even know if we're happy together anymore, or if this is just some stupid fucking habit where we've been together so long we think we might as well keep going. But I can't keep going if I have to spend my entire fucking life being humiliated every time I talk to someone else, always being dragged away to be *scolded* like—"

"Emily."

"—like some little girl who doesn't know how to act. I'm not cheating on you! I'd never cheat on you, but sometimes

I want to, sometimes I wish you'd just walk in and see me making out with some other guy so it would finally make you break up with me and leave me the fuck alone!"

"You don't know what you're saying."

"I do know what I'm saying." She cried now as if someone were knocking her in the back again and again. Jacob's body was so alive, so alert, that it was practically pleasurable—he looked out and around at the patio and down the steps at the cars and felt both entirely present in this scene, where his girlfriend might well be in the process of breaking up with him, and also absent from it, a stranger to both of them. He had his hands on her shuddering back, and for want of anything else to do he massaged her shoulders, which he knew he never did particularly well. She had her face in her hands and all he could see of her head was her hair.

"Emily, I love you. I love you. Look at me."

She fought with surprising strength to keep him from prying her head up.

"Can you just say it?" he said. "Can you just say I love you? I'll say it. I love you."

Jacob thought that his feeling that someone was watching them might be an artifact of all the activity in his mind and body, but when he turned to look he saw something as unwelcome as a ghost: the school's computer expert, Mr. Brower, stood lit up in silhouette in the lounge window. Mr. Brower was a gray-skinned, slack-bellied man, obscurely lecherous, always peering over the top of his monitor with something between contempt and shyness. On his face now was an expression of predatory calm—it seemed to Jacob the most frightening face he had ever seen. The computer lab was next to the art room, but the lights had been off in there, hadn't they? No one had been upstairs.

"Let's move, I think someone's watching us," Jacob said, in a voice different from the ones they'd been using.

Emily didn't respond but the tone of her crying changed so he knew that she was listening.

Jacob led them away from the table and down to the front steps, out of view. He was careful to sit so that their knees touched, and she didn't move away. Her face was a mess and one nostril was blocked with clear snot, but she looked him in the eyes without self-consciousness. "I really don't think I should, but I guess I love you," she said.

"That's good." For a second the news that she was not going to break up with him turned him deaf and senseless.

"I don't ever want to go to a dance or anything with you again, though. It's stupid. I should be with my friends and you should be with yours. We can meet up afterward."

"Okay."

"You like Charles more than me anyway."

"No I don't."

"Yes you do, but it's fine. Now I have to go inside and go to the bathroom," she said, standing up unsteadily. "But I don't want you to follow me. Now who was watching us again? Where were they? Were you just trying to distract me?"

One night that winter Arthur picked up the phone and, without acknowledging that Emily was on the line, told

Jacob to come downstairs for a minute. Arthur's voice sounded full of purpose, and as Jacob thumped down the stairs he wondered if his father might be about to announce that he had cancer as well. Jacob smelled before he saw that Arthur had built a fire—something he'd once done fairly regularly but not since Alice had died. He was on his knees on the marble hearth, poking between gray smoldering logs with a section of bark. Will and Cara sat side by side on the couch wearing the same look of glum captivity.

In the year and a half that Arthur had been in therapy, he had become prone to saying all sorts of embarrassing, frank things. Like someone peddling religion, he seemed always to be waiting for an opening in a conversation, a rich silence. "Here," he'd say, handing over a book, "read this, starting with *Although*. He talks about grief-*waves*, which is exactly the right word, I think. Mine are coming much more rarely now. Like maybe once every couple of days, instead of every couple of hours." "I don't think I've ever talked to you guys about when *Mom's* mom died—did you know she died when Mom was twenty-four? Have we ever talked about that, calling around to see if someone could take the body and all that?"

He'd managed his suffering the only way he could—he'd become interested in it. He'd joined a widowers' group that met Monday evenings. Alice used to say that if someone had been on fire, Arthur would have stopped him to ask if he'd ever heard what Winston Churchill once said when Parliament was burning. Now instead of Churchill it was Pamela D. Blair, PhD, and Granger E. Westberg. "A lot of it's just common sense, but good to hear, I think." On one of these books' recommendations he asked the kids what changes they would like to see in the house, ideas for how things ought to run. Will, who in the evenings was busy with the school paper, suggested that they have family dinners only on Sundays. Jacob suggested a policy of no questions about homework so long as their grades stayed all right (Arthur didn't know when to check the mail for report cards). Cara proposed that Finney start sleeping in her room.

These differences and dozens of others, spoken and not, had been so readily accepted that it was only on the rare occasions when they did something normal—spent a Saturday afternoon at the Air and Space Museum; drove after dinner to Baskin-Robbins—that Jacob was able to mark how much their lives had changed. Alice had known all of the kids' teachers names, and known too whether they were enemies or allies. She had known which friends Cara was likely to invite to her birthday party and which she couldn't bear to hear mentioned. Arthur, running the house, had an air of someone cooking without a recipe, adding salt when he'd meant to add sugar and then saying *Yes, exactly*. Their family life had been inching toward chaos ever since Alice had first gone into the hospital, but now it seemed to have become permanently disordered, which—depending on the day—either mortified Jacob or delighted him.

Now, sitting in front of the dry, blazing fire, he was flustered and irritated and determined not to be soothed until he'd paid his father back for interrupting him on the phone.

Arthur coughed into his fist, then said the kids had probably noticed that he'd not been home some Thursday evenings lately. (No, but they kept silent.) Well, he'd made a new friend.

The words hung in the air in front of Arthur's face. He knitted his brow, as if considering whether to draw the sentence back and try again. Then suddenly he noticed something in the fire and leapt down onto his knees to resume prodding. ("Is there smoke going into the room? Do you guys see smoke?")

He squinted up toward the ceiling. "She's actually one of your old pals," he said, and at that moment Will and Jacob exchanged a look across the room of such sympathy— disbelief, embarrassment, dread—that it was nearly intolerable, it was as if they'd kissed on the mouth. "Remember Charlotte Chassler? We ran into each other at the store one day and—well, we just started talking about you guys and whatnot, then went out for coffee, now we've made sort of a weekly thing of it this past month or so. She actually got divorced about a year ago. Did you know she's not at Waggoner anymore? She's teaching somewhere in Silver Spring now. Her own class of fifth graders."

Charlotte Chassler. Mrs. Chassler.

"Are you . . . saying you're interested in each other?" Will asked. He sat forward, neatly shredding a piece of the waxy starter wood from the basket under the mantle.

Arthur paused for long enough that he could have been considering the question for the first time. "We're not 'a couple,' or however you want to put it. I think one of the nice things is that we're both happy getting to know each other. She's—well, you guys know—she's very nice to talk to. I wouldn't have said, but I didn't think you'd want me keeping secrets." With his expression he folded that last thought out of view, like a stain on a napkin. "Hand up?" Will gripped his hand at the wrist and hoisted him up off the ground—a playful and not quite necessary thing Arthur liked to do. "Are any of you hungry? I was about to put Tater Tots in."

They didn't talk about Mrs. Chassler again that night or for the rest of the week, and Jacob surprised himself by deciding not to mention her to Emily. He told himself that this was out of respect for his father, but really it had more to do with shame; he liked when Emily marveled at the freedom of his family, how he could leave the house and not even write a note about where he was going, and he wasn't inclined to complicate the picture. But he did tell Owen, whose family life meant Jacob could tell him anything. "I think my dad might be dating Mrs. Chassler."

"Huh," Owen said. "Are you going to have to see her?"

"I don't know, probably."

"Uh-oh."

(For Owen all problems, particularly those regarding adults, came down to social problems. Awkward interactions, embarrassing confrontations—these were to be avoided like electrocution.)

To Jacob's surprise he found that he—or a part of him— did want to see Mrs. Chassler. Another part of him, the sensible part, the part that understood how it would feel to see his father touch someone else's knee, wanted never to see her or even to hear her name. But Mrs. Chassler—was she still beautiful? Did she remember him? Jacob hadn't known her very well—she'd only come to his class for a year, once a week. But Will had known her, and so she had smiled at Jacob in the hall, asked how he was doing, told him to tie his shoes.

In the way he'd loved many of his first teachers, he'd loved Mrs. Chassler, however briefly and incoherently. This had been before Owen, before Marek, before he and Will had even moved into their own rooms, when he'd worn corduroy pants and plain-color turtlenecks, when for a few months he'd been missing his left front tooth. On the occasions when she came to teach his class he was shy to the point of invisibility, but in his fantasies—he'd forgotten so much of this!—he would save her from a fire, or perform on the piano while she applauded in the front row. She was the youngish part-time art teacher, red-cheeked and quick to smile, who appeared with her rolling cart to lead them in building gingerbread houses, making pinch pots. She seemed constantly, cheerily distracted, as if distraction were in fact her natural state of being (for an unpleasant second it occurred to him that she was not unlike his mother in this respect). He remembered when she'd gotten married, or rather he had an image of her standing in the front office taking an enormous red bouquet from one of the secretaries, grinning with joy and embarrassment.

Emily certainly didn't need to know about any of this.

Now that his father had told them about Mrs. Chassler, Jacob did notice that Arthur wasn't home on Thursday evenings, and soon he noticed Tuesday evenings too. And then, by December, he noticed that Arthur was coming home from movies on weekend afternoons with a particular playful expression that Jacob didn't like to study too closely. "I'm going to go see that new portrait exhibit." "I think I'm going to go watch them light the tree on the Mall tonight."

"It's been a long time since I had a friend like this," he said one day, in a tone at once apologetic and boastful.

Emily was over one afternoon and she and Jacob were watching *Full House* while Will, in the armchair, made red marks on a set of newspaper proofs. Cara rocked in the rocking chair, her feet hooked around the chair legs. Will and Cara could have been anywhere in the house, of course, but when Emily was over she often drew the family into the room as if by gravity. Will asked Emily how she was liking Mr. Firenze's European History class—a class that was like a secret society, and whose members treasured their sleepless nights and impossible workloads. Emily, irritatingly pleased, said she loved it, and asked whether it was easier or harder than Mrs. Larue's Honors Physics. These conversations seemed to Jacob designed to leave him out, and in defiance he fixated on the TV—Uncle Joey and Uncle Jesse were playing with hand puppets in the basement—and turned the volume up so loud that they could hardly hear each other.

He did hear, though, when Will, enjoying himself, said, "So what do you think about Mrs. Chassler?"

Jacob turned to scowl at Will but it was too late—Emily was tenacious in this way, she would root out the truth from the tiniest slip.

Will explained, and Jacob talked over him. "I didn't tell you because it's nothing and because it's not my business. I was going to. I was going to tell you if it was actually anything, but we don't know anything. Thanks, Will. Thank you very, very much."

Over the next few weeks Emily gave Jacob good reason to wish no one had told her. The prospect of Jacob's father with a girlfriend was for her a bottomless mystery. "Do you think they make out and stuff?"

"I have no idea."

"Isn't it weird to think of adults making out? Like who makes the first move? Do you think he feels her up? Sorry."

Jacob had half an inclination to turn himself into a hermit. Even kissing Emily, and the usually irresistible maneuvering to find time with her and a door that locked, had been tainted. He imagined, as if in a grimy mirror, his father pressed against Mrs. Chassler, his thick hands in her hair. He found himself revising his old fantasies, considering the likelihood that Mrs. Chassler had gotten fat by now. He prayed, many nights in bed, that tomorrow Arthur would say, as he unpacked groceries or gathered the dishes, that he and Mrs. Chassler probably weren't going to be seeing each other much anymore. A little melancholy and guilt in his voice. Just us after all.

But it didn't happen. Occasionally Arthur brought with

him now into the house the smell of peach perfume. He hummed while he toasted pine nuts in a pan, reading the sections of the newspaper he'd missed that morning. In compensation, he began to make a point of having them all visit Alice's grave every week. It was no longer something he would let the kids weasel out of—they were all to go together, every Saturday afternoon; more as witnesses to his presence than for their own good, Jacob felt.

It was a Saturday in February, a day as warm as spring, and the four Vines stood around Alice's gravestone, on sod so neatly laid that it was hard to envision digging ever having taken place here. The curb and grass and stones all looked plump and wet. For Jacob his mother's gravestone, in the two years that they'd been coming, had changed in his mind from something having to do with his actual mother into something purely scenic, like the plaque that stood at the corner of Jefferson and Pinyon (THE TOWN OF WAGGONER: INCORPORATED 1896). A glossy black stone with plain gray letters read:

ALICE LOBEL VINE, WIFE AND MOTHER
June 4, 1952–December 11, 1993

Those numbers, which had once seemed to him blunt and astonishing, no longer had much power. Now it was February 16, 1996. December of seventh grade—when he had never seen a girl naked, never set foot in high school—seemed prehistoric. He sometimes thought, absurdly, that if his mother were to see him now, she might not recognize him. He shaved once or even twice a week (at night, so any cuts would have time to heal before school). His armpit hair was now beyond dispute, a pair of dense black tassels. Her son the man. To bring her back he would have had to bring back a self who seemed to him small, timid, skittering. By dying she had grown him up, and grown him away from her.

Or so he believed most of the time. It would occasionally happen—though never at moments he could anticipate or court—that someone would sneeze just the way she did in the next aisle at the grocery store. Or he would walk into the playroom, looking for his science binder, and realize that he'd been just about to call out to ask her for help. At these moments he got a feeling like waking up from a dream of falling—a cold ghostly plunge. She'd recognize him after all.

The question of how long they would stand over the grave was delicate. After a minute Cara would begin to fidget, or to ask if she could go look for older graves; Will and Arthur would frown at the ground; Jacob would listen to a traffic helicopter whapping overhead or watch another family laying down a photograph and hope that his father wouldn't make them hold hands. Today he did. Their jackets lay bunched at their feet. Arthur's hand felt heavy and dry. "Why don't we go around and give a little update? Will?"

"I just got put in charge of lights for *Macbeth,* which is pretty cool. I'm working a lot on the paper. I miss you."

"Cara?"

"Hi. I got a ninety-one on my Reading quiz last week. I

moved my bed so it's facing the other way and I like it a lot better. Um..."

"Jacob?"

"I'm fine. I'm good. Everything's good."

Ordinarily this might have been when Arthur let their hands go, but today he held on and continued to look down—and a little timer of dread began to tick in Jacob. "Well, for me, I just wanted to say I'm feeling happy. I really wasn't sure that was going to happen again." He squeezed Jacob's hand so hard that his knuckles cracked. Arthur's lips buckled and his face threatened to break, almost as if he were about to sneeze, but his features collected themselves. He cleared his throat, a sound that drew a ring around all of them, and they walked slowly toward the car. He put his arm around Cara, who didn't mind. "How does that go? 'The trees are coming into leaf...'" Arthur knew perfectly well that they would have no idea, especially Cara, but he was hardly talking to them. He tugged a low branch, sprinkling himself. "'The recent buds...' something something... 'Their greenness is a kind of grief.' I remember I never understood what that meant."

For Jacob there was real benefit in not having a parent's full attention, and it had to do with the ongoing dreary crisis that was school. The network of crises. As a freshman Jacob felt he had begun to understand what it must be like to owe money—hardly a day, hardly a period, passed in which he didn't have to lie to one teacher or another that he'd left his assignment sheet at school, or that he'd written down the wrong date, or that he'd been out of the room during some crucial discussion. He had become adept at searching prolongedly through his backpack. On any one day a few of his teachers could be held off, but never all of them, and always there were new demands piling up, new books he was meant to have finished, new lists of vocabulary words culled from new articles he hadn't read.

He and Emily had no classes together. She had been placed in honors courses, with fifteen-page-paper assignments and teachers who boasted that their reading lists were college level, and his schedule had come to be full of Introductions. Even a place like Vernon Day had kids who read car magazines under their desks and drew nipples on their binders. Who, when Mr. Vesell asked them to name a family of organisms other than animals and plants, mumbled "Minerals?"

Jacob's teachers were peppy, overmatched Vernon Day alums, or else they were human pieces of antique classroom equipment, twenty-year veterans whirring away behind blank eyes. While Emily took Honors European History with Mr. Firenze, Jacob, in Mrs. Dunn's American History, played the part of a soldier in a mock trial about the Boston Massacre ("I heard a great commotion and then I felt something strike me from the direction of the crowd, sir!").

One morning as Jacob sat in the lounge during his free period, a boy named Ian Robeck, his hands stuffed in the pouch of his hooded sweatshirt, asked if Jacob wanted to go to Safeway. Not many people happened to be free during third period, so over the course of the year he and Ian had become something just short of friends. Ian was known for having to wake up at five because he lived an hour and a half from school. He loved pro wrestling—or anyway he talked with unusual passion about it—and he listened to heavy metal that made Jacob, when Ian dropped his headphones over Jacob's ears, feel incredulous and old.

They walked to Safeway together under a sky the same color as the sidewalk, talking about whether Jamie Kim or Ellen Mosello was the hottest girl coming to high school next year. They knew both girls—regarded throughout the high school like athletes of unusual promise—from middle school. There seemed to Jacob something slightly murderous in Ian's brand of lust; he wore the same smirk, talking about whether Ellen's breasts would have grown, as he did when he talked about the Undertaker putting Steve Austin in a sleeper hold.

Ian lit a cigarette and, out of politeness, offered one to Jacob. An SUV full of juniors holding Tropical Smoothies bounced past. Everything was fine as Jacob and Ian plucked stale bagels out of the plastic bins and paid with change. Everything was fine as they strolled, chewing, past the Salvation Army woman and her clanging bell, and as they noticed from the dark spots on the stairs that it had begun to rain. Everything was fine until suddenly, and for no reason Jacob could immediately discern, it wasn't.

Jacob had had a vision, or a flutter of nausea. A moment outside himself. It was 10:30 on a gray morning and he was walking back from Safeway with Ian Robeck, talking about thirteen-year-old girls to whom he had never spoken. He had a throbbing pimple in one corner of his mouth, and next period he had a biology quiz during which he'd been planning on hiding in the lounge. Exhaustion was such a common feature of his life, of everyone's life, that he had to be careful not to mistake its symptoms—a slight ache, a feeling that his brain had been replaced with damp cotton balls—for emotion. A nap might scrub everything clean. But this didn't feel like exhaustion; in fact his heart was racing. He told Ian he had to print something in the computer lab and raced inside and up the stairwell to stand outside Emily's French Literature class.

Jacob knew Emily's schedule as well as he knew his own. When he needed her to come out of class, as he did now, he coughed and held up his pinkie. She was so capable an actress that often he wouldn't realize she'd noticed him until she stood up from her chair.

She led them now away from the door, out of Mr. Moldeaux's sight. Mr. Moldeaux had gray curls that rested on his shirt's collar, and Jacob had never heard him speak anything other than French, even in the halls. The way Emily held her mouth when she spoke French—a concerned-looking pursing of the lips—both irritated Jacob and made him want to press his mouth against hers. Now she slouched impatiently, clicking the end of her pen.

"Something weird happened," he said.

"What?"

"I don't know. I had an idea when I was coming back from Safeway. I think I really want to start trying now," he said.

"Okay. In school?"

"Uh-huh. I shouldn't just...drift anymore. I want to actually work."

"Good. Are you okay?"

"I think so. Yes."

"I have to go back in. We'll talk more later. *Je t'adore.*"

Next period in Mr. Vesell's Introduction to Biology, Jacob sat up unusually straight on his stool. Mr. Vesell, who'd only come to Vernon Day that year, was an able but uninspiring teacher who gave off the deadly smell of genuine kindness. He walked on the tips of his toes, and rode his bike to and from school in a helmet that doubled the size of his head.

Since no one feared Mr. Vesell, and since the class met at the end of the morning, the room almost always featured a student or two asleep. Even today, despite the quiz, Brooke Reilly had made a nest of her sweatshirt and laid her head down on the desk. When Mr. Vesell touched her shoulder and asked, apologetically, for her to please stay with them and, if she needed to, go buy a Coke from the vending machine, she scowled and stared ahead.

Isaac Demby stood looking along with Jessica Braun's notes, glancing every few seconds toward the front of the room. Sarah Moy flipped through the textbook murmuring to herself. Jacob—who had lost the textbook two weeks earlier and who had never quite designated a notebook for Biology—sat before a counter clear of everything but a single Uni-ball pen. He was like a samurai clutching his sword. Mr. Vesell drifted around the room, handing out sheets of paper that seemed to have hardly any writing. Everyone pushed their books onto the floor and sank into silent intensity. Fine. There was nothing that Jacob couldn't manage.

The quiz was just one question long.

Describe, IN DETAIL, and using drawings if necessary, the process by which the information stored in DNA is expressed as a protein.

Jacob lifted his pen and crisply wrote his name and today's date.

Well, first, of course, you had the DNA. Which had to do with mitosis. And when the cell was ready for that, first everything sort of bunched together inside the little circle. And then the cell started breaking into two, or actually the little circle started breaking into two...

Martha Willis, in the seat beside Jacob, had drawn a row of careful hatch marks and something that looked like a snowman. David Goldstein's paper was covered already in dense tilting script, his pencil point trailing powder. It took all of Jacob's strength not to stand up and leave the room. Mr. Vesell, sensing Jacob's disturbance and seeing his blank page, came hurrying over. "Is everything all right?"

"Mm-hmm."

"Are you going to get writing?"

"Yup. Here I go."

"Okay, good."

What Jacob finally wrote, in a neat, cramped hand was:

Mr. Vesell—

I didn't study for this quiz, so I'm afraid I'm not able to answer this question. I completely understand that this means I'll receive a zero, and I also know that I deserve it. But I want you to know that I'm determined to start taking my work more seriously. I know this is something that's expected of me so I don't deserve any special congratulations, but you're going to start to see a real difference from here forward.

I'm very sorry about the quiz.

Jacob

Passing this paper in, Jacob felt solemn and proud, a repentant killer marching toward the gallows. Mr. Vesell quickly read the note and then, with what looked like embarrassment, shuffled it to the bottom of the pile. For the rest of the period Jacob listened zealously as Mr. Vesell demonstrated what a correct answer would have looked like. The DNA unzipping, the RNA neatly assembling...

That night Jacob found his textbook—it had been in a pile in his room all along—and began with the very first page. *Simply put, biology is the science of life.* It took him less time than he would have thought to catch up. Taken in order, the lessons had an almost ridiculous coherence. Soon enough the readings they discussed in class were the very readings he'd done the night before. School is so simple! And at some point in those first weeks of new resolve, like the first faint flexing of a new muscle, Jacob experienced a shiver. This was during the unit about the scientists who had discovered the structure of DNA. Mr. Vesell told the story well—Watson and Crick and poor doomed Rosalind Franklin; Linus Pauling in his study with his Tinkertoys—and at some point as Jacob sat there, he realized that he was simply, and without effort, listening. Twenty-five minutes had passed since he last checked the clock. From then on he related to everything in the class a little differently. He'd be looking at a diagram in the book of the potassium-ion channel in a cell wall, and he'd experience a momentary loss of scale. He was cells. Each one felt palpable, bustling. Undoubtedly his epiphanies contained more than a bit of wishfulness, and even so they were fragile; as soon as he trained his attention on the sensation it began to fade. But so long as he let the feeling blossom out of sight, he could sustain the most extraordinary feeling of spaciousness and of clarity—it was more than understanding, it was embodying.

One night on the phone Jacob explained to Emily what he'd learned. This wasn't so unusual. They talked so much—as many as five or ten times each night—that they rarely had anything they actually wanted to convey; their conversations had a quality of resignation, as if they happened to be riding beside each other on an overnight train. She would read him the Notable Quotes from her mother's *Newsweek,* he would recount for her the plots of movies he'd watched the night before (the Barleys had no TV, so he would have to describe Keanu Reeves or Morgan Freeman as if to a grandparent). Tonight he told her about the chemical assembly lines in their bodies, and he was paying such attention to getting the details right that he had no idea whether she was raptly listening or if she had put the phone down and was tending to a grilled-cheese sandwich. (Neither, as it turned out—she was listening while correcting a Trig test from the week before).

More and more insistently in the coming weeks, as Mr. Vesell led them through a chaotic lab in which they simulated fruit-fly matings on the computer, Jacob came to believe that he'd finally discovered a subject that he might care about, a forum for his latent greatness. He wondered if he could have found history just as engaging, if he had happened to have his vision in the afternoon rather than in the morning. No matter. He presented his interest to Emily—he would never have talked about it with Charles or Owen or even his father—as something destined, a natural outgrowth of having watched his mother in the hospital. He decided he was going to be a doctor, quite possibly a surgeon. "It's how *everything* works," he said. "It's how your body... knows how to make your body. And when the instructions screw up, that's when people get six toes or cancer or whatever."

"How do the different parts work, though? How do, you know, these cells know that they're supposed to make a hand and these cells know they're supposed to make a brain?"

"It's all... in there. It's an instruction manual. It's like an instruction manual with a part about making an instruction manual."

They had this conversation while waiting, a bit stiffly, for

Emily's mother to come to United Artists and pick them up. It was a Saturday night in February, warm enough that they held their coats in their laps. They had just watched *Seven* (though they'd bought tickets for *101 Dalmations*). The end, when Gwyneth Paltrow's head arrived in a box, had both unsettled Jacob and provoked in him a ferocious, delicious love for Emily—if she were to die, then he, like Brad Pitt, would be reduced to babbling and sobbing in the desert. He would shoot Kevin Spacey in the head. He had gripped her hand so hard that she'd winced.

They sat on the edge of the courtyard where, a couple of years ago, they'd lingered and teased each other. The space was full now of people who seemed young and unsure, giggling and shrieking and making fools of themselves.

"Do you think I'm stupid?" he asked.

"Shut up."

"Honestly. Do you think I'm stupid?"

"Honestly, shut up. Yes, I think you're very stupid."

"You used to say you thought I was one of the smartest people you'd ever met."

"When did I say that?"

"When we were first going out. You wrote it in a letter."

"I must have been trying to flatter you."

Emily's mother's maroon minivan pulled to a stop and they both climbed in. Mrs. Barley had on NPR, a lighthearted program with music that sounded as if it had been recorded in a barn, and to announce to them her intention to go on listening she nudged the volume knob higher. She was unsmiling, with pale eyes and fine silver hair pinned tightly back. Emily said she was funny and free-spirited, especially when compared to her father, but around Jacob she seemed as cold as a stranger.

She had driven Jacob home enough nights now that she knew where to turn, and knew too that although the Vines' house would look abandoned, there was no reason to wait outside. Arthur would be out; Will would be at Kate's or at rehearsal; Cara would be at gymnastics or else sitting in front of the TV with her babysitter, working on a friendship bracelet in the near dark. No one should expect the usual things of them.

But Mrs. Barley wasn't as awed by his situation as he would have liked. Her eyes were never entirely focused when she looked at him. She was thinking of her own father (who had Parkinson's disease), or she was thinking of money (her husband's retirement, Emily's college). Jacob was used to being found charming by adults, and it bothered him—felt as if he were being mistaken for Ian Robeck—to knock against this crucial adult's sympathy without gaining entrance.

They pulled up in front of the Vines' dark house, and just as Jacob was climbing out Emily surprised him by saying, "I think I forgot my necklace last weekend. Can I go in and look for it for a minute?"

She was out the door before her mother could respond, and they were inside, up in Jacob's room, before Jacob realized that she hadn't forgotten her necklace at all. Emily pulled the bedroom door shut behind her.

Another scene for the memory loop.

She peeled off her shirt and bra and jeans and under-wear and left them in a tidy pile beside the bed, working quickly, smiling at her daring. And with stunning, slightly frantic speed she let them kiss and rub and grab at each other, and then suddenly, just as Jacob felt the first help-less warming, she pulled away and looked at him with wide eyes.

"Jacob Vine, I want us to make love."

"You feel bad for calling me stupid."

"You're brilliant."

"You're just saying that."

"Yes I am. Now make love to me."

The room was so dark that their naked bodies looked black and white. He felt unusually aware of his own breath-ing. Here, physically present and touchable in his bed, no less miraculous than the first time it had happened, was a naked girl. Small pointed breasts, damp springy tangles, lengths of leg and stomach.

"I don't have a condom."

"It's okay, I just had my period."

Jacob wasn't sure what bearing this had on the question, but he took her word for it.

"I don't think we have time," he said.

"We do. I want you."

"I want you too. I don't know. I really don't know."

As it turned out he shouldn't have worried about the time. She took hold of him and eased herself over him, and before she'd had a chance to move or moan, before he'd had a chance even to reflect on what he was doing, he was crackling, he was wilting, he was through. He had made love to the thought of making love. She was bewildered only for a moment, before she realized what had happened and leaned over to plant a single salvaging kiss on his lips.

Afterward she dressed as quickly as she'd undressed and then kissed him again as he lay in bed, drained and dazzled.

"I'll be better than that," he said meekly.

"You were great, my love. Be quiet. But I need a necklace. Can I go steal something from Cara?"

"I don't think Cara has any normal necklaces. They're all just beads and stuff."

"Are there any of your mom's old ones around?" She said this with a hesitancy that Jacob understood, but he was happy, even eager, to violate this particular taboo for her. He pulled on his pants and together they crept down into Arthur's bedroom and over to Alice's old side of the bed, where her engraved wooden jewelry box stood untouched. The lights in the room were off and, to acknowledge what they had done upstairs, and to distract somewhat from the awkwardness of what they were doing now, they kissed again. Emily chose a thin metal necklace with a blue stone hanging from the center. "I'll give it back," she whispered, but he waved her away.

They made their way downstairs in a cloud of elation, and they were just kissing good-bye in the dark hallway by the door when they heard footsteps on the porch. Arthur, coming up the steps, pulled the keys from his pocket, and kept his attention directed over his shoulder at a smiling woman in a long gray coat like Paddington Bear's. A trap-door beneath Jacob swung open—beneath him and inside him.

"Hey, you two!" Arthur said heartily. "Emily, I think that's your mother's car out there."

"I know! I was just leaving."

She held the necklace behind her back. Jacob had never seen her turn this particular shade of red.

"Before you go (are you going, Jacob?), why not say hi to Charlotte!" Mrs. Chassler was shorter and broader than Jacob remembered, less radiant. The edges of her nostrils were red, as if she had a cold. Her hair, which had as many colors as a loaf of multigrain bread, went only to her shoulders. Jacob noticed that he hadn't yet managed to say anything.

"Jacob Vine," Mrs. Chassler said, extending her hand formally, playfully. The voice hadn't changed. "And is this your friend I've been hearing so much about? Hi, I'm Charlotte Chassler." Such voltages of awkwardness buzzed between the two couples standing in the hall that everything else—the car outside, the coats on the hooks—temporarily disappeared. Until Jacob got outside he felt that he couldn't breathe.

On the freezing patio, shaken but buoyant, Jacob touched Emily on the shoulder rather than kiss her good night. He was barefoot with the cuffs of his pants pinned under his heels. She ran out to her car, and Jacob watched her pull away before he turned back toward the house.

He hurried past Arthur and Mrs. Chassler, facing each

other over the kitchen counter, and up to his room, where he lay in bed and directed himself not to think about his father, and instead to bask in the fact that on these very sheets, in this very air...

He didn't succeed. After a few minutes he was standing at the top of the stairs, listening to the voices below and trying to gauge from their tones what they were doing. It was hard to say. A faucet was running, and he heard his father talking in the voice he used when he was trying to be funny. After fifteen minutes Jacob's pager hummed deep in his pocket.

4°5683°968

He kissed the screen, in the automatic way he did when he was alone, and went into the bathroom to study his face. If he died tonight, his life would not have been entirely a waste. The toilet was running. He plunged his hand into the freezing tank, tugged the chain, and pressed down on the rubber stopper. The first time he'd fixed the toilet as a nonvirgin. The first time he'd realized there wasn't a towel in here as a nonvirgin. With his hand still wet, he sat on the ledge outside the bathroom, under the angled window directly beneath the full moon, and called Owen.

"Do I sound different?"

"Why? Did you and Emily have sex?"

"Do I sound different?"

"You had sex! I deplore you. I really and truly deplore you."

Next he called Emily, resolved to hang up if either of her parents answered.

"I just wanted to say I love you too," he said.

"Good, okay."

"And thank you for..."

"Don't *thank* me."

His recognition that she wanted to be off the phone made him determined to stay on.

"Are you positive you're not going to be pregnant?"

"Shush. Yes."

With the back of his hand he tented out the waistband of his boxers and studied the matted spirals. "Should we get tested for things, like AIDS and stuff?"

"Jacob, we've never done anything with anyone else."

"How do I know that?"

"I'm hanging up."

"Don't, I'll stop, I'll stop. I think my dad's pathetic."

"Why?"

"He's like a dog. Why can't he ever just be alone? Mrs. Chassler was our *teacher*. She taught us how to make cotton clouds."

"So? She looked nice. Maybe he's lonely."

"He's supposed to be lonely! His *wife* died."

"Well, I'm sure he is lonely. Whatever else happens, I think you can probably count on that."

One night that spring, Charlotte (she was Charlotte by then, even in Jacob's mind) came to the Vines' for dinner. Jacob had seen her occasionally since the night with Emily, a nod and hello in the kitchen or on the porch—but never for dinner, and Jacob had begun to imagine, to hope, that his life and his father's might travel on parallel tracks, the relationship of each unexamined on the periphery of the other's vision. No luck.

It was only April, but for a week it had been as hot as summer, and Charlotte arrived in a white dress embroidered with blue flowers. "Is this what they call a sundress?" Arthur said, hugging her as if after a long separation (they had seen each other that afternoon), taking from her a bottle of wine.

Emily was over too; most Sundays she and Jacob ate at one or the other of their houses. She had come over earlier in the afternoon and, carrying conspicuous loads of notebooks, they'd retreated to Jacob's bedroom. The familiar starving delight had given way to disaster—the condom burst. She must have nicked it with her fingernail taking it out of the package, or he must have forgotten to squeeze the air from the tip. Her period was starting in three days, and Jacob now understood what that meant. The two of them, Jacob in particular, came back downstairs too much in shock to mind having to eat with Arthur and Charlotte.

Dinner would be outside, although it was just hot enough that this wouldn't be entirely a treat. The garden, left to its own devices over the past year, had become dense and tousled from all the rain they'd been getting. Mosquitoes had begun to circle endlessly, almost invisibly.

Cara slowly carried three full water glasses over the threshold onto the patio ("Careful, careful!"), and then, on a separate trip, the white plastic silverware rack that was the emblem of outdoor dining. The pieces clinked together like wind chimes. She was ten years old and, though she still wore plain T-shirts and shorts that had belonged to her brothers, she was just beginning to experiment with the powers that came with being a young woman. She had braces that were now green and white, for the softball team. She baby-talked with her girlfriends but could sound as haughty as a teenager when she talked to boys. She loved guests, loved occasions.

Arthur had mentioned the day before, haltingly, that Charlotte would be coming over for dinner, and he'd like for all of them to be home to spend some time with her. Immediately they'd all schemed to get away. Jacob had called Emily to plead especially for her to come, and if he hadn't done that, then Emily wouldn't have come over beforehand, and if it hadn't been for that…

Arthur stood now in the middle of the kitchen, a glass salad bowl cradled against his side, and nodding toward the colander full of spaghetti, he said to Charlotte, "Grab a plate and get started, before the hogs get in here and eat it all. Pesto's in that bowl. Hogs? Come eat!"

Jacob piled a tangle of spaghetti onto his plate and, when Arthur gave him a look, said, "What? You said to eat." Emily stood against the stove with her plate flat against her chest, wearing a convincing expression of calm. Being an only child had taught her how to make her concerns invisible among adults.

There was some awkwardness as Charlotte decided where to sit. There were seats next to Arthur, at the head, and next to Emily. In a rush of discomfort Arthur steered her directly to Alice's old place. Carefully, like someone using props in a play, she served herself salad, poured herself water, laid her napkin on her lap.

Cara said, "Dad, can I tell you Mr. Janublis's puzzle from today?" She looked at Arthur but all her attention was on Emily, with whom she was half in love. "So picture a hallway full of lockers. And somebody goes down the hall and opens every other locker."

"Don't baby-talk."

"I'm *not*. So someone opens every other locker. And then someone else comes along and opens every fourth locker, but if he comes to a locker that's already open, he closes it. Or no, wait. *First* the person goes along and opens every fourth locker, and then someone else comes along...Wait."

Just when she began to laugh, hoping that everyone would join her, Will said, "You have pesto in your braces." Her smile vanished like an eel into a rock. She turned red, raised her napkin to her face, and set to work with her tongue, nearly tearful with embarrassment.

Will neatly sliced his entire plate of pasta, as Alice used to tell them not to do, and managed to convey by his posture and by the quality of his attention—friendly but detached—that this was for him not nearly so consequential as it was for his siblings. He had his own responsibilities elsewhere.

"So you've got to indulge me," Charlotte said, tearing a piece of bread. "Who from your class are you still in touch with? I want to hear what Jenny Dunham is doing, Peter Benthart, Jeremy...what was his name?"

Will sipped his water. "I haven't really kept in touch with that many people, but let's see. Jeremy Salnikoff?"

"Yes! What's Jeremy doing?"

"His family moved to Dallas. I think his dad got a job at some school there. And I haven't seen him, but someone told me last year about Nick Casanderos. He got in some sort of car accident and he's fine but his little brother's legs were apparently all smashed up. I ran into Jenny Dunham a little bit ago—she's at Spillerton, seems the same as ever, still says she's going to be an actress."

Jacob, unable to think of anything to say to Emily, instead served her a second helping of salad. Cara sat on her knees in her chair, as was her habit, and she now practically climbed onto the table in the hopes of being included. "Have I ever met Jenny?" she said. "Is she the one who was in the golf commercial? Is that her? Hello!"

Arthur and Emily had a peculiar ease in conversation with each other—peculiar because Arthur's main feeling regarding his children's relationships seemed to be an embarrassment that verged on disavowing responsibility entirely. He had never knocked on a door to see what Jacob and Emily were up to, and when he'd once surprised them in the living room, unbuttoned and straining, he'd quickly turned on his heels and pretended to have forgotten something upstairs. He and Emily talked easily now, though, about whether Vernon was becoming too much of a prep school, and whether it made sense to put so much focus on AP courses when lots of colleges didn't even honor the credits anymore. She was four months older than Jacob but at these moments she might have been his older sister. Emily looked so placid and ordinary—she was describing for Arthur the tour of the Capitol her class had taken the week before—that Jacob found himself beginning to recover from the shock upstairs. He spun the spaghetti on his fork and invented some statistics. There was probably only a 5 percent chance that this was the right time for Emily to get pregnant. And even if it was, there was probably only a 2 percent chance that he had actually managed to do it. Couples tried for years and never got pregnant. It was the same as when he'd been terrified of storms, dragging his parents down into the basement whenever he heard thunder, certain lightning would seek him out. They'd get a home pregnancy test, maybe even tomorrow, and end all this. He put a hand on Emily's knee.

"We rode on this little train," she said, "like a mini Metro, but it just runs between the Senate and the Capitol. All these senators were standing there talking, waiting to get on. We saw Ted Kennedy coming out of the bathroom."

"Did you? You aren't old enough to remember all that Chappaquiddick stuff, but my God, was that a big deal when it happened. Remember that, Charlotte? How does he look? He used to be very handsome, believe it or not."

Cara turned to Charlotte and said, "Look, Finney's trying to catch a bug."

"Oop! Did he get him?"

"Cara, Finney shouldn't catch *bugs*. Bobby Kennedy was one of the first jobs I ever had. I went door to door handing out buttons with my parents—this completely awful neighborhood. That was in Chicago."

As soon as their plates were empty, Will stood up and, pulling the keys from his back pocket, said he was sorry to duck out but he was supposed to go over to another editor's house that night to do some layout. Charlotte looked up at him with large-eyed fondness. Jacob had long since given up on complaining that the rules didn't apply to Will. There were hardly any rules, and if Jacob had joined the newspaper or anything else he would have been free to go as well. Will carried in his plate, and after a minute they all heard the engine start and the car pulling out of the driveway.

"Jacob, can you drive yet? I can never remember when all that starts." Charlotte's attention was like a pitcher of water and she made sure to keep everyone's glasses even, never to overfill them by a drop. It was the first time that night, possibly the first time since elementary school, that he saw a flicker of what he'd loved in her when he was seven years old. His strongest impression of her until then had been of an uptight, too-sweet matron—more like a nurse to his father than girlfriend, and more like a stranger to Jacob than like the glowing teacher he'd once watched drink from the water fountain.

"Let's see hands for lemon sorbet," Arthur said, pushing back his chair. Finney rose to attention and wagged eagerly. "One, two . . . With or without berries?"

When he brought out the bowls, Charlotte was talking to Emily about how law school really wasn't just for lawyers anymore.

"You don't actually know if you want to go to law school though, right?" Jacob said.

"I don't *know*, but I think I probably will. It seems like a good thing to do."

Before she took a bite of the sorbet, Charlotte—quickly but not so quickly that Arthur didn't see—plucked a mosquito out of her dish and flicked it away. Arthur hadn't noticed that they were one spoon short, so he wiped his fork and ate with that. It seemed to have gotten dark in just the time that he was in the kitchen. Finney, his ears raised, glared at a patch of air beside the table. "My legs are getting *eaten,*" Emily said to Jacob, and as if by agreement everyone at the table began to smack at their ankles and necks. Cara said, "Me too! Look at my arm!" After a few minutes something black swooped past Cara's head and Jacob said, "Is that a bat?" which made Cara shriek and rush to the door, finally winning the laughter she'd been working for all night. "What do you think, enough of the great outdoors?" Arthur said, and he laid a hand on Charlotte's lower back as they filed inside, each carrying a bowl and glass. He leaned forward so that his chin touched her shoulder and whispered, too quietly for Jacob to hear, something that made her posture soften.

Emily lingered outside, looking down, clearing the table as thoroughly as if she weren't a guest but a waitress. She put the salad bowl in the pasta bowl, piled the silverware inside, stacked the leftover plates, even wiped at a corner of the table where a tomato had spat its innards. "You don't need to do that," Jacob said, reaching to take the napkin from her. She turned so her back was to him. "*Stop cleaning up,*" he said, "I'll do it later."

Keeping her face pointed down at the table, she said something that Jacob couldn't hear. It was not her usual voice—it wasn't much more than a squeak. He came around to face her. It was too dark for him to see if she was crying. "What are you doing?" he said. "Come inside."

"I'm *scared*," she whispered.

"Me too. I am too," he said, but he realized that until just that moment he hadn't been, or that what he'd thought was fear was in fact a mild and bearable cousin. Emily had been acting. She didn't have a plan. This was nothing like lightning at all. "I love you," he said, putting a hand on her arm.

Inside, in the unnatural light of the kitchen, Cara was giving Charlotte a tour of the pictures on the fridge, and Arthur was doing the dishes with his sleeves rolled up.

Emily threw the napkin at Jacob's chest but didn't raise her voice. "Why do you always tell me that?" she said. "Who cares how you feel? Who fucking cares how you feel at all?"

Related Material

In eighth grade a girl named Claire Frunt left Vernon Day and everyone knew, claimed already to have known, why: she was pregnant and was going to get an abortion. At twelve she dated boys from high school, or boys who had dropped out of high school—they waited for her like stray dogs in the parking lot. Until sixth grade she'd worn headbands and played flute duets at talent shows, but one fall she came back with half of her hair dyed black and sudden familiarity with pot brownies. Still—pregnant? Wouldn't her stomach have been bigger? (According to most people she'd been at least five months pregnant.) What about the birth control she made no secret of taking? It didn't matter. From then on she was Claire Frunt, the girl who dropped out to have an abortion.

At one of his many desperate moments that spring, Jacob had found himself on his bed with the old Vernon Day phone book open in front of him, working up the nerve to ask Claire—with whom he hadn't spoken in years, and never about anything more personal than Social Studies—where and how she had gotten her abortion. He gave up, woke up, when someone who sounded like an older brother told him Claire wasn't taking any calls.

It was now a Thursday afternoon in May, that last part of the school year when everyone, teachers and students, looks better and acts kinder. Even the weather seemed to be saying, *Oh, all right, enough with pretending that school matters. Go out! Sleep in the grass! Ask a teacher if she wants to come to Free Cone Day!*

On the occasions that Jacob noticed it, the weather seemed to be mocking him. He stood in the crisp chill of a CVS, peering down the aisles and praying that a pregnancy test wasn't the sort of thing that you had to ask for specially, locked under glass. For four intolerable weeks Emily had been refusing out of fear or stubbornness to take one, but now, with her period still not arrived, she had given in—frightening Jacob almost as much as if she had continued to hold out.

Jacob had never experienced anything like the month of April. He might as well have spent it underground. Every night, as if by appointment, he had a dream in which Emily would tell him that she was pregnant, then tell him she'd been kidding, then that she was actually pregnant, and so on, back and forth, until he woke up and saw with dread that he still had hours more to sleep. He tolerated school as he would being stuck in an elevator while needing to use the bathroom—breathing deeply, shutting his eyes, glancing toward the door, checking his watch. He left classes and wandered the halls. He stood alone in the music room, tapping his temple with a drumstick.

But a few times a day he'd have a fit of giddiness, deliverance. He'd sit up straight and look around, all the world transformed. She wasn't going to be pregnant! He was insane! What the hell was he doing to himself? He was fifteen years old!

Then hopelessness, despair, like water slowly filling a beaker. She is pregnant. I know she is. We'll have to commit joint suicide, like Romeo and Juliet.

The pregnancy tests were in aisle seven, past the chewable fiber supplements, the cold medicines, the wart removers. They had two brands, Clearblue and e.p.t, boxes as innocuous as thermometers. He chose a three-pack of First Response—OVER 99% ACCURATE! DIGITAL! RESULTS IN WORDS! (Those words, printed in black on a small gray screen: *Pregnant. Not pregnant.*)

The man who checked Jacob out didn't, as Jacob feared he would, ask for an ID. He didn't even seem to look at what Jacob placed on the counter, but once he'd dropped the box into a white plastic bag, he said, "Let me tell you something."

Jacob waited.

"Do you know how many kids I've seen come through here with the exact same look you've got on right now?" He had uncombed graying hair and a mustache. He was always encouraging the students who came in, particularly the girls, to come hear him play bass in his band. "And can I tell you how many of the girls, of the ones I know, ever ended up being pregnant?" He made a zero with his craggy hand and raised his eyebrows.

Back at school Jacob glanced in all directions before passing the test to Emily in the hallway behind the theater, as if they were exchanging drugs. She slipped it into her backpack without expression. For most of the past month she'd been cool to him, touchy. He'd coped with this by asking her five or ten times in every conversation why she was mad, what was wrong, why she kept making that face, et cetera.

Lately she'd reminded him of her father, though Jacob wouldn't dare say it. The ferocious staring, the sneer. He, Jacob was convinced, was psychologically the key to Emily, the person she lived to please or defy. This theory bothered her more than she could say.

Her father—whom all of Emily's friends called Mr. Barley—seemed to wish both that Emily would transform back into the four-year-old who clamored to be carried on his shoulders, and that she would become, now, a Supreme Court justice. The messy middle stages were hardly tolerable. He was behind the near-weekly groundings, the insistence that she bring home nothing lower than an A-minus, the fact that she said "Pardon me?" even in conversation with Jacob. He was a lawyer with a specialty in cases to do with international finance, but he was a good deal older than Jacob's parents—a good deal older than Emily's mother too—and now he was in semiretirement. Jacob was aware, without quite knowing how he'd learned it, that Mr.

Barley had grown up poor and been the first in his family to go to college. He conveyed just by the way he walked across the room that he believed his success was distinctly earned. He had thick black hair, heavy eyebrows, a narrow scolding mouth over surprisingly derelict teeth. Most of the time he spoke softly, one leg crossed over the other, a mocking prance in his voice. "Is that what they said? Really?" That was his dinner-table self, his church self. But his anger was extraordinary, not something Emily often talked about. Seething, red-faced, tearing the phone out of the wall. When he had once smelled cigarette smoke in her room, he had kicked over the chair on which she kept all her papers, then exhausted himself ripping apart her bed.

Their house, crisp white-painted brick, looked so orderly, so conservative and proper, that Jacob had a hard time imagining the scenes Emily described. Inside her house it was nearly always dark, whatever the time of day or the season, because the wooden shutters were closed and the windows were small. The house didn't seem to have been designed for light, or air-conditioning, or a microwave, or television. It was older, and you knew without asking that the people inside never peed on the toilet seat and that they would prefer that you take off your shoes.

When Jacob came for dinner Emily insisted that he not wear his jeans with the rip in the thigh, and always Mr. Barley greeted him at the door with a scrutinizing look that lasted a moment longer than it should have before giving way to greetings and offers (insistences) to hang up his coat. They ate on plates larger and more ornate than anything in the Vines' house. Above the center of the dark wooden table hung a brass light fixture with a ring of white plastic candles. Behind Jacob's seat the heavy sliding doors that led to the rest of the house were always shut. Flitting around their legs and under the sideboard, more like a spirit than an animal, was Mrs. Barley's beloved gray cat, Nikki.

Jacob was unaccustomed to using cloth napkins, and when, at one of those early dinners, he blew his nose into one, he saw with dawning humiliation the expressions on Emily and her parents' faces. The food, cooked entirely by Mrs. Barley, was heavier than what Jacob ate at home. Slabs of roast beef beside dark, leaking greens. Creamy mashed potatoes. Emily was newly a vegetarian, but Mrs. Barley made no concessions, so Jacob would eat his portion of meat and then Emily's. Mrs. Barley served and cleared the table—it all felt to Jacob stiff and bizarre and made him want to leap up and help with the dishes. (He tried once, but the look from Mr. Barley made him sit back down.) For dessert there were usually chocolates sent to Mr. Barley by an old client—everyone at the table would make a show of inspecting the box before plucking one out, then sighing with pleasure at the first liquor- or caramel-oozing bite.

At some point during each of these dinners, before Jacob and Emily would be excused down to the basement (where they were forbidden to close the door), Mr. Barley and Jacob would have a conversation that was, in its ritual and lightness, like a dance. The subject always had to do with school. Mr. Barley had taken it upon himself to encourage Jacob to work harder, and Jacob took pleasure in being not quite under his thumb.

"Did you get back your math test this week?"

"Mm-hmm."

"And?"

"I did pretty well. Nobody got an A."

"What's pretty well, then? A B?"

"Only three people got a B. I got a B-minus."

"A *B-minus is pretty well*?"

"In Mrs. Derren's class it's actually pretty much the average."

"Well you shouldn't be 'pretty much the average,' especially not if 'pretty much the average' is a *B-minus*. Emily, you've studied this stuff, haven't you? Why don't you help him and see if they'll agree to a retest?"

"Good idea," she said. "Did you do something new with these potatoes, Mom? Lace them with an addictive substance perhaps?" She was, in her parents' presence, the courtly wit, the charming jewel. You would never have known, seeing how they beamed at one another, that she regularly sobbed "I hate them so much" after a fight, or that she feared that if she were to be pregnant they would throw her out of the house.

And what would they do to Jacob? Jacob occasionally imagined a steely standoff between himself and Mr. Barley, a wrestling match on a rocky ledge...But, more often, he pictured much worse: a tricky legal maneuver to have Jacob expelled from school, blacklisted, possibly imprisoned.

God, why had it come to this? Envisioning a world in which that single condom hadn't broken was for Jacob like trying to imagine a version of the world in which his mother hadn't gotten sick. Irresistible, excruciating, useless. That first stretch of his and Emily's relationship seemed now to have been pure delight, an inhabitable montage.

He tortured himself regularly with a memory from the ice storm last winter, before high school, before they had ever had sex. Jacob had been over at Emily's for dinner, and they had contrived, as soon as they saw what the weather was doing, to delay and delay until Jacob couldn't possibly have gone home. Emily had explained to her mother that it was so dangerous out, really it didn't make sense for anyone to leave the house in weather like this, so why didn't Jacob just sleep over in the basement? Don't say no before you've thought about it! We'll make him up a bed on the couch, there's that little shower down there, I'll be up in my room with the door locked. We won't see each other from the moment he goes downstairs.

Jacob still couldn't quite fathom how Mrs. Barley had agreed—and much less how she'd convinced her husband. But before he knew it he was calling home ("Just tell Dad I'm sleeping at Charles's") and then accepting from Emily, who could barely keep from laughing, a set of folded white towels and a travel toothbrush still sealed in its crinkling plastic wrap. Once he was alone downstairs he took advantage of his unaccustomed freedom by falling to his knees to sniff the carpet, to see if he might decode the damp, bready components of the smell that was so bound up in his mind with seeing Emily naked. He washed his face and brushed his teeth and climbed into the bed whose springs pressed into his back. How strange to be in this room, in this house. He considered masturbating, thought better of it. He lamented, and tried to accept, that there would be no secret visit from Emily tonight. He turned on the lamp, stood up from bed wearing just his T-shirt and boxers, and went over to inspect the bookshelves. *How to Talk So Kids Will Listen (and Listen So Kids Will Talk). Reviving Ophelia.* An entire shelf full of copies of the NYU *Law Review. Mastering the Art of French Cooking.* And, under that, some of the books that Emily must have read, or been read, as a little girl: *Miss. Nelson Is Missing, Dominic, Grover Goes to School, Matilda.*

Across the room his pager buzzed in his pants, and when he saw Emily's code—585—his first thought, absurdly, was that she had meant to page someone else (Charles?) and that he had caught her. His heart hurried. A minute later she paged again. He went to the phone on the low table in the corner of the room, but when he lifted the receiver there was no dial tone. *"Hi!"* he heard Emily whisper, a happy, tiny voice.

"Hi!"

"I was worried you wouldn't figure out to pick up! How are you down there?"

"Good. Just, you know, looking around and stuff. How are you up there?"

"Good! I miss you!"

"I miss you too. I like being in the same house with you."

"I like it too! I want to say good night. Come up to the bottom of the stairs on the first floor!"

"Now?"

"What time does it say on the clock down there?"

"Ten-twenty-five."

"How many seconds?"

"Forty-eight. Forty-nine."

"Let's meet at EXACTLY ten-thirty, by that clock. But be VERY QUIET. Okay?"

"Okay."

At 10:29, Jacob crept up the carpeted stairs on the balls of his feet and then out onto the cold wooden landing. The house was perfectly dark, and it took all his concentration to hold in mind the exact arrangement of furniture in the hallway: the satin-covered bench, the marble-topped table, the glass case full of ornamental pipes. His attention was so focused, and Emily was so silent, that he didn't even realize she had come down the stairs until he bumped against her at the end of the banister. He opened his mouth to whisper something and she covered it with her hand. They stood pressed together on the wide bottom stair, their noses resting tip to tip, so perfectly silent that they could hear the chips of ice pinging against the windows at the back of the house. Her parents were asleep not fifty feet away. Jacob's eyes were open but they might as well have been closed. They hugged, a soft and complete pressing together of their bodies, as if they were cinched together in a sleeping bag. She pressed her mouth against his ear and said, or warmly breathed, "I love you." He kissed her ear in response, not trusting himself to whisper. They stayed together for what seemed to Jacob a minute but may in fact have been ten. Finally, giving him a last squeeze, she turned—his eyes were just beginning to adjust to the dark—and slipped silently back up the stairs, where she shut herself behind the door as lightly as closing the cover on a book.

Thinking of that night now, as he lay in his sweltering bedroom waiting for Emily to call and tell him whether she was pregnant, physically hurt. Outside birds were still busily chirping. The trees had become so thick with green that you couldn't see any of the neighbors' houses, and Finney, fat and panting, was out digging up the disintegrating toys of last fall. Jacob had come straight upstairs after dinner and drawn the shades, and now he waited with a feeling at the bottom of his stomach like a mattress being walked on. He'd announced that he had a huge History project to work on, and in fact he did, but his binder lay untouched in his backpack. Will and Cara, like everyone in the world other than Jacob and Emily, were over at friends' houses studying for finals (even Cara, just in fifth grade, had end-of-year exams, and she talked about them as seriously as if she were in medical school). He could hear his father and Charlotte in the backyard, talking as they unpacked the boccie set she'd gotten him. Arthur had tried the other afternoon to ask Jacob if he was depressed. *There's a strain of this in our family . . .* Jacob had, to Arthur's visible relief, changed the subject.

Again and again now Jacob moved between lying in bed, staring at the angled ceiling, and pacing the floor. He walked across the room diagonally, nine steps each way, frowning with his hands clasped behind his back. The room was so hot that he felt as if he had a fever, but it didn't occur to him to open the window or to turn on the fan, the heat seemed right for the moment. The carpet was thick and gray and stained in places with ragged ovals where Finney had once pissed or shat. The paint on the walls seemed to be sweating. If she wasn't pregnant, then he would never again have sex. He would never lie. He would never snap at his father or exclude Cara or tease Will. He would never be jealous or irritable with Emily. He would never talk behind anyone's back. He would never read only the first ten, middle ten, and last ten pages of a book for school.

Since his mother had died, Jacob had believed without ever quite voicing it that he had earned a reprieve from true suffering. One way or another things would work out for him. No longer. His old contract seemed suddenly to have been written on ash.

Eventually it got to be 9:44. (Jacob felt that not a single minute had slipped by unnoticed all night; he had inhabited each one like a smelly little phone booth.) His pager leapt at the foot of the bed: 585*911.

Afterward Jacob would say that he'd known right away, but he hadn't. His palms had turned cold, his chest had begun to heave like an accordion, but if you had stopped him, even then, and forced him to say what was the most likely thing, he would have said she'd gotten her period. *I was so scared!* he imagined saying. He'd go downstairs like Scrooge on Christmas morning.

"Jacob, I am."

"You are what?"

"I'm *pregnant*. I'm pregnant, I'm pregnant, Jacob, it was *positive*."

"Oh God. Oh my God."

"I know. I know. I know."

Even over the phone they seemed to be collapsing toward each other.

All three tests had said the same thing. She had no patience for Jacob's line of questioning about whether the word *Not* might just have been too faint to see.

"I have to go."

"Why?"

"I just do."

And like that Jacob was alone in his room and his reasonably promising life was over. He looked at his pager, at the phone, and considered what they'd just done to him. His face was so hot that he felt if he didn't splash water on it he might burn his pillow. For an hour or longer he just lay there, thinking he should get up, thinking he should close his eyes, staring. He began to dial Emily's number a few times but hung up before he finished. He listened, as if he had been buried alive and had no way of alerting anyone to his condition, to Will come up the stairs and go into the bathroom and blow his nose and then go into his room and turn on a Stan Getz CD. He heard the rushing noise in the wall of someone in the house having flushed a toilet. He kept glimpsing some version of the thought, like a shirt in a dryer, *The thing I've feared most is true.* He pitied Emily and pitied himself. He hated Emily for ever having convinced him to have sex, and hated himself for not knowing how to put on a condom.

Somehow, in feverish little jolts, he managed to sleep.

At four in the morning he lurched awake and without thinking fell to his knees in front of the bookshelves. The lights in the room were still on. In his sleep it had occurred to him to look for *Changing Bodies, Changing Lives*. He found it between an eighth-grade world history textbook that he had never taken out of its plastic and a row of Far Side collections. The book's spine was slanted from all these years of standing at an angle, but otherwise it was just the same as he remembered. It fell open to a passage about wet dreams that had once haunted and terrified him (he had prayed, with near-tearful sincerity, to never be subjected to anything like that). He knelt on the carpet to read. The section on pregnancy and abortion began on page 239.

Abortion is legal, and as a teenager you have the right to have an abortion if you want one.

Abortion is also controversial, and you will have to decide what you believe is "right" for you. Here are the different reactions some teens had when we asked them if they would choose an abortion:

—Abortions are okay for other people, but not for me. I don't believe in it for myself.

—I'm worried that I would regret it years later.

—I feel so lucky to be able to have the choice. If I got pregnant now, I would never be able to have the baby...I

don't think abortion is killing. After all, the fetus couldn't possibly live on its own when it's only two and a half or three months.

Useless, useless, useless. What had he hoped for? A manual. Just as the book had once told him what it meant to French kiss and when he could expect to grow pubic hair, he had thought there might be a section on what to do in the event of getting your fifteen-year-old girlfriend pregnant. Not whether to get an abortion, since it hadn't occurred to him that she might not, but how: how to plan it, how to get away with it, how to get over it.

He crawled back into bed and eventually slept again, soaking the bed with such sweat that it was as if he had a tropical infection.

By the time he left for school the next morning he had convinced himself that Emily had confessed to her parents (this was an era when he was riding his bike, but he felt he could no more ride his bike to school now than he could walk on his hands; he let Will drive him, and slumped, not talking, with his head against the window). The idea of Emily's confession had occurred to him somewhat idly during the night, but in the morning it had bolstered itself and bolstered itself until it had seemed that everything he knew about her made it not just likely but certain. It was another warm and clear morning—all the cars on the road had their windows down, and men walked to work carrying their jackets. As Will's car coasted around the loop toward the front of the school, Jacob let his eyes fall shut, expecting—

and maybe even hoping—that when he opened them Mr. Barley would be standing at the top of the stairs, hands on his hips, waiting to destroy him.

A year before Cara had been born, when Jacob was four, his mother had had a miscarriage. He had little or no memory of this, but from his parents or from Will he had pieced together a story. They'd announced they were having a little sister, and taken Will and Jacob to IHOP to celebrate. That he definitely didn't remember, but he could see himself—this would have been a month or two later—sitting on the floor in the living room surrounded by M.U.S.C.L.E. Men, while his mother wept on the phone.

How much of the memory was real? Jacob had no idea. His mom did get pregnant again and did have a baby—here he had actual memories, his mother damp and happy under a white blanket; him pushing Cara, a wrinkly little red-faced potato, in her stroller around and around the driveway—and this experience seemed somehow to cancel out the miscarriage, to scrub it from the record.

Just once, in first or second grade, he had said to his parents in a too-casual voice, "If the baby after me didn't die, would Cara never have been born?" His father had given him a look of such simple horror—no trace of *teaching a lesson*—that Jacob had felt as if he'd been spanked, and never said anything like that again.

Emily hadn't confessed to her parents, but she had decided that they needed to tell someone: Mrs. Rice was the natural choice. Mrs. Rice taught Emily painting, and Emily regarded her—as many girls did—as a confidant. She and Emily and a few other girls often stayed after school in the art room, having steady, wandering conversations, and working together on endless projects like repainting the walls. The cluster of girls around Mrs. Rice tended to be mature, displaced, a little damaged. To them she dispensed her stories, her life, in dollops that she made no effort to connect. Did Jacob know that Mrs. Rice had once lived in California, as the trophy girlfriend in a biker gang? Or that in her twenties she'd been married to a wealthy older man who had insisted that she wear a different gown every night to dinner?

Now her hair was the color of beet juice, she wore cable-knit sweaters coated in dog hair, and she seemed to view the rest of the teachers at Vernon Day, and maybe even the entire spectacle of striving and applying and studying, with a distance that was fonder and less involved than judgment. She found everything funny but also sad. She had apparently told Emily that you had to be careful with high school boys, because their physical need for sex was so out of whack with their emotional need for a mother that everything could get royally fucked up. She cursed freely, even in class.

Emily brought Jacob with her into Mrs. Rice's office one afternoon that week and asked if they could shut the door.

The office, just off the art room, felt smaller than it was, because every surface was covered in drawing paper and stacks of portfolios waiting to be graded. Jacob perched on the corner of a chair and Emily sat on an arm of the small sofa. Jacob's heart was pounding and he wasn't sure he would have been able to speak even if he had wanted to—he felt as if he were sitting in both a principal's and a psychiatrist's office. Mrs. Rice had guessed already that Emily was having sex, and once Emily was able to get out the words *I think I'm pregnant*, she didn't shake her head or glare at Jacob. She pursed her unpainted lips and blinked and sipped from the mug of cold coffee she'd been working on since that morning. Emily, starting to cry, said there was no way she could tell her parents, but she'd heard somewhere that you needed an adult signature to get an abortion, and she was so worried that— Mrs. Rice wheeled her chair through stacks of paper to where she could lay a hand on each of their knees. "This isn't the end of your life," she said. "You guys and a hundred thousand couples around the country are sitting on this secret right now. We can deal. We can deal."

Mrs. Rice said they'd find a way to get signed whatever paperwork needed signing, but for a few days now they should all just try to chill, think, see if they can get a handle on themselves. She talked as if it were happening to her too. "Even if you're sure you want one, it could be smart to just live with it for a little, let the feelings run through you. You never make good decisions when you're just trying to put out the fire with whatever's handy. Both of you can come talk to me anytime, seriously, anytime."

Jacob was so grateful and so overwhelmed that for a minute he thought he'd cry too. He wanted to curl himself

•

into Mrs. Rice's lap and let her cradle him in her sweater. All year he'd hated her because he suspected that she knew it was him and Charles who had trashed the sculptures that night in fall—and who did she think she was, knowing he'd done that and still smiling at him in the halls? No more. He forgave her. He loved her.

Before they left, Mrs. Rice told them about a college student of hers who had gotten pregnant, a devout Catholic girl from Singapore. "She didn't have any friends here, and she actually ended up staying with me for a couple of weeks. Just brutal. This was years ago." Was that an invitation? A reminder that other people had it worse? However she meant it, it soothed them. Walking out of the art room and down the stairs, to the main hall where students in flip-flops offered each other rides home and pulled down the sunglasses from the tops of their heads, Jacob and Emily held hands, something they had done very little of this past month and something Jacob had supposed they might never do again.

They made their way, mostly in silence, out to the parking lot and around the corner to the stretch of sidewalk on Wisconsin where Emily waited for the bus.

"Do you think you'll get it soon?"

"Pretty soon. I'll probably call tomorrow or Thursday."

Here, on other afternoons, they'd kissed gum out of one another's mouth, groped while people in passing cars honked and hooted, mouthed "I love you!" back and forth as the bus pulled out of sight. They had never, though, in Jacob's mind, seemed quite so adult, or quite so certain to be together forever. Catastrophe survivors.

The bus pulled up with a *whoosh* and sunk noisily to the curb. Emily kissed Jacob on the chin and, hoisting her bag onto her shoulder, standing aside to let a man in an inflatable foot cast hobble off, climbed aboard and made her way home in flawless disguise.

That night Jacob knocked on Will's door and let himself in, hoping for what most confessors hope for: shock, comfort, pardon. It was the stretch of time between dinner and bed, and Will was at his desk, squinting into his computer screen, a book of Ovid's poetry flat beside the keyboard. He worked incessantly on translations, which, for reasons Jacob couldn't fathom, seemed to proceed at a pace of no more than a few lines a week.

Jacob lay across Will's bed with his head against the wall. Above Will's desk hung a poster of an old Guinness ad with a toucan balancing a glass on its beak. The shelves Jacob faced showed a mosaic of colorful spines that, taken together, presented Will as he liked to see himself: Kafka's stories, *Zen and the Art of Motorcycle Maintenance*, *Up in the Old Hotel*, a dozen skinny battered plays. As recently as a year ago Will had had that strange, taut, shining look that some pubescent boys have—as if the pimples on his jawline and the cords in his forearms were signs of an impending explosion—but now he had emerged lean and calm, with a voice that made Jacob think of creaking wood.

"So," Jacob began, "this is completely weird and completely secret, but—"

As he listened Will swiveled in his desk chair, one leg folded underneath him, his head at a slight tilt. Naturally they both spoke softly, but just to be safe Will stood up and clicked the lock on the door.

"I think you've got to tell Dad," he finally said.

"Why?"

Will blinked, considering. He looked both less surprised and less troubled than Jacob would have hoped. You tell Dad because your girlfriend is going to have an *abortion*. Did Jacob even know what happened in an abortion, really?

Of course he knew what happened in an abortion! Who did Will think he was?

Well, what was she planning to do, just stay in bed and tell her parents to leave her alone? What if something went wrong? You couldn't just sneak off and do a thing like that.

People snuck off and did precisely that every day, Jacob pointed out, a little shakily.

But it's a *big deal*, Will kept trying to get across, and so Jacob, contrary to everything he felt, found himself arguing that it wasn't such a big deal at all. Judy had had an abortion, Jacob said.

"She's *Judy*," Will said.

They sat silently together, argued out, until Will said, "It was stupid to start having sex before you knew what you were doing."

"Right," Jacob said, "it would have been much better if"—sometimes assembling the correct, cruel words took longer than the impulse behind them lasted—"everyone should be like you and wait until they're forty-five. That would be very smart."

When Will blushed, the color rose in his face like mercury in a thermometer, stopping just below his glasses. "All I meant is you should have been careful."

Jacob winced and said, "Well, we weren't. Obviously."

"Ah, Jacob," Will said, and Jacob was so surprised to hear his name on his brother's lips, particularly in such a sorrowful voice, that he looked up and saw that Will was actually suffering for him. There might have been a moment for Will of feeling that Jacob had gotten his comeuppance, a glimmer of justice done—but it had now given way to the sad, simple fact that his brother was in trouble. You could always half-believe that other people had unsuspected resources, secret reserves, and that in the end they would come out stronger. Brothers knew better.

Will and Jacob had hardly hugged since they were little, and they didn't hug now, but as Jacob slunk out, feeling unexpectedly gutted, Will said, "You know, didn't that girl in your grade have an abortion? People do this, I guess. It's weird but people do."

One afternoon that week Jacob walked into the school library, where only a few of the carrels were occupied, and found the section in the back devoted to women's health.

Most of the books had a 1980s aura—faded color photographs of women with perms, nurses holding clipboards. Inside one book, *The Miracle of Birth*, Jacob found black-and-white photos of a wiry woman in a hospital bed straining and sweating. Another book seemed to be entirely about how best to raise a child in a world full of toxins. Another was about the history of the women's suffrage movement. It was a spottily organized section, rarely visited. Finally, in a book with a plain blue cover, he found a chapter with the heading "What exactly is an abortion?" He read it standing up, facing the wall.

> An abortion is a procedure to end a pregnancy by removing the fetus and placenta from the mother's womb. There are many forms of abortion—sometimes an abortion occurs on its own (spontaneously), and other times a woman chooses (elects) to end the pregnancy.
>
> A surgical abortion, also known as a suction curettage, uses a vacuum to remove the fetus and related material. This is usually done after six weeks of pregnancy. Medicine (sedative) may be given to cause sleepiness. The doctor may numb the cervix so you have little pain during the procedure.
>
> If the surgical abortion is done after twelve weeks of pregnancy, the doctor must first open (dilate) the cervical canal. Small sticks called laminaria . . .

The shiver Jacob felt, the transformation of himself into chilled gelatin, was strongest in his knees and his palms, but not limited to them. He suddenly regretted the barbecue chicken sandwich he'd eaten an hour ago for lunch, and glanced around for a trash can in case he would need to vomit. It wasn't disgust he felt, but rather sharp bodily awareness, inside and out. He could feel small dry sticks pressing against soft walls, tearing and scraping, and he could feel his organs recoiling. Will was right: he'd been carrying along the impression, never scrutinized, that having an abortion wasn't so much a physical procedure as a psychological one—you made peace with the thought of parting with this potential life, shut your eyes tightly, and lived on with perhaps the occasional ghostly regret. But there was nothing ghostly about a fetus and placenta. A wet slap on the table, solid as a jellyfish.

He slid the book back onto the shelf and sunk onto the windowsill, which was not quite deep enough to support him. He was aware of having an ill, anguished look on his face, and also of a distant urge to cry, to melt down and abandon all responsibility.

Outside someone was driving a mower over the soccer field. The sun through the windows had turned each table-top into a bright, reflective square. Somewhere in another aisle a study group was whispering, melting into giggles every couple of minutes. *I don't think I can do this,* Jacob thought, with the clarity and boldness of someone who after all didn't have to do anything.

As he left, the librarian nodded at him from behind her desk, but Jacob avoided her eyes and made his way out and down the stairs to an empty sofa in the lounge where he collapsed and sat staring, touching the cracked surface of his lower lip. Ian Robeck approached to see if Jacob wanted to go to McDonald's, but he turned away when he saw Jacob's face. Emily would be out of class at 3:15, and they would talk then, though Jacob wasn't exactly sure what he wanted to tell her. *This isn't as simple as I thought. Maybe a baby isn't the unacceptable thing, maybe an abortion is the unacceptable thing. Maybe I've been wrong about my life entirely.*

By the next day Jacob had not quite forgotten the scraping and the sickness, but he had remembered other things, such as his intention to go off to college and to meet someone new and to become a famous scientist. There was a path in his mind where he spent most of his days, and on it he and Emily walked linked into the indefinite future, each step following neatly from the decisions he'd made and the people he'd known when he was twelve. But as meticulously and protectively as he tended that path—bristling when Mrs. Barley had once suggested to Emily that they should try dating other people—he believed, and even depended on, it ending well before they finished high school.

He had told Emily, on the phone the night of the library, that he didn't want her to have an abortion, and they had had a dreary, tearful, dutiful fight. He had said (it made him cringe to remember the willed catch in his throat), "I've seen enough people close to me die." They had seemed to speak lines from a play at a sex-ed assembly: it wasn't his decision, it was partly his decision, it was her body, it was their baby, on and on. By the time they hung up he'd begun to hope he would lose out. She could arrange her abortion without consulting him, and he, after the fact, could savor his own useless ambivalence.

They sat now—this was late Thursday afternoon—at a

picnic table in the grass on the side of school that no one ever went to, under the wide golden canopy of a gingko tree. The light and temperature were absurdly pleasant, and a sunset was spread over half the sky. As she began talking, in a voice that sounded like someone concentrating on her posture, it occurred to him that she was breaking up with him. He wasn't prepared for this! She'd been thinking and thinking and she hadn't slept in like two nights and this was probably the hardest thing she'd ever decided in her life, but . . .

To do something he plucked the woody little canoe-shaped seeds from the cracks in the table. She interrupted herself to shout, "Stop! Stop doing that! Just pay attention!"

"You were right yesterday," she said. "I'm not doing this because of you, but you were right." She had just been thinking these past few days about how she would feel afterward. Not like she'd killed something, but close. "I don't understand how someone could do this and be a *vegetarian*," she said, starting to laugh and then wrong-footing them both by bursting into tears.

To his astonishment he found himself calm. Unreliably calm. He felt as if he were underwater, moving in slow, majestic sweeps. He kept saying things like, "Are you sure?" "You've totally thought this out?" As if he'd been sent by the government to assess her readiness. Was it relief at not being broken up with? Shock at what she was saying? Slowly he could feel something heavy rising toward the surface, but it hadn't broken yet.

She breathed in through her nose, squinted questioningly at Jacob, and started talking faster. (Was it his imagination or did she keep touching her stomach?)

Here was the plan. She was going to wait until her parents went to church on Sunday, then she was going to leave a note. She'd pack everything into her camp duffel and catch the bus on MacArthur. She'd ride to Mrs. Rice's house in Silver Spring, and she would spend a few nights on the couch there getting herself together. Eventually Mrs. Rice would put her on a train to Philadelphia, where she would meet her mom's cousins Dahlia and David. They lived in a cabin that David had helped to build, an hour and a half from Philadelphia in the Pennsylvania woods. They grew their own kale and potatoes, kept chickens, built furniture. They had always said, and Emily insisted they'd really meant it, that they would love to have her stay with them anytime.

(Hearing Dahlia's and David's names opened just the tiniest crack in Jacob's feeling of peace. They were mythical figures in Emily's life, wise and attractive and resourceful, the evidence that her family had something going for it after all. Whenever Emily talked about them, Jacob said they sounded like people who smelled bad.)

For the next few months, Emily said, she'd help Dahlia out at the shelter, and live in the guest bedroom where she stayed during summers (Jacob had seen pictures: a small striped rug on a wooden floor, an undersize bed). And in fall she would give birth to her baby, their baby. Eventually she'd look for a place of her own, but until then she would raise it with Dahlia and David's help, feed it, reenroll herself in school there. When she finally felt settled, she would get in touch with her parents, tell them where she was. They won't be able to do anything to me by then, she said.

"And then what?" Jacob said, panic beginning to nose its way out.

"And then I'll live. And that will be my life. Finishing school, raising a child, maybe Dahlia and David will watch the baby—she'll be a toddler by then—while I start college. I'll go somewhere nearby."

"And what about"—Jacob could hardly say the word—"*me?*"

"Well, ideally . . . you would come with me. I know what a huge thing it is to ask this of you, and I swear to God I won't hold it against you if you don't want to come. But if you can, I know Dahlia would be completely happy to let us be there together, and it could actually be so beautiful, finally living together, and getting to see our baby together, and finally building a life together without our parents and teachers hovering over us all the time and yelling at us if we lay in each other's laps. We're already fifteen—I'll be sixteen next year—and my mom was only twenty when she married my dad, and if you think about it there really isn't much of a difference. I know this isn't the officially approved Vernon Day life, where you graduate and go to Yale and get internships and get married at twenty-five and everything's perfect perfect perfect, but this could be our life, we could get away from all that, I hate the idea of living inside these fucking fences everyone's put up."

There was Jacob's terror, breaching like a whale, displaying in an instant its entire enormous body. Although it was seventy degrees his arms were covered in goose bumps and his teeth began to chatter. "But what if—," he said. "What about—Don't you think—"

Who the hell was this girl? He stared across the table into her shining, fanatical eyes and realized that he had never known anything about her at all. Here, beneath the polite smile and five-paragraph essays, was the bare floor of her true self: tenacious, crazed, bold in the way people they read about in history books were bold.

"Okay," he said, certain he was making the biggest mistake he would ever make. "Let's run away."

"Are you serious?" She frowned and for a second Jacob thought she was disappointed, but it was only determination.

"I'm serious. I want to go."

"We're going to start our life."

"We're going to start our life."

"And our baby's life."

"And our baby's life."

Now Jacob was crying too, and since they were holding each other's hands their tears flowed freely, wetting both of their cheeks, gathering on their lips.

"I love you so much."

"I love you. So much."

Mr. Vesell rode by just then and trilled hello with his bell. A squirrel raced across the grass to the safety of a tree. Jacob freed his hand and, laughing, wiped his nose. He would throw out his life like dumping out an old binder.

He would learn to use a lathe. He would dig potatoes. He would stand on the porch on cool mornings and watch the steam come off his coffee (he would start drinking coffee) while Emily slept upstairs. Go to the woods. Smell not exactly bad but different. Yes. His young wife. His new, possibly bearded, solemnly responsible, self. Escape.

Emily got her abortion at a clinic on Fourteenth and U.

She went on a Friday morning, driven by her mother. The waiting room had a brown tile floor and a window that looked into a supply closet. Folding chairs stood arranged in even rows, and on a TV by the front desk, secured to a stand by black canvas straps, the local news played just too loud to ignore. Get ready for a heat wave and some thundershowers this weekend. An accident on the Occoquan, delays in both directions.

At the front of the room, two women who looked like sisters pressed against each other while the younger one filled out her intake form.

Emily had known that something was the matter as soon as she heard her mother answer the phone. Too bright and surprised a hello, then too long a silence. The den door closed. Mrs. Rice wouldn't possibly do that to her, would she? Yes, she would. *She's never going to forgive me, but I love her too much to let her wreck her life.* Emily began immediately to pack, kneeling in front of her closet in a silent stricken panic. Her mother stepped in and closed the door behind her.

"Your father doesn't know and I don't have any intention

of telling him. But there is no question of what's going to happen here. This is not your decision."

And suddenly it wasn't. Emily's expression of outrage, denial, hatred, fell away to reveal a lake of childish shame. "I'm so sorry!" she wailed, but with hardly a sound.

Her mother held the back of her neck, hard enough to leave fingerprints.

The operating room reminded Emily of a dentist's office. Her mother stayed in the waiting room. Every fourth panel in the ceiling was a fluorescent light. The stirrups against her bare feet were as cold as if they had been refrigerated. The nurse, all in purple, disappeared for long enough that Emily thought about running. Instead she cried and trembled and squeezed her eyes shut. When the doctor came in, a man with gray hair and a broad smile, he began blandly narrating everything he did, and only looked at Emily's face to hand her a tissue. *Now you're going to feel a sharp poke.*

Once she was home—the whole thing took less than two hours—Emily burst into tears on the phone with Jacob and asked him why the fuck he hadn't insisted on coming with her. He, helplessly and not quite truthfully, said he thought she wouldn't have wanted him there. He was on the pay phone in the first-floor stairwell at school, turning again and again to face away from the people passing behind him. That night, without even the feeblest hope that it would make a difference, he sent her a sixty-five-dollar bouquet that he charged to his father's credit card.

One of the things that Emily's mother said were "beyond

argument" was that Emily and Jacob were not to see each other anymore. If Emily didn't like it, then she could take it up with her father, who she could be sure wouldn't stop at breaking them up. Nonetheless she and Jacob could have stayed together—they both felt sure of this. It would have been easy enough, and possibly even thrilling, to carry on a forbidden relationship. Every kiss a crime.

But she had her abortion the first week in June, and they were broken up by the end of August. It was her decision— she was the one who finally said the words—but it was hardly necessary: something had changed, as plainly as if one of them had been to war. They began guarding their lives from each other, going to bed without saying good night. When it was finally over Jacob was both shattered and relieved. Their conversations had come to feel sodden and hopeless, enlivened only by the occasional fight.

She took a job that summer at a coffee shop near her house, where she seemed to spend most of her day being told by men that she was beautiful—sad older men with ear hair, married men who worked in the office building across the street, college-age men who passed her their numbers along with their tips. She began smoking in earnest, and looked thinner than Jacob had ever seen her. He spent the summer volunteering in Mr. Vesell's old lab at NIH, usually in a baffled and depressed fog, staring blindly into microscopes, eating cafeteria wraps with European scientists twice his age. He'd go entire days without a clue as to whether it was sunny or raining or what.

"I told you things wouldn't be the same if we had sex,"

Jacob said, stupidly, during one of their endless, aimless conversations in those last weeks.

Emily paused, for long enough that Jacob wondered if the phone had gone dead, and when she spoke again she sounded suddenly much older. "Things haven't been the same for a long time," she said. Jacob understood just what she meant, but like someone kneeling one final time in a church after losing his faith, he said, "Yes they have, don't say that," and hoped she would believe him.

The Knight of the Sad Countenance

When Jacob still thought that he might end up there, he visited Will for a weekend at Harvard. This was the winter of Jacob's junior year, when life at home had started to feel like something worth leaving behind, and college—any college—loomed like an oasis on the horizon. Will's manner, when he came home during that first year at school, added to Jacob's enchantment. Will wore a hooded Harvard sweatshirt, and read books with monochrome covers: *Warfare in the West, Origins of Monotheism.* All this seemed to Jacob slightly obnoxious, as did Will's not-quite smile of anticipation when someone asked him where he was going to school, but it was an obnoxiousness Jacob would forgive if only he could take it up himself.

Will's dorm, made of red brick with concrete moldings above the windows, stood behind a library that looked to Jacob like a building on the Washington Mall. His suite, which he shared with four other freshmen, had wide wood floors, a Chinese board game balanced on a futon, chairs and lamps that could have been dragged in off the street. "Thomas has an air mattress he's not using, so we'll just bring it into my room." Will's roommates wandered through the suite all weekend in towels and flip-flops, sleeping and eating and working as if each one lived in a private time zone. "It's Little Vine!" "Vine Jr.!" They were nerdy in a proud, challenging way. They volunteered for congressmen, wrote essays for *Slate*, applied for fellowships. Their delight in their intelligence, their edgy ambition, was like an accent that they all had in common.

That first night it snowed, and Will took Jacob out for Indian food off Harvard Square with a roommate of his named Tian-Xi. He'd worked the past two summers designing Web pages for a software company. He looked brightly up, trading plates with Will, and asked Jacob what he wanted to study. "Are you interested in economics, like William?" "William said you worked in a lab?" It wasn't until the second or third "William" that Jacob realized he didn't say it because his English came from a classroom. He said it because Will must have introduced himself that way. William Vine.

When Tian-Xi stood up to go to the bathroom, Will wiped his mouth and said, "There was another Will in our orientation group."

"Oh. I was just surprised."

"It's not like I had some—"

But he was back. And Jacob understood, anyway: this lanky young man, with silver-rimmed glasses and a stack of Niebuhr's essays by his bedside, didn't belong anymore to Jacob and Waggoner. He hadn't for years, actually, but until now he hadn't found quite the proper container for the self he'd been constructing. Calling him Will would be the strange thing now, the thing that placed you at a distance from his life.

Back home Jacob felt a claustrophobia that no amount of space could cure. Every leaf and branch, every speed bump and front door, seemed to insult him with its smallness, its complacency. He began reading Harvard course descriptions online, imagining himself eating meals not at the kitchen table but at a window seat on Harvard Square. After Emily, in the second half of high school, Jacob had changed—not so that it would have been obvious to anyone who didn't know him well, but to him it had felt like joining the priesthood. The Order of the Secret Pregnancies. He'd cut his hair short, taken down the posters in his room, started reading *Scientific American* instead of *Rolling Stone*. He dated rarely and never with much conviction. He not only took as many advanced classes as he could but also made a point of cobbling together opinions about things like Whitewater (overblown) and punctuated equilibrium (dubious).

He still saw Owen and Charles, but a bit dutifully. More and more he hung out with the people who ran the school's "alternative" newspaper, and who spent their weekends watching the strange, not-very-enjoyable movies from the cult shelf in Potomac Video. *Space Is the Place. Koyaanisqatsi.* They smoked pot but not the way the stoners and polo-shirt preppies did; they smoked and became introverted, philosophical. *Somewhere in the universe there are three people exactly like us, sitting around a table exactly like this, having exactly this conversation.* Toward his father and Charlotte he cultivated an attitude of bemused detachment. He began to see more clearly what was embarrassing about his father—the pull-ups he'd started doing, the poetry he read to Charlotte in a voice as if he were casting a spell—but somehow he'd become less pained by it. The currency of his and Arthur's relationship became the riches on Arthur's bookshelves: battered red editions of Montaigne's essays, Medawar, Vonnegut, Philip Roth. "Have you read Woolf's essays yet? Try this one where she's watching a moth die." "Look at this thing on how the South justified slavery. Isn't it good?" Arthur passed books on to Jacob, who passed them on to Cara, who changed her screen name to vonnegirl86.

Jacob only applied to Lodwick to spare his guidance counselor's feelings; she'd said her nephew had a wonderful time there and that Jacob reminded her of him so much. It hadn't occurred to him that he might end up there. The rejection from Haverford—yes, well, the interviewer had been kind of a dick. The rejection from Yale—no one was getting into Yale that year. By the time the ones from Brown and Harvard came—two in the same day—he was stuffing the letters deep in the trash, like evidence of a crime.

He didn't quite accept that he would in fact be going to Lodwick until he saw his name (bubble-lettered by his RA) taped to the door of his new room. He had never seen

Lodwick until he started school there, and it turned out to be full of smart, ambitious kids who had wished to go elsewhere. Fleeces and carabiners, engineers and theater directors. The school was on twenty acres at the foot of the Adirondacks, surrounded on two sides by dense gray woods, walking distance from a town called Hagman that had a coffee shop and a movie theater with an old-fashioned marquee. The weather seemed always to be the same: silver sky, bare trees, yellow grass giving way in places to mud crisscrossed with shoe-prints. At first discouragement was a constant threat. On a Friday night early in the year Jacob joined a few people from his floor going into town for pizza, and as they walked along the road that seemed much longer in the dark, their hoods drawn against the cold, they ran out of things to talk about and Jacob believed he could feel among them a dangerous flagging of hope, a slackening sail. They didn't know each other and didn't particularly care to. The wind could die in the middle of a class too, or waiting in line at the dining hall.

But gradually people paired off; bands and improv troupes formed; eccentric personalities emerged. In high school people had occasionally taken bold leaps over a summer—they would come back to school thin or fat, suddenly tall or suddenly gay—but here the freedom to invent or alter one's character seemed as common, and as giddily embraced, as the freedom to drink or to sleep through class.

And freedom really was the rule, even if their beds (narrow as benches) and their showers (hair mats in the drain) resembled the amenities in prison more than the ones in their previous lives. There was no one to stop them from staying up until four in the morning on a Wednesday, and no one to stop them from sleeping until three the next afternoon. Even classes exerted only a faint pull. Jacob had been just twice in two and a half months to a math class in which the professor had announced, tapping the desk with his eighty-year-old fingertips, that he had always believed taking roll to be degrading. In East Asian Civilizations Jacob had managed to write an eleven-page paper on samurai culture without having torn the plastic wrapper on his textbook. Having been told for most of the past decade that he needed to work hard in order to get into college, he now found himself like a believer after Judgment Day.

Suddenly the dismal weeks, the dreams of transferring, seemed distant and unserious. He wasn't the only one to go through this—they all had their stories of doubts and relief, their hard-won wisdom. *I think you should never make friends with your roommate. I think it would be weirder if you* weren't *having second thoughts about your major. Long-distance can work so long as you see each other at least once a month.* Most of these conversations were with Andrew, a friend from Jacob's East Asian Civilizations class. Andrew had grown up in Chicago and had begun and quit smoking by age sixteen. He taught Jacob to play the guitar. One night they took a six-pack onto the library steps and recounted their sexual histories to the tune of "Sweet Caroline." Jacob hadn't been certain of finding people like that here—but Andrew introduced him to Wallace, who introduced him to the people in the other freshman hall. Now Jacob spent many nights, past three or four in the morning, slumped on someone's futon, talking to Andrew and Wallace about Clarissa and listening to them talk about the girls they loved, all scheming and relishing their suffering.

Will called every couple of weeks, regularly enough that Jacob wondered if he had it written on a calendar somewhere. Jacob told him about Immunology, the only class he truly liked. He told him about Clarissa, recounting their latest progress like a long-awaited episode of a TV show. He had a feeling that conversation needed constantly to be kept in motion, or else the gap between them—Harvard hosted Al Gore while Lodwick held its annual Laser Tag Weekend—might come into view. But Will just listened, laughed, and always ended by saying, "So, when can I come down for a visit?" He was friendly but insistent, and Jacob was equally firm (though less friendly) in putting him off. At first he said he needed time to settle in, and then he said it was too close to Christmas. The thought of Will visiting— of Will seeing Lodwick's "student center" or witnessing a numbingly basic freshman lecture—made him itch with embarrassment.

But the truth was that Jacob could now go entire weeks without remembering that he hadn't wanted to be here. Academically, this had mostly to do with his Immunology professor, Rakesh Mehra, who was the type around whom students became a little nutty. They'd ask him to make lists of the books they ought to read; they'd laugh in hard nervous bursts at things that turned out not to be jokes; they'd linger after class, slowly closing their notebooks and tucking away their pens, as if they were hoping to be asked on dates.

Rakesh was the youngest tenured professor in Lodwick's Biology Department and one of the youngest in the entire school. He wore ragged plain T-shirts and threadbare jeans over a body that weighed barely 120 pounds. He spoke softly, exhaustedly, in a faint British accent, running his skeletal fingers through black-and-silver hair that stood in unwashed clumps. In the middle of a sentence, in front of the class, he'd pause and say that he'd had an idea and needed to be alone to think it through. Did anyone mind if they picked up here next week?

In October, when they were cleaning up one day after lab, Rakesh asked Jacob if he'd like to join his "loyal band of servants." "I like *the cut of your jib*," Rakesh said, smiling in a way that teased but didn't undermine the kindness. Was he impressed by Jacob's work? Worn down by his admiration? Jacob nodded and promptly lost hold of his notebook, spilling a lake of loose pages onto the floor between them.

From then on he and Rakesh spent hours each week together in the simmering chaos of the lab. All the counters were piled with pipette-tip containers, boxes of scratchy Kimwipes, paper towels on which someone had written a crucial insight in shorthand. Jacob learned to use the microscopes, each one as heavy as a small desk, and to operate the enormous, clammy centrifuge. The question Rakesh had recruited Jacob to study had to do, as everything Rakesh studied had to do, with the maturation of T cells. How, with only their limited DNA, did they learn to defend us against everything from the flu to a bad blood transfusion? How did they know what was part of us and what wasn't? These subjects, which Jacob always presented to his family and friends as laughably minor, had in fact come to seem to him central; organisms were immune systems with bodies attached. Unfathomable that he'd gone the first eighteen years of his life without understanding.

His attitude toward science wasn't entirely reverent, though—he did still want to be famous. This was something he never mentioned to anyone, and would have denied fervently. But in bed at night, or walking between the library and the lab, he would imagine presenting some startling find to Rakesh. Future renown consumed not much less of his mental time than did Clarissa, the girl he'd found to love. His notion was to be a scientist and a writer, a public intellectual: Stephen Jay Gould, Richard Feynman, Jacob Vine. He imagined himself being interviewed on public TV, in magazines, explaining his discoveries in brilliant accessible detail (and possibly with a faint British Indian accent of his own). Eventually, as lightly as snowfall, he would reveal the story of his mother's death and then turn shy when the interviewer asked if he thought there might possibly be a connection between her death and his work. The Humble Genius. Grants and panel discussions.

At least once a week, Jacob and Rakesh ate dinner together on the dining hall's narrow balcony, Rakesh with his waterproof jacket draped over his shoulders as if he were recuperating. (In public he managed to look especially fragile and eccentric.) Rakesh ate most nights with his students—his wife, Amita, studied bat diseases in Uganda and was nearly always away—and he talked in just the same hesitant, meandering way to all of them. He told how carbon monoxide poisoning explained ghost sightings; how the patterns of bombings in London during World War II matched the incidence of sunspots; how the parting of the Red Sea had in fact been a rare but predictable phenomenon of the tides. Starving and crazed after hours of work, Jacob ate whole plates of stir-fry, salty brown gloop coating chicken and cashews and green peppers, mounds of white rice. Not for Rakesh. Rakesh ate just a blueberry yogurt, and used a wooden stirrer for a spoon. He also drank astonishing quantities of the cafeteria's bitter, scalding coffee, whatever the time. He needed to go finish up some work, he said. Also, he needed something to warm him up—was there a window open somewhere?

Once they were finished eating, Rakesh would take out a pen (all his jeans were stained with royal blue blooms) and continue that day's lesson. "This will be very helpful for you to understand," he said. Mouse A and mouse B are injected with antigen Q. We know that mouse A's thymus has been removed, but not before his immune system developed immunity to antigen Q. How could we find out, without opening them up, which mouse was which?

Crisp angular drawings, lovely tilting script. Boarding school education. Jacob sometimes practiced drawing mice the way that Rakesh did, but he could never manage the smooth automatic motion: a small triangle for the head and a larger one for the body. So simple.

"We've worked too long," Rakesh would suddenly say, capping his pen. "Your mind is turning to mush. You're thinking of Dulcinea." Jacob had had to look up Dulcinea—Rakesh loved *Don Quixote, The Three Musketeers, The Count of Monte Cristo.* "I was twelve years old and those were the only books my grandfather owned. I was going to be a *swashbuckler.*" He hesitated before *swashbuckler;* he'd learned thousands of words from print without ever hearing them pronounced.

Jacob was thinking of Dulcinea—that is, Clarissa, whose actual name had come to seem no less enchanting. It was just before ten o'clock, and she would be coming back soon from the library, showering, changing into her pajamas. She lived in Gordon Hall, across the courtyard from Jacob's building.

Early in the year, at a party in the student center basement, Jacob and Clarissa had kissed. She'd had three shots of tequila beforehand and arrived in an ecstatic, loose-limbed mood. A sophomore band played David Bowie covers while all the freshmen stood around the edges of the room waiting to be introduced to one another. Not Clarissa. Dancing by the soda table, she lassoed Jacob around the neck with her weightless striped scarf and said, "Cute bio-lab boy, I command you to kiss me!" The room was dark except for the emergency lights that no one could figure out how to turn off. Jacob, sober and stiff, considered the possibility that she was joking before he put his hands on her hips and stepped nervously closer. *College!* he thought. Her lips tasted like rubbing alcohol. Such happy, hilarious freedom. Such promise.

She was both wilder and more girlish than Emily, or than anyone Jacob had ever wanted to date. She wore makeup every day of her life (Jacob had learned this only when he'd happened to see her one night fresh from washing her face). She giggled. She'd experimented with drugs. The first time Jacob saw her he thought she was Iranian or Egyptian— pale skin, delicate sharp features, enormous eyes. No. She was from California and so were her parents. One grandmother was Israeli. He spent a lot of time asking for her life story, mining for closeness. She'd grown up in an LA suburb with divorced parents, in the shadow of a dazzling older sister (high school valedictorian, London School of Economics). At home she'd been the jester, the tomboy, until that moment in high school when she'd realized that her sister's friends—men three and four years older than her—were paying her attention too, and that they were eager to take her out, buy her drinks, take her along on weekend camping trips in the mountains. From then on she was trouble, and she alluded occasionally to suspensions and to mandatory community service. She had broken up with one of these older guys—Steven—just before coming to college, and still on many nights her phone would be busy for hours at a stretch.

Clarissa was taking Immunology because she'd heard it didn't have a midterm; she was going to be a film director or a photographer. In lab she and Laura, her roommate, were always partners, both with their goggle straps loosened so as not to mess up their hair. Rakesh almost never called on or even looked at them, and when he had to—when, for instance, Clarissa couldn't manage to load the slide during the cell-counting lab—he behaved with brisk embarrassment. He became clumsy and irritable, and had a look on his face as if he were defending himself against mockery. And he may have been right—in dealing with men, particularly older men, Clarissa wore a teasing suggestion of a smile, raised her eyebrows, touched too much. Once, in the middle of a walk across campus, Rakesh had said to Jacob, "Men like us are doomed to love women like Clarissa, but fortunately only when they're young, and only once."

The security guard at Clarissa's building knew Jacob by now, and no longer required him to call upstairs. "Sign your name," he said automatically, clacking the clipboard onto the counter. (Leaving the building at one or two in the morning, Jacob had seen porn on the guard's small TV—his expression, watching, was impatient and businesslike, without a hint of pleasure.)

Upstairs Jacob found Clarissa cheery, her legs folded underneath her. It was the middle of November, and Jacob had become fixated on the idea that he and Clarissa should go away together for a weekend before the end of the semester. A romantic escape to the countryside. (They discussed it mainly through teasing—Jacob would point to all the shoes in her closet or the row of makeup on her radiator, and she would insist that if you just set her on a trail with some gorp she was as happy as anybody. Well, prove it, he'd say, and there it would usually end.)

She seemed to spend all her nights working on a paper that had been due the week before or on a test that the professor had agreed she could take home. Now she let her hands float above the keyboard and asked Jacob, by way of greeting, whether it sounded better to say *the painting's masses narrow into ribbons* or *the painting's ribbons thicken into masses.*

"How about you finish this paragraph and then we take a walk," he said.

"No, I hate walking. Walking's overrated. Laura? What's a fancier word for *hyperactive*? *Frenetic?*"

On the other side of the room, Laura sat wearing reading glasses, making a point of minding her own business.

Clarissa and Laura were so close that many people assumed, incorrectly, they had known each other before coming to school. Laura was from Wheaton, Ohio. They always sat together at meals, and on weekends they came into bars and parties arm in arm and then danced together, using each other to block off clumsily advancing men. It had been Laura whom Jacob approached to find out whether he had any hope with Clarissa. He had leapt out at her like a mugger by the salad bar. "Does Clarissa have a boyfriend, do you know?" Jacob had done his best to make his voice sound idle.

"Not at the moment," Laura had said with less meanness than she might have, spooning a hard-boiled egg onto her plate.

When Clarissa finished her work for the night, she lay back on her bed and let her bare feet fall into Jacob's lap.

Although the hallway they lived off was, like all freshman halls, a mess—music spilling from open doors, torn flyers, people shrieking and shouting and laughing—as long as he was in this room Jacob had the feeling of being in an enchanted seashell. Clarissa wore a tank top and a pair of plaid pajama pants. Her toenails, as tiny as a baby's, were painted deep red. (Jacob wasn't put off, but rather curious, to notice the few black bristles on her big toes.) Someone who sounded like Rufus Wainwright sang quietly from Laura's computer speakers. A string of Christmas lights hung above the window, and beside Clarissa's bed, on the floor, stood a tall white bottle of the lotion that gave Clarissa her smell of strawberries. Girls made better use of their rooms than boys did; they made their beds and bought imitation Oriental rugs and stood dried roses in empty wine bottles.

"See, look how beat up my feet are and you're trying to make me walk."

The soles of her feet had dry white cracks. Cautiously Jacob took her left foot in his hand.

"Your hands are sweaty! Don't you use baby powder?"

He laughed, reddening. "So, going away," he said.

"We don't really have to talk about that now, do we?"

"Just for a minute. I looked at a couple of places online, and there's a town called Mathusine. It's like forty minutes from the bus station, and there are a whole bunch of places we could stay, very cheap, and all these hikes around, a waterfall that's supposed to be very pretty when it freezes. We'd go on that Friday and come back Sunday afternoon."

"Oh, I don't know, don't you think it would be . . . boring?

Staying at some little inn somewhere? Would it be all sixty-year-olds? Bird-watching societies? Why don't *you* come, Laura?! We could tell them we're a threesome!"

"We should decide about a reservation, though. They really might fill up. If we're going to do it I want to call this week."

"I don't know, I don't know, don't reserve anything. I need to talk to my mom. I think we might be going away earlier than I thought. Why does everything have to be such an ordeal? Can't we just see what we feel like doing? Come back! That felt nice!"

Such a scrap as her saying that his hand on her foot felt nice was enough to cancel out all the rest, and to send him, at one in the morning, back across campus feeling elated and fluish with desire. He imagined himself and Clarissa alone in a room with a tall soft bed, a fireplace, an old-fashioned lock on a heavy door. They'd share wine from the bottle and share a slice of chocolate cake. Sex, yes, but it seemed to him sacrilegious, or simple bad luck, to imagine it too directly. A different Clarissa would emerge if they went away, one who talked to him without glancing around the room, one whose love he could depend on like a gold brick in a safe. His entire happiness seemed to depend on it.

The idea of taking Clarissa away had actually come from Peter, Jacob's roommate. Peter was large and red-faced and Christian. He and Jacob treated each other impersonally, with mutual distaste. Peter spent half an hour each morning on the toilet; Jacob kept a permanent fermenting heap of laundry at the foot of his bed. A few nights each month Peter came home drunk, his shirt unbuttoned and gel in his hair, and he'd sit sweating on the bed, glugging tap water and multivitamins, pledging never to go out again. He had a younger girlfriend back home—North Carolina—and Jacob listened to them most nights on the phone, Peter speaking in a high, artificial voice, talking about what they'd do when she visited. Take the bus into the city for a play. Go camping. Go to the outlet malls. Jacob had never thought of going to a bed-and-breakfast, or even of a weekend away, but as soon as Peter mentioned it, it seemed to him the solution to all the problems he was having in winning Clarissa's love.

And for reasons Jacob didn't quite understand, he couldn't get enough of enumerating these problems. At the bar in Hagman where he and his friends spent most week-end nights, where the bouncer was a junior they all knew, Jacob would lean against the edge of the pool table and drink cloying Jack and Cokes until he achieved a certain happy disembodiment in which he would direct a friction-less stream of talk at Andrew or Wallace or even a stranger. "I honestly wasn't sure that people actually felt like this, but it's like…it's like with everyone else I've been…talk-ing in sign language wearing boxing gloves. And with Clar-issa I'm not! We're just talking, face-to-face, and I actually don't even care if we start going out now or ten years from now because I know it's going to happen. I just know. You know?"

The only person Jacob didn't like to bring up Clarissa around was Rakesh. It wouldn't have fit with the tone of their relationship, and Jacob had the sense that Rakesh wouldn't approve of his expending such hope and energy on her. It wasn't *serious*.

Around Clarissa's roommate, Laura, Jacob had no such compunctions. Poor Laura. Jacob would buttonhole her as she walked quickly to her chemistry class, then follow her up the stairs. "Did Clarissa say anything about me after I left?" "Do you know if she's talked to her mom yet?" "Did you hear her say anything to him about getting back together?" On and on and on. Laura was polite, patient, even indulgent. She never exactly encouraged Jacob but neither did she extinguish his hope entirely, which she could have done easily enough. She had dark hair cut just below her ears, ruddy cheeks—something about her appearance made Jacob think of books like *The Scarlet Letter*. Though she laughed easily and played intramural soccer and was known above all for being *kind,* Jacob sensed in her a deep and unshakable seriousness, as if she'd grown up on a farm.

Through her Jacob believed he had a pipeline not only to the innermost thoughts of Clarissa, but also to the hidden workings of the female mind and body. Freed by his lack of romantic interest in her, he felt he could ask Laura anything, and she never turned him away. Sitting in her and Clarissa's room while Clarissa was in class, or sitting on the grass outside the library, they would talk for hours. Do orgasms feel the same for women as they do for men? How often do women masturbate? Why are women like Clarissa so attracted to older men? Is it rebellion against their parents? Is it something evolutionary? Is it (the thought made

Jacob queasy) sexual experience? Is Clarissa afraid of having a boyfriend who actually treats her well? What does it feel like to have your breasts touched? What does it feel like to get your period? Would Clarissa like Jacob better if she saw him less?

Jacob imagined Laura, back in Ohio, taking care of elderly parents, bathing baby siblings, scrubbing floors. She could maintain her cheer through anything, he thought, but would probably never be truly happy. Whenever, out of politeness, Jacob asked about her life, for details about the ex-boyfriends from home to whom she occasionally alluded, Laura would turn vague and clipped. *Nothing worth getting into. I don't want to talk about that stuff.*

Her strongest advice, and to Jacob the most disturbing, was that he should find another girl. Nothing would bring Clarissa around faster. "But I'm not *interested* in anyone else," he said.

"You don't have to actually be interested. How many hookups here do you think involve people who are interested in each other?"

"But I don't think I could just make myself hook up with someone. It's like I hardly even see people other than her. They're blurry or something."

"Well, I'm just telling you what would work."

As it turned out, Jacob could make himself. In a dorm room party celebrating the birthday of someone he had never met, while Clarissa and Laura played poker on the floor, Jacob downed two cups of the punch the hosts had mixed in a recycling bin, and then set all his attention on a girl from his philosophy class. Tatiana Oshanski was older than the rest of the freshmen, though no one knew quite how much older. She'd started school a few years earlier, dropped out, gone somewhere out of state, reenrolled. The details were murky. But she had an adult woman's confident sexuality and ease. She wore dark lipstick and, to class, business suits (perhaps she was coming from a job?). Now, though, she was dressed for the weekend, a glittery tank top and tight jeans and golden hoop earrings, and she held her punch with one hand, grinning at the feeblest joke, and with the other took hold of Jacob's wrist when she wanted to emphasize a point. The music was loud. They climbed out onto the fire escape and she burrowed under his arm to keep warm, then pretended not to be able to see the constellations. *This is so easy*, Jacob thought. Did she want to go get an extra sweatshirt from his room? She did. He twisted the dead bolt (Peter was back in North Carolina for the weekend), shut off the lights, waited for his computer to awaken so he could find something appropriate on Napster. And soon they were peeling off shirts, shoving dirty socks out of the way without breaking their kiss or opening their eyes. Once she was gone—it was three in the morning when they finally detached—Jacob flip-flopped down the hall to the communal bathroom and showered so long under water so scalding that he emerged looking like a boiled ham, pink and blameless.

A week later he was in the library, in the high-ceilinged reading room where students came to stock up on the feeling, contained in the green glass lamps and tall shelves and leather chairs, that they were truly in college, when Laura gestured across the room for him to come here. All over the library people were whispering—it was, in its way, as social as any bar. He knelt beside her chair, hanging from the armrest, and she said, in a voice both triumphant and irritated, *"Clarissa will say yes."*

Immediately Jacob thought he might tip over. "Yes to what?"

"The weekend away. She'll go."

"What did she say?"

"She said she thought about it and she wants to go. Go ask her. She's home now."

Nodding, packing his bag as he sped down the marble stairs, Jacob ran across campus to Gordon and, when he found a workman in the elevator, up the six flights to Clarissa's room. She'll say yes! Should he kiss her right now? Better to wait.

She lay on her stomach on the bed, the Immunology textbook open on her pillow. As soon as she turned to look at him he realized that she'd been asleep. A glazed private dopiness clung to her face.

"I thought you didn't like visiting me anymore."

"I've just been working a lot at night. Rakesh is working on a paper."

"How's Tatiana?"

"I don't know."

She grunted, in derision or just acknowledgment, and rolled onto her back. "I was having the weirdest dream. You were trying to kidnap me."

"I would never do that."

"Sure you would." She blinked and yawned, then laughed at the droplets that leapt from her mouth.

"Well, did you think any more about me taking you somewhere for a weekend?" he said.

"See?"

"It would only be *kidnapping* if you resisted." He sat down beside her.

"Resistance is futile," she said, smiling. "Who said that? Okay, fine, let's go." And like a puppy she shifted her body against him, nuzzling her head into his lap. "What are we going to do there?"

"Sleep. Go for walks. Watch movies."

"That sounds so *nice*. What else?"

"We could…rent bikes, I guess? Ride horses? I don't know."

She slipped one of her hands under the bottom of his shirt and lay her cold palm against his back.

"Will you call now? Call from here."

Jacob, moving carefully so that she wouldn't take her hand off him, tugged the phone close and pulled from his wallet the card on which he'd written the Arbor Inn's phone number. So this, Jacob thought, is what having Clarissa's love would feel like.

A bothered-sounding woman answered just as Jacob was going to hang up. "And you're not going to need us to pick you up at the bus station, are you?" she said. "You don't mind dogs? All right, so I've got you and your wife down here for early afternoon on Friday, then. December eleventh. We'll see you then."

Rakesh really was hoping to submit a paper by the end of the semester, and so Jacob really had been working more than he ever had before. The possibility of having his name on the paper, which Rakesh had hinted that he would, felt to Jacob like a present making its way slowly toward him in the mail. Published at age eighteen. Even Will and his roommates would have to be impressed with that.

He was working so much now that when he wasn't in the lab, his mind carried on experiments without him. Like feeling the motion of the waves after getting off a boat, he would continue to feel the gloves on his hands, the tweezers, the pipette, see the data streaming by. When he was in the lab— where, curiously, the prospect of publication meant less to him than it did anywhere else—he was thinking of how soon he could leave, and decorating another invented scene with Clarissa. It was as if there were two news tickers running simultaneously along the bottom of his mind:

If we stain these cells for that, then we'll find out whether... Unless we were really seeing... So maybe instead we should...

If we take the blanket onto the floor, we can... Unless the floor's too cold... So maybe instead we should...

One morning when Rakesh and Jacob were studying Jacob's data—meditating on might have been more accurate than studying—Rakesh looked up and said that he wanted to go for a walk. "Come with. Let's expose the old carcasses to a bit of oxygen," he said, stretching like a cat. "I haven't breathed actual air since Tuesday."

It was the beginning of December, and the ground on either side of the brick walkway was covered in a shell of snow. The sun and snow combined to give the sky a color like a camera flash, and Jacob had to shade his eyes. Any weather is overwhelming after enough hours in the lab; to stand by a patch of dirt with a bare tree was like watching Niagara Falls rush by. They started to walk, as was not unusual, in silence.

"Do you know what I've been thinking, my dear boy? I've been thinking that once we've finished, you and I will rent a boat and spend a few days at sea." Rakesh lay a square of peppery-smelling nicotine gum in his mouth. "We'll eat only what we catch. With the exception of rum—that our provisions will allow. What do you say?"

"Sounds pretty good."

"You sound unenthused. Piracy is not for everyone, I understand."

Jacob had gotten used to these reveries by now, but he never knew quite how he ought to respond. He'd resolved finally to tell Rakesh that he was going away for the weekend. He'd let it go too long and now it would be—not a crisis, but a disappointment. There was a look of Rakesh's, irritation and willed self-control, that Jacob did all he could to avoid provoking. "So, this weekend," he began to say.

"I believe," Rakesh said, "that I would benefit from a dose of caffeine. Shall we?"

All right, Jacob would tell him after they got coffee. As soon as they were back outside.

In the dining hall Laura sat camped with her books and a thermos at a table, and Rakesh gave her a stiff smile and nod. "Ms. Brinkley," Jacob said, only realizing afterward that he was imitating Rakesh, and that he was hoping to preempt any conversation. He led them out a different door than the one they'd come in so she wouldn't have a chance to mention the weekend.

"Perhaps you were wondering," Rakesh said, holding the door, "why I pulled you aside." It hadn't occurred to Jacob that Rakesh might have a particular reason for pulling him aside. "And perhaps you've also wondered why I'm not my chipper self."

"You're not?"

"Well." He stopped and turned to Jacob meaningfully, and Jacob realized that he had not one idea what Rakesh might be about to say. The cold was such that Jacob found himself scrunching together his features as if he were about to sneeze, to protect himself from the wind. "Amita, I am sorry to say, has deemed me unfit company."

"Rakesh, I'm so sorry. You mean she's left, or—"

"Yes. Well, she was already away, so I think really it's just that she isn't coming back. Which I supposed everyone might have guessed by my attire? They haven't?"

"The people in the lab? No, I don't think so. If they have, they haven't said anything to me."

"Good, good," he said, starting to walk again. For only the second or third time since they'd known each other, he put a hand on Jacob's back. "It seems to me that I'd forgotten that basic maxim: we can succeed at love or we can succeed at work. I'm afraid Amita knew too well how I would tend."

Jacob could only manage to nod and sip his coffee, so Rakesh went on. "I think when we do put out to sea, the only sensible thing would be a ban on the fairer sex. Agreed?"

"Mm-hmm."

"We shall call our vessel the SS *Simplicity*. Now," he said, "what was it about this weekend?"

"Oh. Just that I have a huge philosophy paper to write, so I wondered if I could—"

"Of course, of course." He peeled the lid from his coffee and began to stir it with his finger. He looked so lightened that Jacob felt he could have told him anything. "I shall tell your mice that they've been granted a stay of execution. They will be Dostoyevsky and I the capricious czar. Now go think brilliant thoughts."

On the bus out of town the next day, Clarissa fell asleep curled against the window. Jacob gazed out from his seat that was as high as the back of a brontosaurus, watching Albany speed smoothly by. Across the aisle a middle-aged man with no luggage but a plastic bag ate a roast beef sandwich slathered in mustard. Every few bites he burped sourly, then glared sideways at Jacob, as if challenging him to be disgusted.

Everyone who knew Clarissa would have understood how Jacob felt. On weekends she bestowed her time on one friend or another, and for as long as she was at the party, at the bar, the space and occasion felt blessed. Her attention, never dependable, felt like a shaft of sudden sunlight. And here it was encasing him. What did it feel like, he wondered, to be so sought after? The bus, in spite of the curtains, was as bright as a prism on a table, and Jacob studied Clarissa more closely than he ever had, more calmly. Was she really so extraordinary? Look at the faint dark down at the edges of her mouth. And the place on her chin where she's painted over a pimple. And the odd angular tip to her nose, like a pebble.

But there was something extra, as there is in a tiger or a peacock. She demanded display, protection, worship. She was made of something different from everyone else on this Peter Pan bus headed north on Route 60 on a Friday afternoon in December.

The woman who answered the door at the Arbor Inn was broad, with thick brown hair cut just above her shoulders, work jeans, and a flannel shirt. A wirehaired terrier stood in the doorway, tail stub whirring the air. Jacob's glasses fogged over as soon as they were inside. He recognized the woman's voice from the phone, loud and rough. "I'm Annabel, and this is Mookie—he'll settle down in a minute. My dad's in there sleeping, is why I'm being quiet. He runs it when I'm not here." She wasn't being quiet, but she did seem beleaguered, pulling the key to their room off the row of pegs. As she slowly climbed the stairs, her wide bottom filling Jacob's view, she explained that she'd twisted the hell out of her knee a few months earlier and still wasn't walking on it right.

Here's the bathroom. The shower takes a minute to

warm up. The tub leaks if you let it fill up too much, so don't. This is the library, there are movies on that bottom shelf there—just sign out anything you want to watch. You're in the Sage Room, second one here. To dial out just hit nine and then the area code. Tell me before you do any long distance.

"You guys need anything else?" she said, holding open the door.

They shook their heads, with expressions like orphans in the house of a fearsome aunt.

"Well, I'll be downstairs in the office. Breakfast is six-thirty to nine-thirty, no eggs after nine. Find me if you need anything."

The room seemed not much warmer than the air outside, and they were slow to take off their coats. The bed was high, though not as high as in Jacob's imagination, and there was in fact a fireplace, but no wood, and no sign that it had ever been used. The carpet was thick and brown, and the walls were a grayish purple that made Jacob think of a funeral parlor. A painting on the wall of a duck in flight had a paper tag that said, "Robert Brover, Mathusine Art Gallery, $150." Draped over the bed was a white woven coverlet, weighted down by beads. The only light was the lamp on the desk, beneath which lay a rumpled brochure: *Bed & Breakfast Inns—Rest Assured of Our Quality!*

"Do you think anyone else is staying here?" Jacob whispered.

"I think this whole place is a plot to get our organs. We're going to wake up in a tub full of ice. A leaky tub."

There was an awkwardness they were papering over, a possibly sweet trepidation about being there. It seemed to Jacob incredible that he hadn't given better thought to what it would actually be like once they were alone together. He concentrated on figuring out the coffeemaker.

Once they'd unpacked and brushed the staleness from their teeth, they did discover other guests. Across the stairwell, in the Lavender Room, was a couple from England, Philip and Marian. Why would you come all the way from England to a place like Mathusine? They seemed to think no explanation was necessary—they could have been emissaries from the Mathusine Tourist Board. "You like to hike? Absolutely lovely. Found a lake yesterday, just twenty minutes' walk from here. Frozen solid enough we walked out on it a bit." They were thirty-something, soon to be married, traveling all over the East Coast. Philip, with heavy freckly features, wore a biking shirt brimming with pockets, and as he talked he seemed to be making a point not to stare at Clarissa. "Are you in university? Is it holiday already?" Marian, paler and more reserved than her fiancé, held a folding map—she'd pulled it out to show them the way to the hike—and looked patient, kind, prematurely old. "Are you two on your honeymoon, or...?"

Clarissa smiled brightly and took Jacob's hand. "You guys are actually the first people we've gotten to tell," she said. "Jacob just proposed!"

Philip, momentarily gut-punched, formed a smile. "Is that right? Cheers! How old are—"

"Oh, that's extraordinary!" said Marian. "Just now? Right

here? You'll have to celebrate, won't you? Are you going to race us to the altar? We're not till August."

"We're not sure—sometime in spring, we think. We haven't even told our parents!"

"Oh, they'll be thrilled, won't they? Do you think Annabel's got champagne downstairs? Shall I ask her?"

Jacob and Clarissa walked out, arm in arm, and said to each other in British accents, "Wonderful, isn't it?" "Oh, grand, absolutely grand."

Carrying their key attached to its coaster-size piece of brass, a little giddy, they left the inn and wandered back toward Main Street. Clarissa wore a fleece jacket and, for the first time Jacob had ever seen, ordinary sneakers and jeans that a mother might have owned. Marian had recommended the Riverfront Inn for dinner—*heavenly* pasta, she said. She and Philip had already eaten there twice.

The restaurant, just where the road met the highway, had a dining room with a green carpet and a Ping-Pong table under a dustcover. The only other people inside this early were a pair of platinum-haired women drinking white wine and chatting with a man who seemed to be the manager.

"Do you ever think," Jacob said, "about how weird it is that there are so many places like this in the world, and they're all there, whether you ever see them or not?"

"I think about the people, mostly. All the people you'll never meet. That's what I think I like about the idea of making movies. Talking to all those strangers."

Jacob had only now, chewing a piece of stale bread, realized that he wasn't hungry, and he thought that this probably had to do with his nerves. It was as if he had never, until now, had to consider the question of whether he and Clarissa actually enjoyed each other's company. Who could bother with such stuff, when love was on the menu? There was an air to their being here together that was like the first night of an arranged marriage, politeness and wary warmth. Jacob hoped someone would turn down the lights.

By the time their food came, though, something had happened, thanks to luck or to their first glasses of wine. The possibility of honesty had opened up for them.

"Tell me, Jacob Vine, do you always fall in love with people like this? It's intense! Don't you ever worry that maybe you don't know me?"

She dipped her fingers in the glass candleholder between them and peeled off the finger-caps of wax, dangled them in the flame. It was the first time either of them had ever mentioned Jacob's feelings for her directly. Jacob's lack of appetite wasn't such a bad thing, after all—it meant he could pick at his salad, nibble pieces of chicken, while reserving most of himself for thinking of what to say.

"No, I mean I know that we don't know each other very well yet, obviously. But I just have a feeling that—I think in some cases you see the whole relationship laid out from the beginning, and whether you get to know the details about each other right away or afterward doesn't matter so much. And we do know each other *pretty* well."

"And you really think you love me? That's a pretty serious thing."

"I do. Yes. Or I know that I could love you, which I think is almost the same." ·

She nodded, looked not quite convinced but not quite skeptical either—it was more as if she had been assigned to make inquiries on a friend's behalf.

When they were nearly through their meal Philip and Marian walked in, now wearing evening clothes. "Hello again!" Jacob thought he could see the idea of joining tables together being born and dying, all in the space of a second, on Philip's face. A few more people had come in by then, a family with two well-behaved boys and a foursome of older couples. Jacob and Clarissa were into the last third of their wine bottle and everything seemed warm and entertaining.

"Don't they look," Clarissa whispered, flicking her eyes in the direction of Philip and Marian, "like they have the politest sex? "

" 'Shall we go again, love?' "

" 'I believe so, yes, we shall.' "

"And what about Annabel? Don't you think there's something so sad about her?"

"Sad? No, not really—she just seems like one of those grouchy, competent people. I bet she's pretty happy."

"She had a framed picture on her desk of her dog."

"Did she?"

Talk like this was the punctuation in a long, easy, serious conversation in which they exchanged stories from their lives—experiences they were only now learning to transform into stories—as if they were taking off clothing, matching each other piece for piece. Clarissa told him, with only slight somberness, about the pale crisscrossing scars he'd long noticed on her upper arms. In middle school, when her parents were getting divorced, she used to cut herself with her dad's old razors. Not to kill herself, just to bleed. She'd gotten the idea—she laughed at herself, covered her eyes—from a handout in health class: *Why Are America's Girls Cutting Themselves?*

Jacob—who had told her already about his mother's death, in an earlier, probably premature bid for intimacy—now talked about his father, trying to create a character both sympathetic and absurd. He described the hardware store, the strange glamour Jacob had attached to it growing up, the pride Arthur took in knowing everyone. He talked about that period after his mother had died and before Charlotte had come along, when his father had seemed a few seconds slow, as if his skeleton had become heavy. He told her the strange thing Arthur had said to him only last week, and that Jacob hadn't yet told anyone or even quite thought through himself: " 'Charlotte's reminded me, I think, why people get themselves into these setups in the first place.' "

"Did he mean 'relationships'?"

"I'm not sure."

"You didn't ask?"

"I think when it comes to Charlotte my policy is pretty much not to ask."

It seemed to Jacob that they had broken through something and that the rest of the weekend was going to be much easier. He shifted his chair as close as the table would allow.

"You know, you're a very romantic young man," Clarissa said at one point, tracing his palm with her fingers.

"I don't know about that."

"I'll bet you've memorized love poems."

"So?"

"Am I right?!"

"We had to read e. e. cummings! It was high school!"

"Tell me. Say it."

"Your slightest look easily will unclose me / though I have closed myself as fingers..."

By the time the waiter, apologetically and a bit desperately, came around to say that if they really weren't interested in any dessert or coffee, then ... Jacob realized that he was quite drunk. He stood up and held out Clarissa's coat before picking up his own, and bumped his hip into the corner of the table, knocking over an empty glass, feeling just as if he were on board a swaying ship.

They crossed the dark cold street pressed against each other, shivering, feeling already that the town was theirs; the restaurant, the inn, the British couple—these settings and characters belonged to them. Jacob found himself laughing, making his way up the porch, struggling to guide the key into the lock. What a contrivance, coming here. What transparent, silly scheming, and how gloriously it was working out. Mookie barked from behind a door somewhere in the house and Annabel's voice called out, "Mook! E*nough!*" Inside their room Jacob reached to unzip Clarissa's coat.

He thought of it as following naturally from helping her on with her coat at the restaurant. And of course he thought of it too as the first step toward the lustful undressings to come. Instead, from within her own drunkenness (though she may not, he glimpsed, have been quite so drunk as he was), she withdrew half a step, took off her own coat, and turned to hang it over the back of the chair.

"I'm going to go shower, okay?" she said.

Ah, female mysteriousness! Yes, of course. She needed to shave or primp or scrub or something that only a woman would have known must naturally precede sex. Or maybe she wanted him to join her? Right here? Right above Annabel, asleep with Mookie nestled against her back? What if Philip and Marian came home and needed to use the bathroom? What if someone heard them? His heart and his crotch swelled in synchrony. With a stack of nubbly yellow towels Clarissa stepped out and disappeared down the hall.

Drunk and suddenly aware of being bloated, Jacob hopped up onto the bed and turned on the TV. The red-lettered cable box said that it was 10:19.

On CNN Miles O'Brien nodded seriously as a correspondent in Palm Beach County reported that both camps are preparing for the possibility that this could go to the Supreme Court.

On ESPN a college football band played with wild, slightly out-of-tune joy.

On *Entertainment Tonight* a woman in front of a panel of screens said that up next Mariah Carey would be stopping by the studio for a special Christmas performance.

At 10:41 Jacob rolled over—his whole visual apparatus seemed just slightly loose—and picked up the phone. He knew the number as well as he knew his own. Andrew answered on the third ring.

"I think it's going to happen. It's going great. She's been in the shower a while, though. What should I do?" He spoke quickly, quietly, glancing toward the door.

"Just wait for her to come out."

"Should I go in?"

"No, don't. Definitely not."

"Why not?"

"Too risky. Don't."

"I can't believe this is actually going to happen!"

"Are you drunk?"

"No. Well, yes, but it's fine. I'll call if anything happens."

Now it was 10:47. Clarissa *had* to be waiting for him to come to the shower, didn't she? He wouldn't do anything, he'd just see if the door was open. With a cupped palm he checked his breath. He tugged at the hem of his boxers to unstick himself. Feeling that his heart was sitting higher than usual in his chest, he walked lightly out into the hall. *It's me,* he imagined saying. The door was closed. The water was running. He touched the knob. What was he thinking? Back to the room.

When she hadn't come back by 11:01 he began to get the first chilly apprehensions that something had gone wrong. Maybe a pipe had burst and she was in there mopping up the floor. Or maybe (he handled the thought professionally, dispassionately) she'd clogged the toilet and in shame spent the past half hour futilely plunging. He would go into the hall and call her name with warmth and humor, not a hint of concern.

Through the door he could clearly hear the water running, steadily as before, and the sound of her shifting in the shower, her feet on the tub, her body under the stream. And what else? A whimper, a catching of breath. He stood stern and alert, and when he saw Philip and Marian, pausing at the bottom of the stairs to take off their coats, he hurried back into the room. She was almost certainly just shaving her legs. Girls took extraordinarily long showers. Forty-five minutes long? Yes, forty-five minutes long. Maybe she hadn't gotten in right away. What, was it not enough for him that they were about to spend the night together? Leave her alone.

He turned off the too-bright lamp and lit both of the candles that stood, along with a new box of matches, on the mantle. Yes. Just dark enough for unself-consciousness, just light enough to see. He felt ridiculous alone with the candles, so he turned back on the TV.

Dick Gephardt says we are a country of laws and we need to respect them. With a historical perspective, let's hear now from Doris Kearns Goodwin.

At 11:12 Jacob called Andrew back.

"She's still in the shower. What should I do?"

"Nothing. Just stay there."

"Why not? She's been in there fifty minutes."

"I don't know, but just wait. She'll come out."

"Why? Oh! I think I hear her, here she comes! Bye."

And suddenly, faster than Jacob was ready for her, here Clarissa was back in the room, one towel-corner-tuck away from nudity, holding her clothes in a ball at her chest. He'd never quite appreciated before just how thin her shoulders were. It only took one look at her face, even in the candlelight, to understand that the course of the night had changed, and not in his favor. Her hair hung in wet strips down her back, and her expression was calmly slain. Jacob could feel his drunkenness wearing off like a spell. "Sorry," she said. She tilted her head and shook out an ear. "It didn't really get hot for a while." She sat stiffly on the edge of the desk chair and, holding her towel tight with one hand, dug through her suitcase with the other.

Jacob watched her from the bed, the remote control balanced on his stomach.

"Are you okay?"

"I'm fine."

"No you're not. What happened?"

"Nothing."

"What happened?"

"Can I turn on the light?" she said.

"Okay."

Once she was fully dressed—in the same pair of pajama pants she wore at school and a long-sleeve Pixies T-shirt—she leaned against the edge of the bed and said, with no detectable emotion, "Jacob, we can't do this."

"We can't do what?"

"*This*. Jacob, the candles and everything, it's too much. I thought I could but I can't. I made a mistake. I need to stop doing things like this."

"Things like what?"

"You're incredibly sweet, and I really like being with you, but we can't. I can't."

Of *course* she'd had a wonderful time at dinner, of course she'd meant the things she'd said, but once it had come time to actually...actually *do something* with him, something in her had just frozen up. He felt too strongly about her. She wasn't over Steven, she couldn't just bounce from guy to guy. Jacob was too fragile, it wouldn't be fair.

"I'm not fragile!" Jacob said, in a voice higher than he intended.

"It just wouldn't be right. Trust me. I'm sorry."

And with little more than that she pulled the throw blanket from the foot of the bed and curled up on the arm-chair and ottoman under the window. For a few minutes they lay there, fifteen feet apart, the silence between them like a taut wire. "I'm going to sleep," Clarissa said, and sure enough when Jacob finally stood up to take off his pants and the sweater he had so carefully chosen for tonight, her eyes were shut. She looked like someone pretending to sleep in a play. The blanket wasn't big enough to cover all of her, and where her bare feet poked out they were demurely folded. The radiator was on—Jacob touched it—but the heat wasn't making its way into the rest of the room. The unreality of the situation kept Jacob awake as surely as if they had been having the sex of his fantasies. For an hour he lay on his back under the covers, twitching, chilled inside and out, asking himself what he could have done so wrong, whether there was anything he could do to correct it, what they were going to do tomorrow.

In the candlelight (he hadn't remembered to blow out the candles) he could make out Clarissa's face, and for want of anything else to rest his eyes on, and still unable to sleep, he watched her. There's a thing that happens sometimes when you've been at a dinner party or some other cheery social event with someone, and then afterward, just after both you and she have left, you happen to see her again, sitting in traffic or boarding the subway or just walking down the street. Her face looks so different from how it looked at the party: you suddenly see her anxiety, her inwardness, her unfriend-liness. You realize that the self she gave you and everyone else at the party was a kind of performance, a gift, and that for the world at large the gift is not available. You were seeing one side of a curtain and now you're seeing the other.

Jacob understood—he'd understood it the moment she came back from the shower—that now he was on the wrong side of the curtain with Clarissa, and that he wasn't likely to get back. Playing with his hand on the dinner table, asking him to recite a poem. All now taken away.

The longer he lay there, the more he felt that he needed to go somewhere and call Andrew, maybe even Laura. She would be able to explain, and to reassure him that all wasn't lost.

At 2:30 he went down the hall to find a phone and to pee, so cold and in need of swaddling that he took the comforter with him, wrapped over his shoulders and trailing on the floor. He stepped into the "library," where a gooseneck lamp stood lit all night, but where the phone on a side table seemed not to be connected. Rarely had simple consciousness felt to him like such an ordeal. On the shelves was the usual collection of what travelers leave behind: paperback bestsellers from the past year or two, battered detective and serial killer novels, biographies of presidents and guides to the wildlife of New York state. At the bottom of one of the stacks was a tattered slab of a copy of Carl Sagan's *Cosmos*. Like everyone who stands in front of a bookshelf, Jacob found himself drawn to the one book he'd already read, all the more so for its being difficult to get at. He let *Cosmos* fall open to page 107:

> *But Lowell's lifelong love was the planet Mars. He was elec-*
> *trified by the announcement in 1877 by an Italian astrono-*
> *mer, Giovanni Schiaparelli, of* canali *on Mars. Schiaparelli*
> *had reported during a close approach of Mars to Earth an*
> *intricate network of single and double straight lines criss-*
> *crossing the bright areas of the planet.*

Lifelong love. The words were like cigarette butts in Jacob's mouth.

There was a four-pane window by the bookshelf, and when he noticed that the window was actually set into a door leading onto a balcony, Jacob had the idea that a few minutes outside under the sky might settle him down. A moment of vastness. To get out onto the balcony Jacob had to first move the lamp, then undo a swinging plastic dog gate, and then open the door that felt as if it hadn't been touched in months. The air felt much colder even than he'd expected it to. On the ground, along the railing, was a row of empty flower pots. This was no place to have an epiphany, or even to sit comfortably; the only place for him to settle was a small diamond-gridded metal table. Still Jacob perched on it, wrapped in the blanket, twisted sideways so as to keep his knees from pressing against the railing, and tried to empty his mind of everything but the strange silver-red landscape around him. The balcony overlooked the front yard—a cluster of bushes divided by a cement path—and beyond that was the road out to the three-lane highway where cars headed God knows where sped by. Above him the sky was low and damp, like fog. No stars, no infinity. His feet were bare, but oddly they weren't nearly so cold as the bits of him that were covered, or mostly covered, by the blanket. His leg hairs stood in a dense useless forest. His thoughts, failing at vastness, wandered along his life's own intricate network of crisscrossing lines. He had screwed up in high school so he'd gone to Lodwick so he'd met Clarissa so he'd invited her to go away, and now here he was in the middle of the night on the balcony of a house in a town he would never have suspected of existing. Or, his mother had died so he'd started dating Emily so he'd gotten her pregnant so he'd never been serious with anyone else, so now he lurched after love like Frankenstein's monster after townspeople. There was a little *hum,* a wobble of incipient ache, in his left temple. He realized that if he didn't sleep, tomorrow was going to be even more miserable

than it was destined to be already. He nodded good night at
what he thought might be the moon—a whitish glow where
the clouds pulled apart—and turned to go back in.

It took him surprisingly long to accept that the door was
locked. He huffed hot breath onto his hands, in the hopes
of making the knob unstick, then twisted again and again,
with breaks of a few seconds between attempts. Probably
the mechanism is just stiff, he thought. Bracing himself
with one foot against the wall, he gave the door a powerful
set of shakes. Maybe the top or bottom was just jammed.
First standing on his toes, then bent at the waist, he pried
at the top and bottom of the door with as much of his frozen fingertips as he could wedge between the door and the
frame. Worse than useless. Okay. Think. The sun comes up
in four or five hours. Fine. He considered elbowing out one
of the windows, moving the lamp in front of it, leaving it
for Annabel to discover. He considered forming a ball and
wrapping himself entirely in the blanket, braving the night
like someone trapped in an avalanche. Clarissa would think
something had happened. Something *had* happened. Their
room, his and Clarissa's room, was on the other side of the
house. This nearest bedroom here, the one whose window
ledge was about four feet to the left of the balcony—Jacob
pictured the layout of the house—was the British couple's,
then. Well.

It took five minutes of lying like a ball for Jacob to realize
that he would rather break a leg leaping from the balcony
than spend the night like this. The cold made deep, struc-
tural parts of his body ache. With the pad of his pointer

finger and the tip of his thumbnail he pinched the top of his ear as hard as he could and he felt nothing at all.

And that was how, wearing just boxers and a T-shirt, leaning way out into empty space, teetering on the balcony's railing as if it were the fulcrum of a seesaw, Jacob found himself knocking on Philip and Marian's window at a quarter to three in the morning. Understandably, it took more than a few knocks for them to realize that someone was there, and another minute of explanation for them to see (it was Philip who poked out his startled square head) that the person was not a burglar but Jacob. Less understandably, it didn't occur to any of them for either Philip or Marian to go into the library and try the door themselves. Instead, as if he were easing a heavy sack of frozen goods off a high shelf, before he had any idea how Jacob had come to be there, Philip leaned out of his bedroom window and lay his thick bare arms under Jacob's torso. It was as strange and as helpless as Jacob had ever felt. He went limp as a doll. He could smell Philip's stale dark breath. Their communication, inasmuch as they communicated during those few seconds of maneuvering Jacob through the window, was like a pair of sleeping lovers adjusting to each other's bodies in bed—*Mm? Uh. Er. Egh? Mm.* And he was inside. Back on carpeted ground. Philip had laid him down on his back, and for a few seconds Jacob stayed there, with his eyes fixed on the ceiling. When he climbed to his feet he found Marian sitting up in bed wearing a billowy white nightdress, her mouth forming a perplexed and silent O. "You're all right? What the hell were you doing out there?" Philip said quietly, holding his hip in a way that made clear he'd hurt his back.

"I'm so sorry. I just went out on the balcony for a minute, and the door locked."

"Well, but. Why did— Your girlfriend, then—" Philip's voice expressed, in a way that his face didn't, just how recently he had been deeply asleep.

"Our window's on the other side, so I couldn't reach anywhere else."

"But why, in the first place—"

"Come back to bed," said Marian, and Philip did, so that for a second Jacob had the peculiar feeling of being Philip and Marian's father, making sure that they had no monsters under the bed. Thank God for strangers, Jacob thought. Thank God for unaccountability. "I'm so sorry," he said again. "I'm really, really sorry," and he shut their door with a gentle click.

Back in his room he found that Clarissa had blown out the candles and moved onto the bed, where she now seemed to be truly asleep, greedily sprawled in the middle of the mattress. He leaned close and lay a hand on her back. "I just got stuck outside."

"What?" She sounded newborn.

"I got stuck outside."

"What? Where? Wait, what? Why is your hand so cold? Stop."

"Forget it."

"What's going on?"

"Forget it. Good night."

And she did forget it—she collapsed back onto the pillow, sighed in irritation, and pulled the sheets back over her shoulders. Strangers everywhere, he thought. He felt adrenaline more acutely now than he had outside—only now did the dizzy midair moment begin to seem real. He could still feel the places on his sides where Philip's hands had dug into him, and the place on his stomach that had scraped the window frame on the way in. Philip had touched more of his body than Clarissa ever had or would.

He sat down on the chair by the window and, looking back out at the highway, had to suppress the urge to laugh. *Why, in the first place...?* Eventually he settled in with his legs on the ottoman (he could see why Clarissa had moved at the first opportunity) and looked at the still fan on the ceiling while he waited for his mind to slow down. He felt as if he'd just learned of *canali* on Mars. He felt as if he'd just gotten engaged. He had, for no reason he could identify, a distinct and unsteady feeling of triumph.

His and Clarissa's decision to leave the next morning was a more impressive feat of unspoken communication than anything in their courtship. They tiptoed downstairs, dreading a conversation with Annabel (Clarissa) and with Philip and Marian (Jacob). Lucky for both of them, Harry, Annabel's father, was feeling good enough to hold court. Through the closed doors of the breakfast room, they heard a booming male voice. *"...It's fantastic!...onto a ship...my two older sisters..."* At a round table they found an ancient man, in a wheelchair, waving a fork while addressing the air between

Philip and Marian, who wore identical expressions of defer-
ence and despair. *"And it's all luck! That's what it all comes
down to! I was analyzed, psychoanalyzed, this was when
I was trying to save my marriage, and the doctor said to
me..."* Annabel came in from the kitchen, took the plates
from the table, brushed something from her father's sweater.
He had silver hair still surprisingly thick, and an enormous
tanned head that must once have been handsome. His eyes
were bright but clouded, and his skin was like stained wood,
rotting in places. Inside the enormous pale caverns of his
ears were patches of dirt or decay, as well as beige plastic
contraptions not quite lodged in place.

He turned to Jacob and Clarissa—his body turned as a
single unit—and his face expressed a fear of being interrupted along with a more general bafflement. They smiled
at him in assurance, and then went into the kitchen to tell
Annabel they were leaving. A friend back in Hagman, a
last-minute change, so sorry, they would have to come back.
It was as if Annabel were seeing them for the first time. "I
can't just not charge you for the second night, though," she
said.

"Well, but we already paid you the deposit. What about
if we just pay half of the rest of the bill?" said Jacob, imagining what his father would say. "Is that fair?"

"All right, half." She resumed dropping silverware into
the rack, and Jacob felt the rare and painful jolt of being
undisguisedly disliked.

Outside, the morning was as dark as evening and large
flakes of snow shook out of the clouds. Jacob was so pleased

at having escaped Philip and Marian that he had to fight down the temptation to tell Clarissa about the balcony—he needed to get out of the habit of hoarding his life for her. She said, "Where did you go last night?" and he just said he'd taken a shower. "Who was that old man?" she asked.

"Annabel's dad, I think. Remember?"

After a few minutes on the bus they moved a row apart, ostensibly so Jacob could lie down. There were only a few other passengers, and every few minutes Jacob was roused—though he was never really asleep—by the driver coughing with a sound like crumpling paper.

When the bus stopped to refuel outside of Albany Clarissa said, "Do you want anything? I'm going in to get Tylenol." And then, when Jacob shook his head, she added, "I'm not sorry we came, you know. I hope you're not either." Jacob nodded; it felt as if, in being forced to give up on her, he had somehow for the first time gained the upper hand.

Back at the Hagman station—the trip home felt half as long as the trip out—they stepped onto the curb where bearded homeless men sat all day drunk on the edge of the dry fountain, sobering up with coffee from Dunkin' Donuts. Jacob felt in need of some sobering up himself; his body had an achy unreal feeling. A few gray-and-purple pigeons approached, hopped out of the way, rooted in the sidewalk cracks. The snow was falling here too, but the sun had come out, so the golden dome on the town's big bank shone prettily. Jacob was just turning to tell Clarissa that she didn't need to wait for him, he was going to stop and buy a few things, when across the street he saw something so strange that he thought he had to be imagining it. Will and Laura walking together out of a café, as if they'd known each other all their lives. Someone who looked like Will? No, actually Will. He and Laura both saw Jacob, though they were too far away for Jacob to interpret their expressions. The bus had pulled away and left Jacob and Clarissa facing Will and Laura as if the two couples were staging a duel.

"Hey!"

"Hey!"

Jacob's first thought was that something terrible had happened. Someone dead in a car accident, news too dire to be delivered over the phone. But by the time they'd crossed over to his side of the street, Jacob saw that it was nothing like that—Will had the awkward, good-natured bounce of someone trying to seem at home. "Clarissa? Hey, I've heard a lot about you. William." Will had finally gotten fed up with being put off, he explained, and had just decided to take the train down. Hadn't Jacob gotten his messages?

On the walk back to Jacob's room, Will told the story of looking for him yesterday—a search involving professors and security guards and finally Laura, who'd recognized him from the picture on Jacob's bulletin board. He talked in a way that made clear he'd been telling the story all weekend. Clarissa smiled and made polite conversation until she took the chance to slip away outside Jacob's building, sheepishly calling out that she'd probably see them later. Will knew enough not to ask just then what was happening between them. "I'm actually having a really good time," he said. "Last night we went to—what's it called? That bar with Pac-Man? I met Rakesh in the dining hall this morning. I feel like a spy."

Jacob expected Laura to excuse herself too, but she seemed not even to be considering it. What was it that he saw on her face? Satisfaction. At having spotted Will, or just at being woven into Jacob's life in this way. She must have known the trip with Clarissa was a failure. And now Jacob thought he knew something too. It was her recognizing Will from a picture that finally told him; but all that would come later. First he had the rest of Will's visit to contend with.

They sat together in Jacob's room—Will's bag lay open beside the bed—and Jacob thought one by one of the things he'd dreaded Will seeing. His too-small room with its cracked tile floors. The dark, muddy quad. Peter's beer-tab collection. But having been caught by surprise, he felt pleasantly detached. In certain lights, under certain influences, Lodwick had its charms.

Jacob winced and blushed through a description of the weekend. "Just...kind of a last-ditch effort, I guess. The place was nice, though. This old house in this weird little town. Last night I actually got...forget it."

Laura and Will told a story, one picking up when the other laughed too hard to go on, about something that had happened at the bar, something to do with the bouncer and a freshman, Serge, who had never touched alcohol until that weekend.

When Laura did finally stand up, saying something about the library, she shook Will's hand and told him how nice it had been to meet him. When they were alone—Will on Jacob's bed and Jacob on Peter's—it took a minute or two for the talk to regain its rhythm. Jacob wondered if Will and Laura had kissed, if that was the satisfaction.

"It actually seems really fun here," Will said.

"Yeah, it's . . . Well."

"Laura's cute—she's Clarissa's roommate?"

"Yup."

"And Rakesh seems great. One of those people you can just tell, within thirty seconds, he'd be amazing to know."

"Did he ask at all about where I was, or . . . ?"

"No. He seemed to know you were busy. He said you guys are working on a paper together?"

Jacob told him, proudly, what the paper would be about. The trial infection and thymus transplant—Jacob realized, possibly for the first time, that there was finally a subject he knew well that Will didn't know at all. "And how do you know if the mouse is actually becoming immune?" "Does it matter how old it is?"

The pleasure of knowing the answers, along with its somehow having become the afternoon, made Jacob hungry. They walked down to the dining hall and Jacob piled his plate with scrambled eggs and roasted tomatoes and an English muffin. "Hey, this is my brother." "This is my brother, he's here for the weekend." It seemed as if Jacob knew everyone who walked past.

So profound was his relief, and his enjoyment of his food, that he hardly paused when Will put his elbows on the table and said, "I also wanted to say—" So he did hook up with Laura, Jacob thought. Good for them. "Yesterday was the eleventh."

Ah. Oh. Jacob choked on a piece of egg. His body recognized the date before his brain did.

"I know!" Jacob said. "I know. I just."

"It's not a big deal."

"No, I know, I didn't forget, I was just going to say, actually…"

But it didn't matter what he said. Will could see, as plainly as Jacob's face, that the floor had momentarily opened up underneath him. December the eleventh. Jacob remembered when the date had had a taste in his mind, like a heavy brown lozenge. All those afternoons with Arthur in the cemetery, and here Jacob hadn't even bothered to call home. The taste had been masked by lust and the second-cheapest red wine on the menu.

"I'm really sorry," he said. He felt now as if he and Will were all alone in the dining hall, though people from his class continued to stream by.

"No, don't."

"Really, I'm sorry." Sorry for leaving Will alone here, sorry for always screwing up. Sorry for getting so caught up in himself that he needed his brother to reach in, like an arm into a stream, and pull him onto solid ground.

"My first year at school I forgot Cara's birthday, and there was this whole big stupid thing," Will said.

"It's different though, I…"

Had Will chosen this weekend because it was the eleventh? Jacob couldn't bring himself to ask. Instead he said, "We should see if there's a service or something we could go to tonight."

Will shrugged and finished the lemonade in his glass for the second or third time.

From the dining hall they went to the lab. Will had suggested that they go see it in an attempt, Jacob understood, to shift the emphasis from their mother. No one could shame Jacob like Will, and no one could relieve his shame like Will. They walked without talking, except for Jacob to direct him through one door and another. At first Jacob thought that someone had left the lights on in the lab, but Rakesh stood at the counter in his corner. He held a pencil-thin tube up to the window with his hand in a rubber glove. He acknowledged them with a nod. He might have been standing there all weekend, as content and inscrutable as a deer. "The Brothers Vine. It sounds like a magic act, doesn't it? Well-known at all the least reputable fairs?" Even with Will, he couldn't help exercising his strange, weightless charm. In another era he could have started a religion.

Jacob walked Will over to the mouse cages, the incubator, the desk where he had his instruments arranged like silverware at a restaurant.

"May I reserve your services on Monday for a quick stain?" was all Rakesh said before they left, and the question managed to contain the promise—which Jacob had already understood—that Rakesh would never ask him why his brother was visiting on a weekend when he had had to write a philosophy paper.

"So you guys stain the cells and then they get sucked up through that machine?" Will said, walking outside.

Jacob felt the first hint of condescension from Will—this was the interest a parent shows a child—but it didn't bother him nearly so much as he'd expected. Will could have his adventures with school; Jacob would have his with life.

That night they didn't go to temple—instead they went to a party at a frat where someone had hired a pianist in a tuxedo. They came back to Jacob's dorm at two in the morning, tipsy and embarrassed in the way they were always embarrassed after being their adult selves together. While Will was getting ready for bed, Jacob stood alone in the dark in his room, thinking of whether his other set of sheets were clean, mentally blinking. The heap of clothes on Peter's bed began to speak, so startling Jacob that he yelped. "You ever see the note I put on your desk?"

By turning on his lamp and rooting around on his knees, Jacob did manage to find it. The receipt Peter had written on had blown onto the floor under the dresser, where it might well have stayed with the Q-tips and pennies for the rest of the year. Jacob read, *Your brother called x2, important, coming in town—Friday AM.*

"You didn't see it, though?"

Will walked in, wet-faced, and asked if he could borrow a towel. "Of course, let's see, I usually have one in here." As Jacob draped his last clean towel over his brother's shoulder—when was the last time they'd seen each other's bare chests? shared a room?—he held the note stuffed deep in his left palm. Even now he couldn't say he wished he'd seen it.

You Know Who You Are

A few weeks before he turned fifty-five, Arthur mentioned to his children that he sure thought it would be nice if they came home to celebrate. This was so unlike him, and he sounded so apologetic when he proposed it, that Jacob wondered if his father had in mind some dramatic scene. Maybe he was cutting them out of his will in favor of Charlotte. Maybe he was selling the house. Or maybe—and this wasn't much less distressing—he was just becoming sentimental and wanted an excuse to be moved to tears.

Still, Jacob and Laura bought train tickets for the Friday in November. When they talked about the exact plans, they avoided mentioning Will—he was like a loose floorboard that they'd learned not to touch.

They were living in Bed-Stuy, Brooklyn, in an apartment in need of renovation in a building in need of paint. They'd lived there for the five months since graduation, and they were just now beginning to have real convictions about where to buy milk, what train to take into Manhattan, when to leave the house in the morning so as not to have to wait for the bus. Their building stood across the street from a bodega and a nail salon decorated with a line of fluttery silver flags.

Wasn't everyone their age supposed to be living in Brooklyn? *Ah yes*, one of Laura's professors had said, *it must be just like Paris in the '20s.* But when they did see people their age—in the grocery store, standing outside a bar—they didn't know them, and this seemed now to be an obstacle in a way it never had been during college. No one dropped in to watch TV or to ask if they felt like going out for a drink; no one chatted with them in the elevator (there was no elevator); no one across the hall threw a party on Saturday night. Instead there was just the emptiness of the bleach-smelling stairwell, and the occasional exchange of hellos with David Dirch, the nervous man who owned the building and lived alone below them. Laura was in her first year of medical school at NYU, which kept her too busy to make friends. Jacob worked as an assistant in an immunology lab at Columbia, where his colleagues, immigrants in their thirties and forties, were busy with families and work, and were anyway too peculiar—too impassioned, in the narrow untranslatable way of scientists—to think of seeing socially. That left a handful of stray connections—college almost-friends who'd moved to the city, people from one or another of their high schools, the occasional promising stranger.

A feeling of playing house regularly came over both of

them in those first few months, but never more strongly than on the nights when they had people over for dinner, which seemed to be what grown-ups did when they wanted to see their friends. They'd spend hours cleaning, arranging the lamps, following a four-page recipe for lasagna...and all they'd have to show for it, once their new friends had closed the door behind them at the end of the night, was an astonishing quantity of dishes and a feeling that something faintly embarrassing had taken place. Maybe the embarrassment had just been their eagerness, their too-naked hopefulness. They'd blow out the candles and crawl silently into bed, where the rain dripping on David's tarp—he had lain a plastic sheet over an empty fish pond in the backyard— would *pock-pock-pock* them to sleep. Weeks would pass before one of them would come home anxiously bearing the names of another couple. Most nights it would be just the two of them. They'd wonder how they could ever have longed to graduate—how anyone could fail to be happy in that dining hall, on that path to the library, on that buzzing and living campus.

As juniors Jacob and Laura, who'd remained friendly but not friends after freshman year, had lived in a dorm called Shapiro. They were in the same neuroscience class, and because Jacob was known—not entirely fairly—for being an expert in biology, she asked if they could study together. They started meeting on the nights before quizzes in the lounge on their dorm's first floor, where they would sit on one of the collapsed couches and compare notes. Laura's were meticulous, evenly spaced, her blue script breaking only where she'd copied down a diagram from the board. Jacob often had to stare frowning at his own notes before they became clear—*tr. er.* meant transcription error; that dash was supposed to have been an arrow. At the ends of these long nights—it would be some astonishing, European airport-lounge kind of time, 3:09 a.m.—he would walk her in his socks to her room, and bow as he said good night.

She turned out to be funny and strange in a hundred ways he hadn't been able to see, or hadn't bothered to see, when she'd merely been his conduit to Clarissa. When talking about something she felt strongly about, she made flapping, chattering motions with her hands, as if she'd like them to form mouths and talk for her too. In conversation she skipped from one subject to another seemingly at random—and then would look impatient if you asked how she'd gotten from, say, her father's way of preparing beets to an article she'd read about the Vatican's postal system. Religion was one of the subjects that made her hands flap. She wasn't conventionally religious, though her parents were. But she called Jacob simpleminded and condescending when he dismissed Christianity as a dangerous set of myths, or when he referred broadly to "midwestern people," as if they composed an enormous, good-hearted monolith. Had he ever even been to Ohio? (He'd changed planes once in Cleveland.) Had he ever been friends with a religious person? (Of course! For instance there was...) Had he ever been in a Wal-Mart? (Well, not *in* one.)

When the class ended, they continued turning up at each other's doors. Their rooms, identical blue-carpeted cubes, were two floors apart. They'd discovered a common love of the curly fries in the one café that stayed open all night, and together they'd cross campus and sit in one of the brightly lit booths, talking, waving fries like batons. The campus never entirely slept. In front of one building they would have to detour around freshmen, giddy with freedom, playing and waiting to play four-square. In Shapiro they would ride the elevator with a girl they didn't know, wearing fishnet stockings and crying, apologizing, crying some more. All the while they would carry on a conversation that felt something like therapy. They'd talked about their beliefs, or what they thought might be their beliefs; now they told each other their stories (with the careful omission, on Jacob's part, of stories to do with Clarissa).

Laura told him about having kissed her boyfriend's best friend in high school. She hadn't been unhappy with her boyfriend, and he had never found out. It had just been a game, she said, a test. Could she get away with this. Also she used to steal money from her mother's wallet, a dollar at a time, to buy a certain kind of bracelet that everyone had worn. And once she had seen her father—her watch-collecting, insurance executive father—bare-assed at his bathroom sink, masturbating, with his free hand on his hip like a flamenco dancer.

Jacob's stories tended to be a bit longer, more dramatized. He had to remind himself, occasionally, that he ought to think more about being honest than about being entertaining. He told her about learning that his mother had cancer, and then about her dying. About Emily's abortion.

About a time, in high school, that he and Charles had gotten to talking to a woman at the bar of a seedy Adams Morgan restaurant only to realize, or to imagine, that she was actually a prostitute.

Something rare and delightful was developing between them, but out of self-consciousness or caution they both avoided mentioning it. Jacob wondered if this was how real love felt—a slow enveloping oven heat, compared with which his feelings for Clarissa (or, for that matter, Emily) had been fitful and half-toxic, campfires stoked with plastic bags.

Laura had begun to look different to him too, though except for her hair having grown longer, he didn't think the change was really physical. Her paleness now seemed to him delicate, almost porcelain. He had no idea what he could once have found to complain about in her face—her upturned nose, her wide-set eyes, her smile that seemed always to be anticipating a joke. He also noticed, now that he was paying attention, that she was followed through school by a small but persistent male harem. There was Hendrik Doyle, with the enormous head and obscure poetry anthologies; John Ascher, tall and British and balding; Phil Latimer, who left CDs like Easter eggs outside her door. She smiled at them, put the CDs in a drawer, thanked them when they complimented her—and then spent her nights sitting up in the lamplight of her room with Jacob. On the night of the Spring Bacchanal (the class committee had hired an accordion band and rented a wooden barrel for barefoot grape-crushing), Jacob and Laura finally kissed.

"I didn't think you'd ever have the nerve," she said, close to his ear because of the music.

"I think it must be the wine. I feel completely nerveless. Also, I can see the future: we're going to get married."

"When?"

"Not for a few years. But it'll be very nice, lots of very moving speeches. We'll put flowers on our dog."

"We're getting a dog?"

That summer they wrote each other daily, almost hourly, e-mails. Laura was back in Ohio, answering the phone in her father's office, and when they came back to school in fall, she moved her clothes into Jacob's closet. They shared the bed that was barely wide enough for one of them, went out to dinner on their birthdays, passed colds back and forth almost gratefully. There were dozens of surprises and disappointments. Laura was prone to bouts of depression, during which she would show all the verve of a bowl of mashed potatoes. She turned out to regard her mother—who worked in the administration of her church—with a protective, slightly eerie devotion. And she often went to bed without brushing her teeth.

The main thing about him that she hadn't known, or anyway the thing she hadn't known that most bothered her, had to do with his siblings. She had assumed that their mother's death would have made them close, and yet the relationships seemed strained and oddly formal. Didn't he and Will ever talk on the phone just to chat? How could he not have invited Cara to visit Lodwick even once? She dwelled on these things in a way that made Jacob wonder if behind her questions there was some bit of churchy wisdom from her mother—*how a man treats his siblings is the surest sign of how he'll treat you.* Or maybe not. Maybe it was that her brothers—twins, high school competitive swimmers—were her best friends. She said "I love you" before she hung up with either one of them.

One night that fall Jacob was washing his face before bed when he heard a phone's electronic trill down the hall. "Is that mine?" he hollered. He came back into his room, still patting his face, to find the phone pressed to Laura's ear. "Hold on a second," she said, "here he is. Good talking to you."

It was Will, calling to ask about Christmas. Yes, Jacob was coming home; no, he hadn't bought tickets. While he talked he was thinking—Will and Laura were on the phone for what, two minutes? That night in bed he asked what they'd talked about.

"Nothing. He was telling me about applying for business school. The way he talks is so funny. It's like he has everything on a little chart. Was he always like that?"

"I don't know."

Another night—this was a week or two later, when they were walking back from the library—she said to him, after a silence, that Will had called her that day in her room. "Isn't that weird?" she said. "I guess he looked me up online. He wanted to talk more about grad school stuff. Does he not have many friends?"

That last little insult was a gift for Jacob, a reassurance. But why did Jacob need reassurance? There was no sensible reason for Will's calling her to have pumped cold liquid into Jacob's bloodstream. Cold liquid was pumping into Jacob's bloodstream all the time. And Will didn't have many friends, now that he was out of school. He lived in Boston, working for the year at a venture capital firm, and his life, from what Jacob could tell, was as bleak as his undecorated apartment and the take-out chicken sandwiches he ate most nights for dinner. He had a handful of friends to e-mail, a few rented DVDs scattered on the coffee table, but just being in the apartment you could smell something close to panic. *Is this my life?* Will seemed to be asking. *Tell me what the missing ingredient is. Add what and transform this into something tenable?* Jacob would have gone to Laura with that sort of question too.

And Will continued to call Laura all through the fall, as if she had been assigned to him, like an elementary school pen pal. But that was only Jacob's disapproving version— Laura herself seemed to enjoy hearing from him. (Jacob had once asked her why she let people talk endlessly about themselves, and she had said, simply, "Because it makes me feel important.")

So now, as Lodwick's paths and lawns acquired a permanent-seeming crust of snow, Jacob and Laura's relationship took on this invisible third. Sitting in the dining hall at dinner, sharing an ice-cream sundae in a cereal bowl, Laura said, "I didn't realize you'd told Will about Emily getting pregnant. He really cares about you, you know?" When Jacob asked why Laura was reading a play by Chekhov, she said, "Will said he saw it. It's actually really good."

He's a community service project for her, is what Jacob thought. She'd seen that Will was unhappy, seen that he wasn't as close as he wanted to be to Jacob, and she'd decided that she would be the one to fix it. And she must have liked the unusual view it gave her of Jacob before they'd met. *Will really tried to be something like a father to you, didn't he? Will's like your dad and Cara's like your mom and you're somewhere in between—is that right?* Jacob enjoyed being read like this, even when the readings seemed to him dubious. And by the time he realized that he was no longer the main topic of their conversation, or even one of the main topics, they were talking often enough that there was nothing he could do about it.

It turned out—Jacob learned through Laura—that Will was going through something of a crisis. He was lonely; he was full of doubts about whether he wanted to go to business school; he was convinced that there was something wrong with him when it came to relationships. He'd seen therapists, he'd tried meditation, he'd taken Zoloft. What romantic success he'd had toward the beginning of college had petered out, and now the solitary months had piled up like empty bottles in a bin (and he was back, incidentally, to being called Will). There were some days, Will told Laura, where he went to the store and bought things he didn't need—a magazine, a pack of gum—just for the sake of speaking to someone. He was tired of putting all his energy into work, into school, but he didn't know how to do anything else. His phone never rang. And when the possibility of dating someone appeared—a girl at his office, perfectly attractive, had mentioned a bar that she and her friends were going to—Will's mind immediately began generating excuses. Why was that? Why did he do everything in his power to get back to his apartment and then spend all his time in the apartment thinking of how he could leave?

Hearing these things Jacob would have to struggle—as when you hear a mundane personal story about a celebrity—to keep in mind that the person experiencing all this was the same brother he'd always known. When they saw each other over Christmas Will acted so ordinary and formal— neither of them mentioned Laura, and Will spent all his time working in the spare bedroom upstairs—that Jacob wondered if the torment was a ruse; maybe Will thought he needed some complicated problem in order to go on bothering Laura. And he would have wanted to go on bothering her, Jacob thought, because he was jealous. Here was Will, twenty-three years old, contemplating a solitary life in his crappily constructed Cambridge apartment, while his younger brother all but lived with a girlfriend. Maybe when Will called he was simply saying, to both of them, *Get up! Stop acting married! It isn't fair!*

One night as they lay in bed—this was January—Laura said to Jacob, "Do you think Will might be gay?"

"No. Why?"

"I don't know. It just occurred to me. You've never thought about it?"

Through the wall they could hear the rumbles and explosions of Jacob's neighbor playing Wolfenstein.

"I've thought about it, but I don't think so. He likes girls, he just has no idea what to do with them."

She made a noise that was like a nod—not entirely convinced, but for the time being accepting. After a couple of minutes Jacob said, "What made you ask that?"

At first Jacob thought that she was considering what she was about to say with special care, but finally he had to reach up and shake her arm.

"*Nnnh.*"

"Oh."

"*Nnnnnh.*" She rolled onto her side, giving Jacob her back, and Jacob did what he always did when he couldn't sleep, which was to carry out an experiment in his mind in the most tedious imaginable detail. First he plucked a hole in the plastic wrap on the package of test tubes, then he peeled the wrapping open in a continuous orange-peel strip, then he ... fell asleep, and dreamt that Will had decided to move into his and Laura's bedroom. In the dream Will made a bed for himself on the floor beside theirs, and laid all his clothes in neat piles under the desk. "Isn't there something strange about this?" Jacob tried saying to Laura, but she couldn't hear him, and when she finally did she just laughed and shook her head. He just wasn't comfortable yet around Will, she said. That was all.

By their senior year Jacob had worked for so long in Rakesh's lab—he'd spent a year and a half on a single project to do with skin grafts—that he felt less like an undergrad than like a professional scientist. He'd apply for a PhD program eventually, but starting anywhere else sounded to him like a step backward. He had a daydream—sometimes it veered toward becoming a plan—that he and Laura would rent a house in Hagman after graduation. He would continue working for Rakesh, and she, rather than applying immediately for medical school, would work in one of the doctor's offices in town. He imagined him and Laura sitting around Rakesh's living room late at night, drinking brandy, complaining wittily about the faculty. This was a fantasy wrapped in tweed, a screenwriter's vision of small-town academia, but still he couldn't let it go.

It wouldn't come true. Laura wanted them to move to the city. They'd gone for a weekend together that fall— they'd walked miles of paths through Central Park, eaten oily red soup and alien fruit in Chinatown—and Jacob had assumed that his conclusion had gone for both of them. New York was good for an occasional weekend, but to live in it would be like living in a pinball machine. They'd lose their minds, or they'd become hardened and snobby and impatient. The truth was that Jacob was scared. At Lodwick he felt accomplished, serene, well-regarded; in New York how many thousands of young would-be scientists were there, and how many of them would be smarter than him? How many of them would have published papers in journals more impressive than the *Journal of Asthma and Allergy*? He could too easily imagine the careful expressions on people's faces as they said, "Lodwick. Where is that, again?"

But Laura ordered an application for NYU School of Medicine and spent hours sifting through apartment listings online. Rakesh—who announced that spring that he was taking a position at Cornell—called a friend who ran a lab at Columbia, and got Jacob an interview for a job as a technician. "Marcel is a very good man," Rakesh said. "He will take you under his Francophone wing. I have instructed him to show you all the subtler charms of the urban life— prepare to drink copiously."

And New York did, on the visit they took that spring, seem like somewhere you might actually want to live. This may have been in part a trick of the weather—the sky was as clear as if it had been power-hosed—but it had mostly to do with the discovery of Brooklyn. Jacob had known nothing about it, except that it was less crowded than Manhattan and surprisingly enormous on the map, but by the end of the weekend he and Laura were talking about which of them would drive the U-Haul. The stoops, the trees, the sidewalk chalk, the dogs, the round café tables with wobbly legs... Never in Jacob's life had he felt that the words *young man* applied to him so well as when he and Laura, arm in arm, stood in front of the window of a real-estate office. *Light-drenched... granite-topped... right in the heart of historic Brooklyn.* Why shouldn't they be able to make it in New York? What could all these people—climbing on and off the subway, waiting in line for the ATM—know that he and Laura didn't? If anyone could be happy here, they could. His pulse sped as smoothly as a horse lightly kicked.

Not long after that weekend, Will announced that he too had had a change in his life. He'd met someone. Her name was Lizzie, and she was in her second year at the law school.

They'd met at a panel discussion about education reform. She was from Chicago, she wanted to be a civil rights lawyer, and Jesus, she just couldn't have been any more perfect. She's so smart, he said, as if in shock. But not smart in an obnoxious or a boring way—she's really funny. She's only had one serious boyfriend in her life too, he said, so we're on pretty equal footing. She looks almost South American, very dark hair and greenish eyes.

"Wow," Laura said. "He sounds like he's on speed."

From the beginning Jacob felt a vague but heavy gloom whenever he thought of Will and Lizzie. He told himself this was because he thought Will was going to get hurt, or because he didn't like Will's self-obsession, but the truth was that he was jealous. He resented the disruption of the natural order. He, Jacob, was to be the romantically successful, sexually experienced one. Personal happiness ought not to arrive like a growth spurt—certainly not for other people.

Will didn't call Laura any less often now that he was with Lizzie, though; in fact he may have called her even more, as if he were reporting back to a proud patron. Lizzie had convinced him that he ought to take a job at a nonprofit, he said, rather than going straight into business school. Also she was teaching him how to cook—that Sunday they'd made a roasted chicken with rosemary and some kind of lemon pudding for dessert.

Another change: now Will was calling Jacob as well as Laura. At first their conversations were like the conversations in a locker room, all carefully controlled gazes. But within a few weeks they were talking more easily, and Jacob had mostly forgotten what bad feelings he'd had regarding Lizzie. They talked about the difficulties of going to class or to work when there was the possibility of staying in bed all day. Will asked what Jacob thought about getting roses— cheesy or nice? He also wanted to know how long this giddy part of a relationship lasted—or was it possible that with someone like Lizzie it might last forever?

One night he said, "And thanks for letting me talk to Laura all the time this year. I honestly don't think I would have ever found a girlfriend without her."

"Nobody has to get my permission. I like having you guys get to know each other." And maybe he really did, he thought. Maybe he'd be one of those people closer to his siblings as an adult than as a child. He had started calling Cara more too, in this new spirit of familial warmth. He told her not to just tell him everything was all right and then recite the names of some classes—actually tell him what was going on. And she did. She hated being home with their dad and Charlotte, so she was spending lots of her evenings at mock trial, where she found that she actually liked speaking in front of crowds. She'd dated a boy in her class named Greg for a few months—her first real boyfriend—but broken up with him that winter because he'd proven himself immature. She came alive for him, as Will did, and it was a wonder to him—one only slightly tinged with melancholy— that he hadn't taken better advantage of their being in his life until now. How had he not appreciated earlier the strange miracle of having people who would know what he was talking about if he mentioned the giraffe painting that had hung in the bathroom at home? Or of being able to say, about his father, "He was doing that weird scowly thing he does when he thinks he's saying something important," and to be absolutely sure of being understood?

When, in April, Will said, "Why don't Lizzie and I stay after graduation and help you guys move?" it was a happy discovery for Jacob, like realizing that a long-sore ankle has healed, that he felt no dread. And when Will said, a week later, that Lizzie wouldn't be able to come after all— she had to go to a friend's bachelorette party that weekend in Chicago—it didn't diminish Jacob's hopes that Will and Lizzie would visit them in New York, become the couple-friends he'd long wanted. They'd sit on mismatched chairs, listen to music, laugh themselves hoarse. Before he hung up with Will now he sometimes had half an inclination (though he never acted on it) to say "I love you" himself.

Moving never fails to surprise you with its unpleasantness, however well you think you've imagined it beforehand. Lodwick had for the weekend transformed into an ant farm populated with parents sweatily crawling under beds, carrying lamps out to cars, fighting for space on the stairs. The air was full of the racket of wheels on brick—bins being dragged back and forth, back and forth, wedged into elevators.

In Jacob and Laura's room there were sweatshirts— pounds of sweatshirts—that Jacob had not so much as touched since coming to school. There were dresses and skirts and sweaters and shoes belonging to Laura—all of which needed to be packed up just so, many of which, now that they were out, she needed to try on. Lamps and pens and checkbooks and picture frames and cords and chargers. Bookshelves and printers, textbooks and old letters, half-empty boxes of granola bars and a tin full of popcorn.

There was no way to look at the detonated room without feeling something close to despair. The mess seemed not just organizational but spiritual.

And yet there Will was at the center of it, tireless. He wore a white V-neck undershirt and a pale pair of jeans, and while Jacob spent an hour wrapping a single extension cord in hopeless slow motion, Will filled boxes with books, trooped up and down and out to the truck, carried an entire tall bookshelf flat against his back. Skinny as he was, Will was strong, sinewy, like an eager young apprentice in a storybook. Looking at him now Jacob thought he would have been more at home growing up in the fifties. Wearing a blazer on a date. Helping his girlfriend's father work on his car on a Saturday afternoon.

Jacob spent much of that graduation weekend—a weekend of sitting in the sun wearing a robe like a blue shower curtain, of listening to speeches that could have been written by a random-cliché generator, of warmly greeting the parents of people whose children he knew hardly at all—feeling as if he had mono. It would take days of motionless solitude to recover from all those hours of packing and standing and chatting.

Every class is told that the hopes of a new generation

rest on its shoulders, but in this case it just happens to be true.

Arthur and Charlotte took them all out for dinner at Chant du Coq in Hagman, where every one of the white-clothed tables was taken up by a graduate's family, and where the prices seemed mysteriously to have risen by four dollars on every dish. Will ate with quiet care, as if he were working on a painting; it was his way of leaving Jacob alone. Cara spent the meal looking at her phone in her lap. Charlotte so mechanically praised everything they'd seen and done—*that looked like a great bookstore; I just loved that song when you all came out; they did such a good job with the campus lawn*—that even Arthur seemed slightly embarrassed. "What are Laura's folks saying about you guys moving in?" he said. (Arthur was mightily, and publicly, disappointed that Jacob had rejected his idea of having Laura's family join them for dinner.)

Not since his first weeks at school had Jacob so fervently wished to escape.

And the next morning, after the last of the packing, they did. Will and Jacob and Laura, crammed onto the narrow brown bench that was the U-Haul's front seat, drove the three hours down I-87 into the city, stopping only to pick up a couch and a bed at an IKEA larger and more imposing than any airport. It seemed as if they'd gone from state highways to the vivid gritty corners of the Bronx in a span of seconds. They arrived at the apartment in time for dinner, though they had no idea what to eat. Their neighborhood hadn't seemed quite so deep in Brooklyn when they'd been there before, had it? Their street hadn't looked quite this desolate. Maybe it was just that they were tired. Maybe it was just that it was beginning to drizzle.

The living room's overhead light shone through a dusty yellowish fixture. The fridge and freezer were, of course, empty, and the bedroom looked small and even darker than the front of the apartment. A car alarm wailed, then stopped. Jacob had the same feeling he'd had upon first seeing his cinder-block room as a freshman: *I've made a terrible mistake.* The spare, handsomely lit life that he had imagined for them could never take place here. They would live with these boxes, stepping over them and weaving between them, until they were carried out in boxes themselves.

But there was a half-full bottle of Jack Daniel's in the truck—a leftover from a graduation week party—and once they'd each had a few sips, a spirit of goofy pioneering took hold. "The Allen wrench, good sir." "You won't mind if the couch is missing a right arm, will you?" Straining and kneeling, twisting and yanking, they fought the feet of the couch into place. Laura stood holding the bottle in one hand and the directions, like a treasure map, in the other. Will and Jacob lay inches apart on the floor, bending a pole with all their might in a direction it had no interest in going.

"How do ordinary people do this shit?"

Jacob had only rarely heard Will curse, and he'd certainly never seen him drink this much. Maybe that was another thing Lizzie had taught him to do.

When it got to be ten o'clock and the couch still wasn't

assembled, Laura dragged the bed-box into the bedroom and began, patient as an elf, to lay all the pieces, screws included, on the ground in an arrangement precisely matching their eventual order. From the front of the apartment Jacob could hear her singing to herself in a high breathy voice as she worked—a pantomime of good cheer, he thought, rather than the thing itself. She was as worried about the neighborhood as he was.

"Why was Dad taking so many pictures?" Will said.

"I think it's just his new camera. He wanted to use low-light mode."

"Did Cara seem okay to you?"

"I think so. She's just weird about Dad and Charlotte. And I think she wanted us to invite her here."

They'd achieved a state, having lain there so long, of odd physical harmony. Jacob twisted one of the couch's leg poles, and wordlessly Will tilted the back frame to meet it. Will needed one of the tiny hexagon-shaped screws, and before he could open his mouth Jacob laid one in his palm.

Jacob was the first to notice that the singing from the bedroom, along with the occasional light clinks of metal on wood, had stopped. "Laura?" he said, walking into the back. She lay curled in all her clothes on the white down comforter in the middle of the mattress on the floor, sleeping surrounded by empty boxes and a screwdriver set. Liquor made her sleep. He shut off the light—how strange that this switch would eventually feel like home to him—and gently closed the door.

"She fell asleep?"

"Yup."

Jacob rejoined Will on the floor, but just having stepped away for those few seconds had taken him out of the work, and had given the Jack Daniel's a chance to travel to his brain. He felt clumsy, as if his fingers had swollen to twice their ordinary size. He wouldn't have minded curling up and going to sleep himself. He sat drifting, watching Will study the instructions, for what must have been a full minute.

"Lizzie dumped me," Will said, in a voice so matter-of-fact that at first Jacob thought he was saying something about the couch.

"I'm sorry. What happened?"

"No. It's not a big deal. It was coming for a while, I think."

"When was it?"

"A week ago. Last Thursday and Friday."

"Why didn't you say something?"

"I didn't want the weekend to become just a, you know..."

"But you sound pretty okay about it? Right?"

Will's face looked so strange, as if he were trying to swallow a mouthful of some metallic liquid, that Jacob wondered if in fact he wasn't okay at all. Maybe this was a new and deeper type of distress than he'd ever witnessed in his brother. Maybe past tears lay this robotic bitter expression.

"She just got sick of all my... stuff, I guess," he said.

"What stuff?"

"Oh, calling you guys, I don't know. We weren't... I

think I might have made it sound like we were more serious than we were."

Will sat up and locked his eyes unevenly on Jacob's, as if he were gauging whether to tell a joke. "I have something else to tell you. I've wanted to tell you for a long time."

He did look almost as if he might tell a joke, but only now did Jacob notice a slight vibration coming through the floor—Will's leg was shaking.

"It's bad."

"What? What is it?"

"Jacob, I slept with Laura. We had sex."

What Jacob felt at that moment had a definite quality of cascading, a shower. Something freezing or burning ribboning down through his body from the top of his head in the pattern of a falling firework. Now his leg was shaking too. He almost, *almost,* had the impulse to laugh, but it was a laugh like being hit with a full-body hand buzzer.

"When?"

"A long time ago. Before you were dating. Way before."

Still the shaking didn't stop, and now the chill was spreading and filling Jacob's chest. "When exactly? Are you kidding? Are you fucking kidding?"

They didn't turn away from each other, but their eyes were fixed on points just past each other's faces. Though he'd never been in a Catholic church in his life, as they sat there in the semidark Jacob thought of a priest and a confessor.

"That first weekend. When we first met. When you were out of town with Clarissa. We went back to her room and—

We were drunk. It was stupid. We didn't have any idea you'd end up together."

"Then why didn't you fucking tell me?"

"I was embarrassed. It was stupid. It didn't mean anything."

"But now you have to tell me."

"I'm telling you because— Because..." Will's body did a slight shudder, a little kick like an engine turning over or someone about to throw up. When he spoke again his voice was both quieter and more emphatic. "Because I'm in love with her, Jacob! I love her!"

His voice, saying *I love her,* was unlike anything Jacob had ever heard, from Will or from anyone. It sounded like something delicate being quickly flayed.

"I've been in love with her all year. I've been crying over her every night, I've been praying. Jacob, I've been fucking *praying.*"

"If I had been trying to imagine the worst thing, the most disgusting thing, I couldn't possibly..."

"I don't think she loves you, Jacob. I don't think if she loved you she'd be talking to me as much as she does, telling me all the things she does..."

"Do you know how pathetic you sound?"

"I don't care how pathetic I sound. We slept together, and just the fact that she never told you probably says a lot more about..."

Jacob realized all of a sudden that he was standing up, and that he was holding in his right hand a monkey wrench. "You are so fucking ridiculous," he said, "tiptoeing around... *Jacob, I don't know what to do. Should I take my dick out before I turn off the lights or after? Jacob, help, I don't know what to do with her tits."*

"You can say whatever you want to me, Jacob. But Laura's only living with you because you're too much of a baby to live alone. You're a *child*, and she doesn't deserve to be..."

"I'm a child?! *I'm* a child?!"

"You are. Everyone has spoiled you all your life because..."

What Jacob felt—suddenly the only thing he felt—was that if he didn't get out of the apartment he was going to smash the monkey wrench into Will's skull or his own. Without waiting for another word from Will he unbolted the door and ran down the unfamiliar stairs and out onto the street, which even in his current state he realized might not be entirely safe. The grates on the nail salon and bodega were drawn, and the only living thing he could see was a rat, walking boldly along the outer wall of a building.

He couldn't call what was going on in his head then *thinking*. It was more like being pelted—a *splat* of realization and then a slow ooze of understanding. He dropped the monkey wrench with a clatter and told himself he'd get it later. So Laura and Will had fucked. So Laura's body had— So Will had been crying himself to sleep. So their talks had meant—what? Everything? Nothing?

When he and Laura had first been dating, he'd told himself that with her, it was never as bad as you thought. With other girls—with Emily—they would seem to be in a bad mood, turning away when you tried to take their hands, and in the end it would be just what you feared: they were mad, they were having second thoughts, they had something they wanted to tell you. Not Laura! With her it had always been just a headache. Or a piece of sad news from her mother. Never anything to worry about. What a miserable fucking joke.

As he walked he saw Will's face, large and clear and seemingly floating in the air in front of him, and he felt hate as strong as nausea. *All my life...* All your life what? All Jacob's life Will had been—politely pulling ahead. *You know your brother got the highest grade I've ever given. Your brother has just been such a gift to your father.* Always celebrated, always correct. A plain respectable building in whose shadow Jacob had grown up crooked, knotty, incapable of happiness or kindness. And here all along Will had been—a monster. A stranger. Was there anything, just then, that Jacob wouldn't have believed Will capable of? He had fucked Jacob's girlfriend, and now he wanted to be with her. Did he also want Jacob's life? Did he think everything would have been fine if only Jacob had never been born at all?

Jacob knew, from movies and novels, that "going for a walk to clear your head" was something that people did at moments of duress, but until tonight he'd never felt the impulse. Now he could no more have stood still than he could have done a handstand. Fast, fast, as if he were racing to a train, he walked to the corner with the mailbox, turned onto the sidewalk of large cracked stones past fenced-in lots, then past the courtyard scattered with benches on which lay either people or piles of garbage. He had no doubt at all that his and Laura's relationship was over, his and Will's relationship was over, his and New York's relationship was over. It was just that he couldn't imagine what came next— home? Homelessness? The mental hospital? Every now and then he froze and reversed direction to keep himself from wandering too far from the apartment. He had good reason to feel that he was seeing the same things over and over, if not quite as many times as it seemed to him that he was seeing them. The same tree sawed off at the knee. The same trash can in which someone had piled bags four feet above the rim. Above all the same sign, which finally seemed to be following him, like a message in a dream:

IF YOU'RE THE PERSON WHO TOOK MY DOG FROM OUTSIDE ASSOCIATED LAST THURS., GIVE HIM BACK.
   YOU KNOW WHO YOU ARE!

The sign was taped to lampposts, tree trunks, stuffed into fences and left on stoops. What suffering! You know who you are. No he didn't, he had no idea—he didn't know this city, he didn't know his girlfriend, he didn't know his brother, he hardly knew whether he was hot or cold.

On what must have been his fourth loop through the neighborhood he noticed a clock on what looked like a bank building, and saw that it was one-thirty. He didn't know if the thing that was happening with his vision—a kind of pulsing outward, bursts of sharpness followed by stretches of blur—had to do with his anger or his drunkenness. He

262 / *Ben Dolnick*

turned toward what he hoped was the apartment. A new thought entered his head: he had made a shocking, elementary mistake in leaving Will and Laura alone. Probably they'd been waiting all their lives for this. By the time he reached his corner he was running, as fast as the blur would let him. Probably right now they were fucking on his newly assembled furniture.

No. The apartment was as quiet and as dark as he'd left it, and Will sat alone at the center of the couch, staring in the direction of a pile of boxes. It occurred to Jacob for an instant that he'd imagined the whole thing. "She came out and asked where you were," he said. "I told her that you knew. She's in the bedroom."

Jacob found her lying on the mattress, awake now, though the lights were off. He stood over her. "You. Fucking. Liar."

"I didn't lie." Her voice was more ordinary, less guilt-stricken, than he had expected it to be.

"You did lie. For this entire fucking relationship you've been—"

"We were drunk! We were drunk and I was bored and you were off with Clarissa! If this is going to be the end of our relationship, then maybe..."

"What am I supposed to think you've been talking about every night for nine fucking months?"

"What, you think we've been talking about our glorious night together?"

"How the fuck do I have any idea? Why do *you* get to be mad?"

"I get to be mad because I *am* mad!" She sat up. "I'm not some vessel for you and Will to work out shit from when you were eight years old! I slept with him, just like you've slept with people, before we were going out. I've talked to him on the phone. I know it's fucking awkward, but it doesn't change anything. It was a stupid mistake. That's it."

At the end of the conversation—a conversation during which they might as well have been spitting at each other, and during which he kept expecting his landlord to come up from downstairs—Jacob sat down on the mattress beside her, in all his clothes, too exhausted to speak, and tried to remember that this night too would eventually end. After a few minutes, keeping himself above the covers, he lay down on the edge of the bed. Twelve hours ago they'd been in his room at Lodwick. Four hours ago they'd been laughing in the living room. Every now and then he heard a creak from the front that could have been a tree or could have been Will on the couch. Occasionally Laura's leg drifted over and touched his—though she couldn't have been asleep—and he recoiled as if from something scalding.

Maybe Will and Laura were the love story and Jacob was a minor character, lingering on stage past his last lines.

Maybe he and Will were still seven and nine years old, in their room. Maybe they had never separated, never aged, never changed. Maybe the past ten years—Emily, college, science, Laura—were the sort of elaborate story, glimmering just on the edge of sense, that the mind constructs as it tumbles into sleep.

Maybe he would wake up in the morning and vomit out everything he presently felt, along with the quarter bottle of whiskey.

He had actually begun to fall asleep—a sleep that was like being dunked in dark water—when Laura woke him up by taking his hand. "I love you," she whispered, in an urgent, almost panicked voice. He wasn't dreaming, although he knew that he wasn't entirely awake.

"I love you," he said back. He had believed, not an hour before, that he would die without ever touching her again, but they kissed so hard now that their teeth touched. He could not have said where he was. He felt like someone other than himself entirely.

By the time they woke up the next morning Will was gone. He'd left just a one-line note taped to the door. *Left for the train.* Laura took her time in the bathroom, and when she came out she and Jacob avoided looking at each other, as they would for most of the coming week.

Jacob went down to get the monkey wrench from the street—he'd expected it to be gone—and then set about assembling the kitchen table. The neighborhood looked better in the daylight, busier and greener. The windows let in light and flies. As he worked he didn't think about whether they would ever eat a meal on this table or whether he would ever talk to Will again—he just matched bolts with screws, fitted legs into sockets. If he didn't think about certain things (*Laura naked and reaching for Will's underwear*), if he kind of squinted and held his breath, he felt something like the beginning of the possibility of almost being okay. Other times the possibility of being okay would seem like an insane joke. At those times he felt that not only would he never touch Laura, but he would never touch anyone. *The things people were capable of.* He would have to become a robot.

From Sunday, by one technique or another, all in silence, they made it to Tuesday, when her school and his work were set to start.

Under ordinary circumstances he and Laura would have talked a dozen times on Tuesday and each day afterward, calling each other in every gap, calling each other without even thinking of whether they had anything to say. But not now. Jacob had no one to describe his new boss Marcel to—his beard that started just below his eyes, his high and happy voice, his way of deciding just before they started an experiment that their approach was wrong, wrong, entirely wrong. The confusion of the subway, of finding a place to eat lunch, of spilling rubbing alcohol on his new keyboard—all unreported, and so all only foggily experienced. Now they lived whole days in utter separation, and when they came back to the apartment in the evening and sat down at the table, they didn't say a word.

And yet they did sit at the table. Night after night they sat in silence—Jacob made spaghetti in a pot he'd bought at Target; Laura made grilled cheese in their only college pan. They both slept in the bed, but they didn't touch, and they didn't face each other. How long could this possibly go on? Was it about the rent? What were they waiting to decide?

Jacob had no idea, but he did notice after a few nights that something in Laura's expression had changed. Or maybe he could feel that his own expression had changed. Anyway, speaking was no longer entirely forbidden. At first it was like conversation in a home for invalids. "Do you want water?" "Okay." "I bought a coat." "Okay."

But then the amazing, ordinary thing happened: time passed. Jacob had heard, when his mother had died and a thousand times afterward, that time made things better, that however he felt today he would feel less so in a week, and yet somehow he had forgotten, or disregarded it. It may have been true of his mother's death, but it wouldn't be true now, not for this. Nothing so knotty could ever come untangled, certainly not just by the passive workings of time. But one night in June he and Laura found themselves laughing as they fought over who had left the shower dripping. Not long after that they hugged. The things people were capable of.

Still there were chilly hours—still there were long and baffling and unpleasant conversations.

I don't understand how you could have kept that secret from me.

I think I was punishing you. For Clarissa. Do you think I like thinking about you and her?

We kissed once! Those have nothing in common at all!

Well, what about you getting Emily pregnant? She was pregnant! You could have been a dad!

They never settled on an answer for what either of them had to apologize for, exactly, and they didn't need to: the thing that demanded an apology was too large to get their arms around. They could hurt each other very badly. They could each keep secrets and lie. They were alone together on a trip no less frightening than if they'd decided to sail across the ocean.

If they were going to stay together, it was not going to be by inertia, but by daily, hourly choice.

By the end of summer they had started calling the apartment home. The couch, the bed, and the toolbox had lost whatever poison had attached to them that night in Jacob's mind. When he walked through the neighborhood each day— the edges of the leaves were beginning to go yellow and red—and saw the lost dog signs, now faded and torn, still hanging from lampposts, he no longer had to look away. And when a single new word appeared, scrawled heavily across the top of each sign—

FOUND!

—he even managed to smile.

With Will the path was less visible. Between Will's leaving that morning in May and their father's birthday in November, he and Jacob had less to do with each other than at any other point in their lives. No phone calls, no e-mails. Just silence so total that Jacob wondered if he and Will had been waiting, without knowing it, for just such a blow to sever them. If, without being able to admit it, all they'd ever wanted was to be strangers.

The e-mail came one night in October.

Jacob,

I don't know how it's possible to do something that's both unforgivable and ridiculous, but that's what I seem to have done. I should have told you a long time ago about what happened, before it had time to take on all the special meanings in my head. And I certainly should have talked to you before, in my loneliness and confusion (and yes, jealousy), I convinced myself that I had somehow come to love this person I hardly knew. I'd explain how it all has to do with Mom, or with high school, or with feeling like a fraud, but the truth is I have no idea.

I know I've made trouble for you in your relationship with Laura, and I know I've made trouble for us in our relationship too. In my anger and embarrassment and whatever else I said a lot of things I didn't mean that night, and I hope you did too (not mean some of the things you said). These past few months have been terrible for me, and I hate not knowing how they've been for you. But I also feel like I understand myself better than I ever have, and I really hope we're able to figure out a way past this.

Anyway, one of the things I've definitely realized is that it doesn't do anyone any good in the long run not to tell you things. I love you like a brother. Exactly like a brother, for better or worse.

Will

Jacob sent a response, short but polite, in which he said that he still didn't think he was ready for them to talk. He didn't tell Laura about the e-mail, and he thought he might never mention Will to her again—the witness protection program theory of emotional healing.

This theory—along with Jacob's composure—held up just fine until the moment Will walked into the kitchen at the Vines' house, bags draped over his shoulders, and found Jacob and Laura standing around the counter with Arthur. This was November, the Friday of Arthur's birthday. Will looked even thinner than he had a few months ago. He and Jacob hugged as gingerly as if they were strapped with explosives. Jacob went immediately to see about helping Arthur figure out his new treadmill. Will spent most of the night with Cara, sorting through old papers from the basement, which Charlotte was hoping to turn into an office.

They didn't talk until late that night—Jacob had thought they might not talk at all—when Will found Jacob sitting alone on the ledge by the window outside their bedrooms. Laura had gone to bed. Jacob had been brushing his teeth as he stared out, but now he was just sitting. The tree in the yard had lost all its leaves, and the street, yellow and black and gray, looked freezing.

"Everything's so slow at home, isn't it?" Will said, in the rhythm of a pickup line. Then he took in a sharp breath and said, "How are you doing?"

"I'm all right."

"How's Brooklyn been?"

"Fine."

"Jacob, I—I honestly don't know what I can say. Are you going to act like this forever?"

Jacob shrugged. "I don't hate you or anything. I just don't know if I care about having a relationship with you."

"Well, that's not any better."

Jacob shrugged again, and continued to stare straight ahead, but he felt—and he knew that Will felt too—that, without his having been aware of it, some part of his resistance had been eroding, as it had after countless childhood fights. A process like a river pulling at a fallen branch, and one that Jacob felt just as helpless to stop.

By the next morning he and Will could be in the same room together, and that afternoon they, along with Cara and Laura, helped get the house ready for Arthur's party. In came the table from the patio, out went the couch. The tablecloth needed ironing. The squash soup needed stirring. Judy and Aaron showed up early and stood wearing their coats in the kitchen, nibbling dough. Aaron was burlier than Jacob had ever seen him—he was teaching tae kwon do in Gaithersburg and looked something like a bodyguard. Arthur and Charlotte's friends—some old, many new— came trickling in at seven, each couple bearing a gift and a noisy greeting. The thing that you hope will happen at a party did: a critical number of overlapping conversations and activities had created a tide that was going to keep the party afloat. Stories became more interesting, jokes became wittier. One of Charlotte's nephews circled the living room with a plate of grapes and cheese cubes, coming up to groups and saying, *"Monsieur?"*

Jacob and Laura sat with one of Arthur's partners from the store, Rudy, a twitchy, red-haired man who seemed to have no memory at all of having ever met Jacob. He'd just been on a cruise to Antarctica and wanted to talk about global warming. In a cheerful tone he described super-viruses being unleashed from permafrost, a desert spreading from Philadelphia to San Francisco. Jacob and Laura pinched each other's legs under the table.

People kept interrupting dinner to make toasts—to Arthur, to Charlotte, to looking around this room and seeing all these wonderful faces. Arthur spent the whole night flushed and wet-eyed, putting his hand on people's shoulders. The next morning, over bagels, he and Charlotte would announce that they were engaged. The wedding would be in spring, and once they were married, well, how would everyone feel if Arthur thought about selling the store? What if they started spending a few months a year in Arizona?... But not tonight. Tonight was just birthday cake on the Vines' chipped plates and music from the tinny brown living room speakers.

At one point Jacob and Will stood talking to Judy by the grandfather clock. "This girlfriend of mine is making a ton of money in organic soaps, detergent, all that stuff, and she says she's looking for someone to help her open a second store. So..." Laura came up and pretended to have something to show Jacob in the kitchen. Over the empty cake box she kissed him, holding his face, and Jacob realized, first, that she was drunk, and second, that they were going to make it. So there was a third thing he'd realized: he'd still thought that they might not.

"I'm glad we live together," she said.

"I'm glad too."

"I'm glad you're my boyfriend." She held his waist with one hand, dropped a bit of leftover frosting into her mouth with the other.

"I am too."

"I think your dad's friend Rudy might have pinched my ass." She laughed and sprayed crumbs over Jacob's sweater. At certain moments happiness was so easy that they seemed sure never to lose hold of it again.

At one that morning, when all the guests had gone and the house had taken on the disheveled stillness of an arena after a concert, Jacob sat on the floor of his room. Laura, still wearing her skirt and makeup, lay struggling to keep her eyes open on the bed. In front of Jacob sat a CVS bag that Arthur had given him from the basement, full of Jacob's old school papers. Usually Jacob dreaded these archaeology sessions, but now, because it was late or because he'd been drinking, he found himself lingering over each page. At first he'd been showing his finds to Laura, who made noises of true but sleepy interest. Now he'd decided to leave her alone.

Here was an old report card from Mrs. Grillet, printed on paper as thin as vellum ("Outstanding" in *Asks questions that show comprehension;* "Satisfactory" in *Completes work in a timely fashion*). A drawing of a blue heron (*Great Blue Herons are 42 in. and there found in many different parts of N. America*). A half-empty worksheet about "Día de Los Muertos." And finally, wrinkled at the bottom of the bag, a two-page autobiography with "My Life So Far, by Jacob Vine" handwritten across the top. The cover was a folded piece of green construction paper, so neatly stapled that one of his parents must have done it.

> *I was born in Sibley Hospital in Washington, D.C. and I have lived in Maryland ever since.*
>
> *I have a brother Will, who is very smart, and a sister Cara, who's only in preschool. We have one dog Finney. I had a guinea pig that died of old age.*
>
> *My best friends are Marek, Owen, and Jack.*
>
> *My dad owns Griggs' Hardware. His favorite writers are William Shakespeare and Stephen King, and he reads to me all the time.*
>
> *My mom works at George Washington University and she is a GREAT cook. When she cooks she goes outside and picks all kind of plants.*

If Laura hadn't been sleeping, or if he hadn't felt at a slight distance from himself, he might have burst into tears there on the floor. Instead he just drew in his cheeks and waited for the feeling—something like having swallowed an ice cube—to pass. His poor mother. His poor brother. His poor nine-year-old self carefully erasing and remaking the loops on his cursive g's, oblivious.

Who was it who had written those sentences? He didn't recognize the voice, or many of the "facts." Had he really once considered Jack Santora a best friend? When had his father ever read Stephen King? What could he possibly have meant—who could he have been trying to impress?—with that nonsense about his mother picking plants for dinner? She was no more a great cook than he was.

> *Jacob,*
> *You are very fortunate to have such a wonderful family. I look forward to our working together in the fourth grade!*
> —*Mrs. Sobolesky*

He'd thought his family needed his protection, even then. Only he, at nine years old, stood between them and an exposure too painful to name. Yes, Will had cried during the talent show, but he was very smart. His mother had never volunteered to be a room mother and she didn't sew his Halloween costumes, but she did pick plants for dinner. Okay? Absolved? He'd stood poised, ready to fight off all threats, but the battles he'd worried most about had never come, and the ones that did come he could never have done anything to stop. He wouldn't make that mistake again.

Laura's eyes sprang open, a jolt in the road of her dreaming. Jacob watched her initial bafflement, at where and when and why she was still dressed, give way.

"Turn out the light," she said, wriggling under the blanket. "Come to bed." She scooted over, clearing a space for him. He clicked off the light. "Enough. Come in. Come here."

ALSO BY BEN DOLNICK

"Ben Dolnick is a writer of incredible sensitivity.
Zoology *explores the tricky journey to adulthood*
with honesty, humor, and generosity."
—Jonathan Safran Foer

ZOOLOGY

Zoology is the story of Henry Elinsky, a college flunk-out
who takes a job at the Central Park Zoo and discovers that
becoming an adult takes a lot more than just a weekly pay-
check. *Zoology* is an "exciting, confident, and thoroughly
endearing debut. Dolnick writes with a maturity that be-
lies his years, and *Zoology*—distinguished by a rare com-
bination of narrative patience and instinctive kindness—is
a real cause for celebration" (George Saunders, author of
In Persuasion Nation).

Fiction/978-0-307-27915-6

VINTAGE CONTEMPORARIES
Available at your local bookstore, or visit
www.randomhouse.com

Meet with Interesting People
Enjoy Stimulating Conversation
Discover Wonderful Books

VINTAGE BOOKS / ANCHOR BOOKS

Reading Group Center

THE READING GROUP SOURCE FOR BOOK LOVERS

Visit ReadingGroupCenter.com where you'll find great reading choices—award winners, bestsellers, beloved classics, and many more—and extensive resources for reading groups such as:

Author Chats
Exciting contests offer reading groups the chance to win one-on-one phone conversations with Vintage and Anchor Books authors.

Extensive Discussion Guides
Guides for over 450 titles as well as non–title specific discussion questions by category for fiction, nonfiction, memoir, poetry, and mystery.

Personal Advice and Ideas
Reading groups nationwide share ideas, suggestions, helpful tips, and anecdotal information. Participate in the discussion and share your group's experiences.

Behind the Book Features
Specially designed pages which can include photographs, videos, original essays, notes from the author and editor, and book-related information.

Reading Planner
Plan ahead by browsing upcoming titles, finding author event schedules, and more.

Special for Spanish-language reading groups
www.grupodelectura.com
A dedicated Spanish-language content area complete with recommended titles from Vintage Español.

A selection of some favorite reading group titles from our list

Atonement by Ian McEwan
Balzac and the Little Chinese Seamstress by Dai Sijie
The Blind Assassin by Margaret Atwood
The Devil in the White City by Erik Larson
Empire Falls by Richard Russo
The English Patient by Michael Ondaatje
A Heartbreaking Work of Staggering Genius by Dave Eggers
The House of Sand and Fog by Andre Dubus III
A Lesson Before Dying by Ernest J. Gaines

Lolita by Vladimir Nabokov
Memoirs of a Geisha by Arthur Golden
Midnight in the Garden of Good and Evil by John Berendt
Midwives by Chris Bohjalian
Push by Sapphire
The Reader by Bernhard Schlink
Snow by Orhan Pamuk
An Unquiet Mind by Kay Redfield Jamison
Waiting by Ha Jin
A Year in Provence by Peter Mayle